BACKHAND SMASH

BACKHAND SMASH

J.M. Gregson

severn
House

This first world edition published 2015
in Great Britain and 2016 in the USA by
SEVERN HOUSE PUBLISHERS LTD of
19 Cedar Road, Sutton, Surrey, England, SM2 5DA.
Trade paperback edition first published
in Great Britain and the USA 2016 by
SEVERN HOUSE PUBLISHERS LTD

British Library Cataloguing in Publication Data

Gregson, J. M. author.
  Backhand smash. – (A Percy Peach mystery)
  1. Peach, Percy (Fictitious character)–Fiction. 2. Blake,
  Lucy (Fictitious character)–Fiction. 3. Police–
  England–Lancashire–Fiction. 4. Detective and mystery
  stories.
  I. Title II. Series
  823.9'14-dc23

ISBN-13: 978-0-7278-8565-4 (cased)
ISBN-13: 978-1-84751-674-9 (trade paper)
ISBN-13: 978-1-78010-731-8 (e-book)

All Severn House titles are printed on acid-free paper.

Severn House Publishers support the Forest Stewardship Council™ [FSC™],
the leading international forest certification organisation.
All our titles that are printed on FSC certified paper carry the FSC logo.

Typeset by Palimpsest Book Production Ltd.,
Falkirk, Stirlingshire, Scotland.
Printed and bound in Great Britain by
TJ International, Padstow, Cornwall.

To Christine and Michael, for their steady and valuable support over the years

ONE

'You'll need to watch her. She's only small, she's fifty if she's a day, and she looks as if she couldn't hurt a fly. But Olive knows her tennis and she's bloody good at the net. She'll volley it straight into your privates if you give her half a chance.'

It wasn't the kind of conversation you'd expect in a police staff canteen. (The bureaucrats had tried 'restaurant' and 'dining hall', but neither had caught on at Brunton Police Station.) The talk here normally ranged only from the latest atrocities of the criminal fraternity to the latest inanities of the decision makers in the police service.

But then this speaker wasn't the typical consumer of dubious toad-in-the-hole or bangers and mash. Elaine Brockman was graduate entry to this distinctively scented eating place. She lived what seemed to most of her fellow officers an exotic life outside the station. Her father was a civil servant and her mother was a nursing sister. Both of them had bitterly opposed their daughter's choice of career, though no one who sat with Elaine in the canteen knew anything of that.

The officer she was speaking to could hardly have had a more contrasting life. Nor could he have been more physically different. PC Brockman was small and curvaceous and had dark blonde hair. She also had a surprisingly crisp right uppercut when it was needed. This had recently been used more amongst her over-amorous colleagues than amidst the town's yob fraternity. But Elaine weighed no more than a trim nine stones. She was fair-skinned, blue-eyed and deceptively vulnerable in appearance: the right uppercut had surprised its victims.

No one would have described Detective Sergeant Clyde Northcott as vulnerable. He was very black and very powerful. At six feet three and around fifteen stones of bone and muscle, he was not a man anyone cared to argue with. He had first-hand knowledge of the criminal low life, having been a small-time drug dealer for three months when he was nineteen. His life-style and his colour had ensured that he had needed from an early age to be very handy with his fists.

Northcott had even been a suspect in a murder case. DCI Peach, his present boss, had cleared him of that and then unexpectedly recruited him to the police service. Now, six years later, he was Peach's bagman and trusted aide, the member of the team whom Peach always described as his 'hard bastard', which added even more to Northcott's formid-able reputation. Whereas PC Brockman crept into the police car park each day in an ageing green Toyota passed on to her by her mother, DS Northcott roared in confidently on a Yamaha 350cc motorcycle.

They made an odd couple, but they enjoyed exchanging their very different experiences of life. It was the third time in ten days that they had sat together at lunchtime. An unlikely pair, and today an unlikely subject of conversation: they were talking about tennis. And in particular about the rather snooty Birch Fields Tennis Club. Elaine was filling Clyde Northcott in on the diminutive middle-aged lady who had been endeav-ouring to recruit him as one of its members.

Olive Crawshaw was her name and Elaine Brockman knew her well. She had known her since she was ten years old. 'She's a lady it isn't easy to say no to,' she told Northcott.

'I found it easy enough to say it. She just didn't seem to hear me,' said the big man plaintively.

'That's Olive. She doesn't hear what she doesn't want to hear. She wears you down. Then, when you show the slightest sign of weakness, she pounces. Just like she does at the net when she's on court.'

Clyde frowned. 'I didn't show any weakness. I'm almost sure I didn't show any weakness. But she just went on with her spiel as if I hadn't spoken.'

'That's Olive,' said Elaine again. A fond smile flicked across her highly mobile lips. 'She likes getting the better of men, likes feeling that they're putty in her hands. The bigger the man, the greater the triumph.' She leant back a little to make it more obvious that she was running her gaze up and down

Northcott's formidable frame. 'She'll enjoy getting her way with you.'

'She won't do that,' said Clyde firmly. 'I'm not going to join. I decided years ago that tennis wasn't going to be my game.'

PC Brockman gave him a sceptical but wholly beguiling smile.

Olive Crawshaw would have been surprised but not at all disconcerted to know that she was the subject of conversation in the police canteen. Very few things disconcerted Mrs Crawshaw.

She was, in fact, fifty-four rather than the fifty years that Elaine Brockman had conceded to her, but she had the energy of a thirty-year-old and the resolution of a Matterhorn scaler: she had climbed that formidable Alpine height to celebrate her fiftieth birthday, exciting wonder and admiration in the Swiss guides who had been reluctant to accompany her when she proposed the enterprise. Olive was a traditionalist: the challenge of the Matterhorn excited her far more than the now fashionable and much easier Kilimanjaro.

At the last committee meeting of the Birch Fields Tennis Club, she had volunteered her support for the new initiative the committee had agreed to after several hours of lively debate. The committee members had learned survival techniques over twenty years; Mrs Crawshaw's offer to head the new scheme had been eagerly accepted. This was a controversial venture, which wouldn't be supported by all club members. If you wanted to ride out a controversy, Olive Crawshaw was your woman. Olive wasn't given to boasting, but she might well have been pleased with that summary of her strengths.

The new policy was both ethically correct and economically inevitable. Those were the phrases Olive had used when she had made her trenchant case for it to the committee. The club needed new members. It couldn't simply go on increasing its subscription as its numbers fell. That was counter-productive: unless they remained competitive, putative tennis players would take their custom elsewhere. Worse still, if membership remained exclusive and the cost of playing rose, hard-up young people might give up tennis altogether and switch their allegiance to cheaper and more welcoming sports.

The new policy, now belatedly approved by the committee, was to look for young members from a wider social spectrum and a wider ethnic background. School-leavers who were not going on to college or university would be encouraged to join the juniors. Seniors would be recruited from the Asian community – not many of the older members could distinguish with certainty between the Indian and Pakistani communities that now made up almost thirty per cent of the Brunton population. Respectable people from the lower ranks of society and even manual workers should be encouraged to join the club, provided that they understood and respected its rules.

Trouble ahead, said the chairman, who had been the chief opponent of this widening of membership. But if there was going to be trouble, let Mrs Crawshaw meet it head-on. As the most enthusiastic advocate of the new policy, she could only expect to be allotted this challenging role.

Challenge was a thing Olive relished. Head-on was very much her mode of attack. You couldn't have anything much more head-on as your first recruit than a former drug dealer, reported to be handy with his fists, who was very large and very black. Mrs Crawshaw had determined that Clyde Northcott would be a talisman for the new policy. He would be a quarry whom she would pursue, capture and display triumphantly to those whingers and doubters who had opposed her will on the committee of Birch Fields Tennis Club.

She would display Detective Sergeant Northcott in his shining ebony glory on the number one court at the weekend, as a slap to the prejudiced faces of those who said such men were not suitable members of the town's most exclusive tennis club.

Clyde Northcott was blissfully unaware of the plans Mrs Crawshaw was making for him. He was concentrating very hard on his professional responsibilities. You tended to do that when Detective Chief Inspector Percy Peach was around.

Peach's real name was Denis Charles Scott Peach, but few save his mother-in-law, who was a cricket enthusiast, understood the significance of that D.C.S. They were the initials of the late and much lamented Denis Compton, the most dazzling and best-loved British batsman of the post-war years – Peach's long-dead father had also been a cricket fan. The police service, with its predilection for alliteration, had christened him Percy as a young, fresh-faced copper and Percy he had been ever since then. Percy wasn't yet forty, but no one at Brunton Police Station remembered him as fresh-faced, whilst the local criminal fraternity saw nothing even faintly comical in Percy.

Percy was scowling his contempt at a particularly obnoxious member of that fraternity at this moment. For a man who carried a small black moustache on a round face beneath a shining bald pate, Percy did contempt rather well. On this occasion, there was nothing feigned about his scorn for the man in front of him. Sean Catterick was twenty-six. He had a record of violence and had already served a six-month custodial sentence, reduced to less than half of that by a judicial system that Peach regarded as absurdly ill-informed and misguided.

In Peach's view, Catterick should still have been in prison when he perpetrated his latest outrage. The DCI gazed into the coarse features on the other side of the small interview-room table with undisguised distaste. 'Robbery with violence, Catterick. Violence against a defenceless eighty-one-year-old man in his own home. You're going down for years for this. The world will be well rid of you. Even in Strangeways, they don't have much that's worse than you.'

'You've got the wrong man, Peach. I was nowhere near the place at the time. We've got witnesses to prove it.' He glanced at the thin-faced lawyer beside him and strove to fling confidence across the table. 'You take us to court and we'll make you look fucking stupid, mate.'

'I'm not your mate. People like you don't have mates, Catterick. They have people who lie for them. Anyone who lies for you this time will go down himself.'

Sean Catterick didn't have a wife. He'd battered the two women who'd lived with him over the last three years, but each of them had been too scared to give evidence against him. The coppers on the other side of the table were glad he'd no woman to lie for him now; no one gave much credit to alibis provided by wives or partners, but they were usually difficult to disprove. This man didn't have that support. Catterick said with all the truculence he could muster, 'I didn't do this and you bastards aren't going to fit me up for it.'

Peach glanced at the lawyer who sat beside his quarry with almost as much dislike as he was showing for Catterick: the law said that even scum like this had the right to be defended, but you didn't have to respect the men who did that. The man stared into Peach's black pupils for no more than a second before dropping his eyes to the clipboard in front of him. 'My client denies his presence in Alexandra Street at the time of this attack. Unless you can produce someone to attest to his presence there, you do not have a case to take to court. You must charge him or release him within three hours.'

'Teaching granny to suck eggs, are we? More chance of that than of getting Mr Sean Catterick back on our streets, I'd say.' Percy hissed his genuine hatred on the sibilants. Just half an hour earlier, he'd been with a severely damaged octogenarian who would never go back to his own home, and he carried the image still in his head. 'DS Northcott will tell you why you are going to remain in custody, Mr Catterick.'

If Clyde was surprised to be called upon without notice, he gave no sign of it. He gave the slightest smile of satisfaction and leaned forward to loom over his adversary, so that Catterick instinctively flinched six inches away from him. Peach didn't quite understand how he did it, but Northcott had the capacity to loom over people whilst sitting. He admired this rare quality in his bagman.

Northcott said in the dark voice that suggested deep reserves of violence, 'We have the best of all witnesses, Sean. The victim of your cowardly and unprovoked attack. Joe Brown himself will be in court to put you behind bars.'

'He won't, you know. You'll never persuade the old bugger to give evidence when it comes to the fucking crunch.'

'He'll be there, Sean. Don't cherish any illusions that he won't. And he won't be back in his own house for you to get at him in the meantime. If and when he's fit to leave hospital, he'll be in state care. His wounds might have healed a little by the time you're in court, but we've got a full range of photographs, taken yesterday. We shall present them as evidence in glorious technicolour. Juries are much affected by pictures such as the ones we shall display to them; they tend to remember images when the words of defence lawyers have tinkled away into silence.'

Catterick was scared now. He offered no more than routine, automatic defiance. 'Fuck off, pigs! You can flash all the pictures you like, but you'll still have to prove it was me who hit the old bugger with that lead pipe. You won't be able to do that.'

Percy Peach said nothing, but allowed the richest and most carnivorous of his vast range of smiles to illuminate his round face; the process took several seconds and struck fear into the hearts of accused and lawyer on the other side of the table. 'Very accurate description of the assault weapon, that, Mr Catterick. And very interesting to us pigs, because we haven't issued any description of that weapon to the media. Very interesting indeed.'

DS Northcott loomed again and Sean Catterick flinched again. Clyde bathed the prisoner in his own smile, displaying a perfect set of large white teeth, which looked to Catterick ready for use and very sharp. 'Very nice set of prints we've been able to lift from that ten inches of lead pipe, Sean. Conclusive, I'd say, with the other evidence we have and the information you've just given to us.'

The white-faced lawyer raised his left hand in front of his client's face, warning Catterick against saying any more. 'Could I have a word with you in private, Detective Chief Inspector?'

'Of course you may. Always happy to accommodate the law and its representatives.' Peach directed the smile of a tiger scenting feeding time at his unhappy adversaries.

In the privacy of his office, he listened intently to what the lawyer had to offer. 'We'd like to do a deal. If my client pleads guilty to burglary, will you forget the charge of assault?'

The man was young. He must also be naive and inexperienced if he thought he could trade in this situation. 'We don't do deals, Mr Picton. Catterick is a violent and dangerous man.

He needs to be locked away for a long time to protect the public. You know that as well as I do, even though the system has landed you with the task of defending him. We're speaking off the record, as you requested, but I'd almost think you were trying to pervert the course of justice here.' He accompanied the legal term with the blandest of his smiles.

'We could throw in a guilty plea for another three burglaries. Help your clear-up rate, that would.'

The man was desperate and that was making him reckless. Peach was enjoying being in control: like most policemen, he didn't have much time for lawyers. They were at best a necessary evil. 'I expect he'll ask for numerous minor offences to be taken into account, once he knows he's going down. I expect his lawyer will advise him to do that.' Percy rocked a little on his seat and smiled contentedly.

'The Crown Prosecution Service might refuse to take the case on, with the scanty evidence you have against my client.'

'With what he's just said on tape about the assault weapon? They'll be happy to get their teeth into this one. Almost as happy as I shall be to see your client in the clink.'

Peach was, on this occasion, as confident of that as he sounded. And when he told the CPS that the scum's brief had been trying to do a deal, that would make even that over-cautious bunch of wankers anxious to put Catterick in court. Villains like this one always depressed him, but the interview and its aftermath had gone well enough to make this a thoroughly satisfactory afternoon. 'I suggest you go back to your client and set about rustling up whatever mitigating circumstances you can. I don't envy you that. And I don't wish you success.'

They told Catterick they would be opposing bail when his case was transferred to the Crown Court on the morrow, as it undoubtedly would be. He flung a few meaningless obscenities at them as they dispatched him back to his cell.

Once the CID men were alone, Peach made Northcott remove the bandage from his wrist and examined the livid scar beneath it. He'd seen a few of these in his time, on himself and on others. 'Healing nicely. What did the quack say?'

'He was happy to let it take its course.'

Peach had noticed the tiny pause before the prepared reply. 'You haven't seen the doctor, have you?'

The DS shrugged. 'We were busy with other things. I didn't get round to it.'

'You got that whilst you were arresting Catterick, didn't you? We might want to present the evidence in court.'

'My arm isn't broken. It didn't seem necessary. We've enough evidence, surely, with the hospital report on old Joe and the pictures we've got of his injuries.'

'Resisting arrest, Catterick was, Clyde. I wouldn't have been surprised if he'd suffered injury himself whilst resisting arrest. I might have been quite gratified, in fact.'

'No need to complicate the issue, sir, is there? We've got him bang to rights.'

'I expect you're right, DS Northcott. But you've got your reputation as a hard bastard to protect, you know. It's a good thing that your non-violent streak is securely hidden with me.'

Northcott flexed his fists and examined his knuckles. 'I'm not sure I want to protect that hard-man reputation, sir. But I don't seem to have much option, with you around.'

Peach smiled fondly at his protégé. 'No option at all, Clyde. Your reputation is in safe hands as long as I'm around to look after you. You're a hard bastard.'

A phone call to the CID section asking for Detective Sergeant Northcott by name ended the conversation at this point. Clyde retreated with the phone to the corner of the room and privacy, expecting this to be a call from one of the snouts he retained from the criminal underworld he had long left behind him.

It was not one of them. It was a light but firm female voice. 'It's Olive Crawshaw here, Mr Northcott – Clyde, if you will permit that informality. Following our conversation of two days ago, I am delighted to tell you that you are requested to present yourself for interview at the club on Wednesday evening at eight p.m.'

'At the club?'

'The Birch Fields Tennis Club, Mr Northcott. I'm sure you won't be late.'

'But I hadn't definitely . . . I don't think we'd—'

But she had rung off and Clyde was left staring stupidly at the mouthpiece. He felt that this small, determined woman was more of a threat to his peace of mind than Sean Catterick had ever been.

TWO

Police officers have private lives like other citizens. The difference for them is that they normally choose to avoid any mention of the day job. It complicates your social exchanges, they say. People begin to watch everything they say when they find you are in the police force, as if they think that you are trying to trip them up. They think you will later review every phrase they use, every statement they make. It inhibits free exchanges and in some cases destroys all spontaneous conversation.

Being recognized as a policeman or policewoman can even be dangerous in some contexts. The overwhelming majority of uniformed officers now travel to work in civvies and change into uniform when they reach the station. In some of the darker places in British towns and cities, police officers do not care to walk alone, whether in or out of uniform. As far as most members of the British public are concerned, policing is not a popular calling.

Yet as far as Elaine Brockman was concerned, these problems were almost reversed. She paraded her uniform in the house in her first few days, as a challenge to parents who wished profoundly that she had chosen some other occupation. Her appearance was designed to remind her mum and dad at every turn that 'This is what I have chosen to do. This is what I am. This is what I am going to be for the foreseeable future, so you might as well get used to it, folks.'

But at work she wished that her uniform wasn't quite as new and that her buttons were not quite so bright. A little blending into the background, a little routine acceptance from her colleagues as just another callow young officer, would have been welcomed. Instead, she was that object of police curiosity and derision: the graduate entry. If she was successful, in a few years she might be fast-tracked to promotion. That was the blandishment the scheme offered to those coming into the service from university. Other officers were envious, and envy brings with it hostility.

Police personnel, despite the lurid views of their criminal opponents, are only human. Human nature meant that there was jealousy abroad in Brunton nick. There was even a desire that these toffee-nosed graduates who now seemed to arrive each year should make gaffes. These privileged young beings had been drinking and shagging their way through university whilst the less fortunate beings who were now their colleagues had been learning the hard facts of life and of police routine on the mean streets of the town. PC Brockman was a realist. She knew that there would be much mirth at Brunton Police Station if she slipped up and fell heavily upon her highly desirable backside. Metaphorically or literally: either would do. Both together would be quite wonderful.

She needed allies, and DS Clyde Northcott seemed not only the most obvious one to choose but the one likely to be most valuable to her. With Clyde on her side, there wouldn't be many mutterings or many snide comments. Not many of the people around her voiced any serious opposition to Northcott. He'd made DS and was in plain clothes at twenty-five. The people in uniform were snide about CID, but everyone knew you had made it when you were in plain clothes.

When Northcott voiced his concerns about tennis to her, it seemed to Elaine like manna from heaven. It might become a bond between them, in fact. She felt the need of a bond or two as she looked around the canteen; her over-vivid imagination told her that everyone she saw was anxious that she should fail.

'How's it going?' Clyde asked, as if he read her thoughts.

'Pretty well really. Except . . . well, probably the problem is me. I feel because I've been to Manchester University everyone here is wanting me to make a right bollocks of everything.'

Her dad wouldn't have liked that. He'd have said that her language was being corrupted by the career she had chosen. But all she wanted was to fit in here. Everyone wanted to fit in when they found themselves in a new place and with new people. And the coppers around her used much worse words than 'bollocks'. They were testing her out, seeing how she would react to the 'fucks' and the 'pricks' and the 'twats' and whatever else they could throw at her. They must have very little knowledge of the modern university if they thought that she hadn't heard much worse than that.

Clyde Northcott was looking at her with his head tilted a little to one side. He might be only three years older than her twenty-two, but they both felt at that moment that he was infinitely more experienced.

'The best thing,' he said, 'is to forget all about them and just get on with it. Decide each situation on its merits. If in doubt, ask for guidance from a senior officer. You're still only a PC. You're learning the trade. There's nothing wrong with asking for advice. It's what junior officers are supposed to do. Plunging into tricky situations on your own isn't mature; it's daft.'

She knew he was right: it was sound counsel. But she said, 'It's all very well for you, Clyde. You've proved yourself. You've made DS. You're Percy Peach's bagman. That's the job everyone here would like to have.'

He grinned ruefully. 'It doesn't always feel like that. Sometimes I think he doesn't realize slavery's been abolished. But he looks after you, does Percy. He'd never admit it, but he's got a soft centre. You'd want him in your corner if you were in trouble.'

'I'll take your word for it. He doesn't acknowledge the likes of me. And I'm too scared to speak to him.'

'He'll know all about you, will Percy. Bugger all happens here without him knowing about it. Even Tommy Bloody Tucker is scared of Percy. And he daren't check him, because it's Percy who provides the clear-up rates he rides on.'

'I thought before I came here that Chief Superintendent Tucker would be a real live wire. When I listen to other people talking about him, I realize what a wanker the man is.'

Dad wouldn't have liked 'wanker' either – not from his daughter's fair lips. It was very mild for Brunton Police Station. Clyde sprinkled salt on his chips, then bit into one rather fiercely. 'You should take police gossip with a pinch of salt, Elaine. But you can assume everything you hear about Tommy Bloody Tucker is correct.'

Elaine finished her yoghurt and studied her spoon thought-fully, not daring to look at the big man on the other side of the table. That was the English way when you were about to offer a compliment. 'I'm grateful to you for your advice, you know. These things might seem obvious to you, but when you're a new girl on the block, you need someone who knows his way around to guide you.'

'They're not a bad lot, you know, when you get to know them. They're not given to sentiment – dealing with the villains of the town soon knocks that out of you. And you've probably already found that they have a rather broad and basic sense of humour. But their humour's mostly connected with rank. Whilst you're still a humble PC, that will protect you. They'd far rather see Tommy Bloody Tucker fall flat on his arse than a humble PC, even a graduate-entry PC. If it's any consolation to you, I had to watch my step when I donned the uniform.'

She raised her eyebrows, wanting to make sure that he wasn't joking. It seemed inconceivable that anyone would dare to take the piss out of this formidable figure. 'Because of your colour?' She'd forced herself to use the word, knowing instinc-tively that the 'ethnic background' phrase that had sprung to mind would be dismissed contemptuously as namby-pamby in the police canteen. In the student community that she had so recently inhabited, it was usually assumed that all police forces were institutionally racist, because that suited student prejudices.

Clyde smiled. 'There was a little of that, I suppose. But not much. It was mostly because I'd been in the other camp, as they saw it. I'd been a petty criminal, on the wrong side of the tracks, before I came here. I suppose some saw it as switching sides, as too big a jump for me to make. I had to convince them I wasn't still working for the other lot. A few Saturday night scraps with the drunks helped. They realized that it was better to have me on their side.' He grinned at her, seeking now to make the whole exchange less serious. 'I don't recommend that solution for you, though the gossip tells me you can look after yourself.'

She answered his smile, as relieved as he was to dispel the seriousness of the conversation, feeling that despite the fact that they were such physical opposites she was close to him. She might even take Clyde home some at some time in the future, if things went on being good between them. Mum and Dad would like that; they were determined and old-fashioned liberals. Good people really. She felt a sudden surge of affection towards her parents that took her by surprise. Mum and Dad were the kind of folk you joined the police to protect.

DS Northcott twisted his paper napkin in his hands and she realized that he was wondering how to phrase something. Eventually, he said, 'I was hoping that you could advise me on something, Elaine.'

It was the first time he'd used her forename, though he'd told her that she should call him Clyde on her first day here. She said, 'It can't possibly be on a police matter. You have all the answers there and I have none.'

He forced a smile and she decided that he was more attractive like this. She liked her men to look vulnerable occasionally. She'd never thought that the formidable DS Clyde Northcott, the 'hard bastard' of police gossip and the talk of the women's locker room, could ever look vulnerable. He said, 'It's this damned tennis club and your friend Olive Crawshaw.'

She grinned, happy to be on ground where she felt at home and he felt uncomfortable. 'Birch Fields is quite an exclusive club. You should feel honoured to be invited – especially by Olive Crawshaw.'

'I don't do exclusive. I'm no good at exclusive.' He looked suddenly like a small boy admitting that he couldn't swim.

'You'll be all right with Olive on your side. It will be like being Percy Peach's man here. She'll see you through any initial difficulties.'

'But I'm not even sure I want to join.'

'You need the exercise. You roar about on that great bike of yours, but you don't go to gyms or play any sports, apart from a few games of football during the winter for the police team.' She was shocked by how motherly she sounded, with this man who was three years older and infinitely more experienced in life than she was.

For his part, Clyde was surprised by how much she seemed to know about him. He would have resented that in a young male recruit to the service, but he found he rather liked it in her. Sexist, it must be. 'I used to enjoy sport when I was a kid. Had a trial with the Rovers, but didn't make it. I was like all kids – I wanted to play in attack and score goals. I should have been a defender.' His torso moved a little at the table and his neck muscles tensed for a moment, as if he was preparing to head away a shot at goal.

'If you're frightened of making a fool of yourself on the tennis court, we could—'

'I've played before. Quite a lot when I was a kid. Only on the public courts in the park – not in a club. But I wasn't bad. Not then.' He was surprised how important it was to him that this lively girl didn't think he was a novice.

'That's good, then. It will soon come back, once you get hold of a racket again.'

'I played a fortnight ago, actually. At Birch Fields, as a guest. A pal of mine invited me along for a game. It was afterwards that Mrs Crawshaw decided I should become a member. She plonked the application form in front of me and signed as my proposer.' He packed all the facts of the situation into one swift speech, as if he wished to be rid of them and thrust the initiative into the hands of PC Elaine Brockman.

She giggled. 'Well, there you are, then. No use trying to resist Olive Crawshaw. You'd be like Canute trying to turn back the tide.'

'That's exactly how it feels. I'm used to making my own decisions; this one's been made for me.'

'Lie back and think of England, Clyde. You might even enjoy it.'

He did not share her mirth. 'It's all right for you. It's not you who has to suffer the agonies. I'm supposed to turn up for interview on Wednesday evening, then play at the weekend if I'm accepted as a member.' He stared glumly at the table and his empty plate. 'I could always mess up the interview, I suppose. If bloody Mrs Crawshaw would allow me to do that.'

'I'm a member at Birch Fields myself, you know.'

'No, I didn't know.' He looked as if he was revising his attitude and reconsidering his reactions.

'I haven't played much over the last three years whilst I was away at university.' She smiled at the big man, wondering how to put this tactfully. 'Are you worried about being made to look foolish on the court? Everyone has to begin, you know. Everyone starts as a novice.'

'I'm not a novice. Well, not really. I told you, I used to be quite useful on the public courts. But I'm out of practice. And I've never played at anywhere like Birch Fields. I don't know the etiquette of places like that.'

'It's the same game, you know, wherever it's played. The court is still seventy-eight feet long and thirty-six feet wide. The net is still three and a half feet high and the service line is still twenty-one feet away from it.'

Things you learn as an enthusiastic child stick with you: the figures came back to her as swiftly and as effortlessly as a Federer backhand. Clyde was impressed. 'I used to have a good serve.' He grinned in fond remembrance, opening his broad chest almost as if he was about to throw a ball up.

'I'll bet you did.' She looked over the empty plates into the large black face, which at this moment looked uncharacteristically uncertain. 'We could have a game tomorrow night, if you like. Just a knockabout to give you a little practice and a little confidence before you meet La Crawshaw on Wednesday.' Elaine felt almost like a tart as she made the offer. She was used to fending off advances, not making them herself. But she knew Northcott would have been far too diffident to ask. Now she'd opened the way for a rejection and a snub.

Instead, he said, 'I'd like that. Just don't expect me to be much good.'

'I'll expect you to be erratic. Will that do? Brilliant in flashes, perhaps.'

'I'll try hard to be brilliant in flashes, Elaine.' He'd used her name again. It had come almost naturally this time.

Birch Fields was indeed an exclusive tennis club, as PC Brockman had said. But 'exclusive' does not mean morally impeccable. Dictionary definitions of the word include words like 'moneyed' and 'snobbish'. You can be either or both of these without being of good character. A few of the club's three hundred members sailed very near the law. And one or two of them went well beyond it.

One of these was Jason Fitton. His father had made his money from scrap metal, surprising even himself with the profits he made from what other people had discarded. Derek Fitton had worked hard, very hard, especially in his early days. But his work had paid off: in the 1950s and 1960s, few people had realized the value of scrap. And the last great boom in the manufacturing industry had raised the value of what the techniques of the time were learning to recycle expertly for new uses.

Young Jason had been sent to one of the best public schools in the country, where he had been educated in all sorts of things. For a start, he had learned to speak very differently from his rough-hewn father. He had learned to play rugby and tennis to a reasonable standard, he had developed a dress sense which his father's money enabled him to indulge, and he had learned how to manipulate people. Birch Fields had seemed his natural environment when he returned to Brunton in the 1990s prepared to make his mark on the new century. The tennis club had been happy to welcome him. His skills carried him along as a young man. His money and his influence in the town carried him much further as the years passed and the trends of the new century became apparent.

It would not be fair to ascribe all of his characteristics to his public school. His Eton reports had said consistently that he associated with the wrong company, though there was no note of why such company was tolerated in this most august and reputable of private educational institutions. Jason was now a womanizer: determined, charming and wholly unscrupulous. In 2005, there had even been a move by devastated women and disaffected husbands to exclude Jason from the tennis club. But he paid for all-weather surfacing of two of the courts, had himself elected to the committee and made himself virtually undismissable. Ten years later, most of the members were unaware of or had forgotten his transgressions.

Jason Fitton's business ethics were very different from his father's. A new generation needed new ways, Jason claimed, and he was the man to introduce them. Even to invent them, when he thought that was necessary. He took over his father's business, gave even more powers to its managing director and instructed him to cut whatever corners were necessary to keep the scrap metal profits flowing. But as the new century advanced, the company became increasingly a respectable front for other and darker enterprises. Jason wanted faster and bigger bucks than those achieved by his father's honest toil.

He spotted quickly that drink, sex and gambling would be the social curses of the new century. That meant that they would also be cash cows for anyone willing to meet demand and develop wider facilities. Fitton was the man behind new casinos in Brunton and other Lancashire towns. He controlled an increasing number of brothels in north and east Lancashire; it was a foolish tart who elected to go it alone and operate without one of Fitton's pimps. If new prostitutes were wise, they saw sense quickly and paid their dues to their controllers; if they were foolish or stubborn, they soon had damage to their faces that ensured that they would need to follow some other and less lucrative trade. Broken noses, stitched foreheads and permanently scarred cheeks did not bring in the punters, as Fitton's enforcers were always eager to point out.

Jason had been keeping a low profile for three months now. He had narrowly avoided arrest on charges related to the procurement and grooming of underage girls. He had been implicated in the scandals in Rochdale and Rotherham, but the lawyers of the Crown Prosecution Service had ruled that there was insufficient evidence to mount a successful prosecution against him. This was much to the disgust of the undercover police who had worked long and hard to trap him. Fitton dismissed with contempt any suggestions that he might have been involved, but he was wise enough to know that he must watch his step carefully for a while.

Jason Fitton played tennis at five o'clock on this late-July day, clothed in the finest shirt and shorts that money could buy, behaving impeccably, sportingly calling any tight line decisions against himself. He was still good enough to win against an opponent ten years younger than himself. He bought drinks in the club bar which had just had its licence renewed after his intervention and then left amidst noisy bonhomie, having explained to those enjoying his hospitality that business called.

Business meant a visit to his office in the private section at the back of the town's casino, where three heavily built men were awaiting his instructions. They knew their place in this world created for them by Jason Fitton. They spoke when they were spoken to and awaited their master's bidding. They behaved like obedient, oversized, highly dangerous children.

Fitton sat down at his desk and glanced at the trio for a moment before gesturing to the chairs in front of it. Then he addressed himself very deliberately to the tallest of the three. 'Have the pigs been bothering you, Abe?'

Abe Lockhart noted the use of his first name. It was a badge of status in front of the other two, whom Fitton had so conspicuously ignored. He took his time, wishing to emphasize that status. The pecking order is surprisingly important to men who live by physical violence; brutality makes the codes more simple but more crucial. 'The fuzz have been watching us, Mr Fitton, hoping to pick things up. We've given them nothing to bite on, as per your instructions.'

Fitton nodded. 'They'll get bored. And if they don't get results, they'll switch resources. They have to: they don't have infinite numbers and they've got other problems. If we give them nothing for a couple of months, they'll be off to deal with other things. They have to produce results to wave at the public. They survive on that.'

'You know best, boss.' The men who paid you always liked to be told that, however big they grew. It was one of the few things Abe Lockhart had learned in the rough trade he practised. There wasn't much call for PR when you dealt in cut flesh and broken bones. 'What should we do about Forshaw and these betting shops?'

'Is he still saying that he won't sell to us?'

'Not at the price you named to him. He says Ladbrokes have offered him more.'

They probably had, but he hadn't yet sold to them. Fear was still a great tool when you were dealing with small-time operators like Dave Forshaw. He owned three betting shops in Brunton and its satellite towns. They weren't especially profitable – online betting was now soaking up much of the market – but their very existence was an affront to Fitton. He wanted a monopoly of the direct betting outlets in the area and he wanted other people to see that he had it. Jason looked at the expectant, recently idle faces opposite him. 'It's time to make a move. Whilst the pigs are busy watching our pimps and the Pakis we've been supplying with girls, they won't have any eyes on Forshaw.'

Lockhart nodded, his face twisting into an anticipatory leer, like that of a glutton thinking of steak. 'We can take him out, boss. How much damage do we do to him?'

The man next to him wrung his hands together and then clasped his fists and pretended to spit upon them. Fitton was filled with a sudden revulsion for these men he employed, as Macbeth had been for the men he hired to kill Banquo. A public school education was not always an advantage when you made your living as he did. 'Leave Forshaw for the moment,' he said. 'Take out one of his managers. The one in Darwen. If he doesn't see the light and take our offer after that, we'll give him the battering he's asking for.' Never go for the big man unless you had to; go for the weakest point in his armoury. Forshaw was small beer compared with Fitton. But he had certain friends in the town. It was better that he capitulated without the pressure being made too obvious.

'How far do you want us to go, boss?' Lockhart spoke like a skilled artisan anxious to exhibit his craft. The men beside him leaned forward eagerly.

'Not too far. Don't go killing the poor sod. Excites too much interest, a death does. You can break an arm or a leg and the odd rib, make his face look like only his mother would love it, but don't see the bugger off.'

Lockhart looked at the others, received nods of acceptance. 'You want me to speak to Forshaw again? Give him the chance to change his mind?' It was the nearest he could come to humour and his squat features twisted into a slow grin.

Abruptly, Jason Fitton needed to be rid of them. They reminded him too vividly of what he was. He wanted the ample riches he now controlled, but he hated the instruments he used to gather them. The men trooped out of the office on his dismissal and he sat silently at his desk for a few moments. He left only five minutes after his enforcers. His manager, who was setting up the gaming tables, was happy to see him go. With his smooth and largely unlined face, his expertly cut dark blonde hair and his dark blue Savile Row suit, Jason Fitton was the most handsome presence here throughout the day.

He was also by far the most dangerous one.

Detective Chief Inspector Percy Peach had endured a difficult day. He'd spent a hectic twenty minutes persuading the CPS that they had a very strong case against Sean Catterick, when it should have been obvious to them that the rawest newly qualified lawyer could put him away. With his temper and self-control stretched to breaking point by this, he'd then spent the end of his day with Chief Superintendent Thomas Bulstrode Tucker, the man in nominal charge of Brunton CID. Tommy Bloody Tucker always annoyed him, and with his nerves frayed by the lawyers, he hadn't been able to summon the resources to bait his chief as he normally did.

He was glad to reach the battered 1930s semi-detached he called home, and even more pleased to see the blue Corsa in the drive, which signified that his wife was home before him. Detective Sergeant Lucy Blake had been his bagman (she objected rather fiercely to being described as his baglady). But she had been made to relinquish that role when she married him: police convention was that partners did not work together. Lucy was still a DS in the CID section, but, as Lucy Peach, she could no longer work with Percy. She missed that connection more than she was prepared to admit.

She was stirring a pan of her home-made mushroom soup when Percy entered the house and took advantage of her preoccupation to stroke her bottom and then slide his hands round to her buxom belly. She twitched a little and then threatened him with a hot pan lid; neither action forced him to relinquish his hold upon her. She waved the spoon at him and said the first thing that came into her head to divert him. 'How's Clyde Northcott getting along?'

Percy was aware that there was a small part of his wife that wanted her successor to fail, or at least not to be as successful as she had been. She was allowed to be human, he supposed. 'Clyde's doing OK. He doesn't offer everything that you used to offer.' He stroked her bottom again, receiving a sharp rap as she put down her stirring spoon, and said as dolefully as he could, 'Everything moves on, doesn't it? Nothing is the same from year to year.' His face darkened. 'Except Tommy Bloody Tucker.'

'You used to use me to play the soft cop. Clyde doesn't seem cut out for that.'

'No. He's the hard bastard. I use my immense versatility to play the sympathetic and understanding role you used to undertake.'

She grinned at the thought of Percy in that guise. He wasn't going to give her anything but jokes, as usual. He was too loyal to his staff to denigrate Northcott, even to please her. That was admirable in him and she wouldn't have wanted it any other way, she told herself firmly.

She had news for him, big news, but she decided he would have to wait for that. She'd choose her moment to make the maximum effect. In fact, she was wondering just what words to use and treasuring these last moments when she could hug her knowledge to herself. 'Set the table and get into your comfortable gear,' she ordered sternly. 'This will be ready in five minutes.'

The soup was good and she had curry ready to follow it. Pretty well his favourite meal, she calculated. Almost as if she was luring him into a good mood to deliver bad news, instead of the news she had. He was good in the house, Percy. Quite the modern man, in fact. If he was home before her, as he was on some days, he wired in to the domestic chores or got a meal ready. He pretended exactly the opposite at the station, of course, but that was his way. He liked to be the caricature of the chauvinist pig who exploited the women around him. But she had realized years ago that he was the opposite in many respects of most of the images he chose to create. They were a carapace to protect the man within.

They took their time over the meal, swapping snippets of

information about their days. They were smacking their lips over strawberries and cream when he judged it safe to speak of his new bagman again. 'Clyde's been asked to join a tennis club. Well, not just *a* tennis club. Birch Fields Tennis Club.'

'Cor! He'll stand out like a sore thumb there.' She grinned at the thought of the huge black man standing awkwardly amongst weedy whites. 'Is that racist?'

Percy affected to weigh the suggestion seriously before shaking his head. 'I shouldn't think so. It's more in the nature of a statement of fact.'

There was a pause whilst both of them considered the image of Clyde Northcott in tight shorts amidst the Brunton middle classes on the immaculate surfaces of the courts at the town's most exclusive tennis club.

Then Lucy was seized with concern for Clyde, of whom she was very fond, despite the fact that he had succeeded her. 'Does he play tennis?'

'Apparently, he was quite good at some time in the distant past.'

'It can't be so distant. He's five years younger than me.'

'You'll always be twenty-three to me, my love.'

'Bugger off! I can see Clyde creating waves at Birch Fields. I hope he knows what he's letting himself in for.'

'He's no fool. He can't be if he's taken your place.' Percy checked his bullshit metre swiftly and carried on. 'He's got specialist advice. Our new graduate-entry officer seems now to be his tennis adviser.'

'Elaine Brockman? She seems a nice kid, from what little I've seen of her.'

'Clyde obviously thinks so. He seems anxious to put himself in her hands.' Percy smiled lasciviously. As his bagman had told Elaine earlier in the day, there wasn't much that went on in Brunton nick without Percy Peach knowing about it.

They watched a repeated episode of *Downton Abbey* on the television – Percy had been sceptical of it when it was first released, but Lucy had managed to convince him to give it a go. Lucy, still full of anticipation of the delivery of her great news, could not concentrate. Percy, with his arm round her shoulders on the sofa, eventually said, 'I know you like the period detail and I can see why. The costumes and the rooms are bloody marvellous. But the dialogue is crap.'

'That's what the *Times* review said – in slightly more eloquent terms.'

'I haven't read it,' said Percy defensively. 'I can't help it if great minds think alike.'

She snatched the remote from him impulsively and switched off the set. He stared at her in surprise, wondering if he was about to receive a connubial bollocking for spoiling her enjoyment.

'I'm pregnant!' she said.

She'd spent much of the day thinking of ways to phrase her news, by turns humorous, romantic and triumphant. In the crisis, she'd simply blurted it out in its most basic form.

Percy's response was equally basic. He turned her towards him so that she looked him full in the face and said, 'Bloody hell, Nora!' Then a beam that said much more than words suffused his face. He took her in his arms and embraced her long and tenderly. He sat and stared into her happy face again and repeated, 'Bloody hell, Nora!'

'You have such a way with words!' she said. But she was more pleased by his silence than she would have been by a rush of unnecessary eloquence.

The late-July evening meant that the bedroom was pleasantly warm, a contrast with the winter cold which made the anti-quated heating system a perpetual source of complaint for Lucy. In contrast with his usual practice, Percy took longer to reach the sheets than his wife, as if the gravitas of the great news he carried was slowing his movements. Once there, he lay on his back beside her and directed what he thought must be a final 'Bloody hell, Nora!' at the ceiling.

Lucy giggled a little beside him, waited a few moments for a movement which did not come, and then said softly into his ear, 'I could do with a cuddle.'

He moved cautiously to comply, stroking her shoulder blades, running his hands gently over the small of her back as tenderly as if it was the first time he had touched it, cupping the ample curves of her bottom as gently he had in their early, tentative days. She threw herself enthusiastically against him, then realized the reason for his unwonted caution. She said rather fiercely into his ear, 'I won't break, you know. I'm in the earliest stage of pregnancy, not recovering from a serious operation.'

'Are you sure? I don't want to—'

'Get on with it, you daft wally! Before I lose the urge.'

'I couldn't let you do that. But you may need to take the initiative.'

So she did. And it was wonderful. Percy wasn't sure how long it was before he gazed at the ceiling again with an exhausted grin. 'BLOODY HELL, NORA!'

'You see, I didn't come apart in your hands.'

'No, you certainly didn't do that. It was quite reassuring really. And several other things as well.' Some time later, when she thought he had dropped into the sleep his efforts had warranted, Percy Peach said drowsily, 'Will it be girls on top all the time now?'

THREE

T he man in charge of the betting shop in Darwen was older than Abe Lockhart had expected him to be.

He watched him for a while to make sure that he was in fact the manager. He was definitely in charge of things; he was issuing orders to the staff and seemed to have a good relationship with them. One of the younger women went and spoke to him in his office, obviously asking if she should accept a large stake on first race of the following day at Goodwood. The manager asked her a few questions, then nodded and smiled at her. She seemed to know him well and there was no hint of any sexual harassment. For a man who made his living by violence, Lockhart could be quite a Puritan when it came to sexual harassment.

Betting is one of the growth industries of modern Britain. The shop did a steady trade, without being at any time hectically busy. The manager left his office and talked to the punters at one point. He seemed quite an affable chap. Pity he was going to suffer, really, especially as he'd done nothing personally to offend Jason Fitton. He was merely a pawn in a very ugly game. Abe told himself that he couldn't be too choosy about ugly games: he'd be out of a job without them.

Abe Lockhart was an executive now, he supposed – he'd always been a little puzzled by what that word meant. He was issuing orders to his subordinates here, supervising the successful completion of an operation. That surely must make him an executive. He went back to the car, which was parked no more than fifty yards from the alley they had agreed upon, and spoke to the two ape-like figures within it. 'Right. Place will be shutting in around five minutes. Time you were in position. Remember what we agreed.' His chest swelled a little with pride as he watched the two big men move swiftly into the shadows he had indicated.

*　　*　　*

Clyde Northcott had been right about his serve. When he got it in, it was a good one. The problem was going to be getting it in with any consistency.

They'd knocked the balls around carefully for ten minutes before they started. Clyde had been conscious of a swelling group of boys in their early teens beyond the tall metal fence that surrounded the courts. They were assembling to appreciate the curves of his opponent rather than her tennis skills. He was wondering what he should do about this, rather than concentrating on honing his rusty timing of the forehand drive, when Elaine Brockman dismissed the boys in this fan club with a phrase that was vigorous, unladylike and surprisingly effective – the youths pissed off as bidden, as they would not have done for him. This girl had hidden depths, even if they were hardly romantic ones.

Clyde was still pondering this when she used a similar expression to him. He was astounded, because he didn't think he'd done anything wrong. Apparently, his fault was that he was treating her with too much consideration. 'I'm not a child learning the game. I'm a woman who's played for years. I'm a bit rusty, as you are, but I shall be highly insulted if you continue to play patball with me!'

Clyde wasn't aware that he'd been doing that. He'd been taking it easy, admittedly, but that was mainly because he wanted to get the ball into the court and avoid making a fool of himself in front of this enchanting presence. As if to emphasize her point, Elaine now timed a backhand perfectly and sent it speeding past his despairing racket to hold her service and claim the first game. Then she stalked back to the baseline, crouched ready to receive his service and gave him a quite annoying grin.

Enough was enough. There were limits, even with a woman who looked like this. Clyde frowned fiercely, tossed the ball for the first time precisely where he wanted it above his head, and produced a serve that recalled his best ones as an erratic sixteen-year-old. It whistled past his floundering opponent and he snarled, 'That one fast enough for you?'

'Not bad. Was it a fluke, though? Are you going to produce them with any consistency?' Elaine walked to the backhand court, danced on her toes in preparation and gave him a smile designed to infuriate. The ball flashed past her an instant later, but it was wild and long, the first half of an ignominious double fault. Clyde found his opponent giving him that smile again as he mouthed a silent oath.

Northcott got the message. He concentrated fiercely for the rest of their hour, telling himself that this girl could play, that this wasn't just the happy social outing he had anticipated when he had accepted her invitation to give him a little practice. And with concentration and honest effort, his muscle memory revived. By the end of the hour, he was timing his ground strokes quite well and the ball was flying away and pitching within court for the most part.

He realized belatedly that Elaine was a considerable player, though out of practice because she had played only intermittently during her university years. When his length was short, she was good enough to punish him; he also did his share of chasing unavailingly after balls into his backhand corner. But he managed to produce a couple of real cannonballs in his final service game, which enabled him to clinch the set with a flourish.

'You'll be OK,' was his mentor's verdict as they left the court. 'There's a pub beside the main entrance to the park which has a garden at the back where we can go in our tennis gear. Do you fancy a drink?'

'There's nothing I fancy more at this moment!' said Clyde. There was one thing, but even big black hard bastards had to be gentlemen on occasion.

'Just don't expect me to make the running all the time. It's not ladylike,' said his companion as she led the way.

Fitton's muscle waited a while to do their business with the betting shop manager. Daniel stayed in his office for a good ten minutes after his counter staff had departed, checking takings and records. It had been a successful day, in his judgement. Only one favourite had won, and that hadn't been heavily backed. The football season had not yet started and there had been neither a World nor a European Cup this year, which meant that the football pundits had been quiet. But betting men got itchy quickly and found other fields in which they could persuade themselves they were experts. With some ingenious combinations on offer, there were quite a few bets on cricket coming in, in this Ashes year.

He'd report his thoughts to his son-in-law. Takings were modest but steady, he thought; hopefully the business could stand on its own feet for a while yet. He was grateful to his son-in-law, Dave Forshaw, for letting him stand in as manager during the regular man's holiday.

It made you feel less useless when you could still take charge of a modest enterprise like this and deliver competent reports on the day's takings to the owner. And it was nice to be trusted, even if you were a relation. Daniel made sure that the safe was securely locked and shut the doors of the shop carefully. You might be a little slower when you'd passed sixty-five, but you were more thorough and more reliable than younger men with different concerns.

Daniel locked the door carefully, looked up and down the street, and found it deserted beneath the lamplight at this late hour. The sky had closed in and the first heavy drops of rain were beginning to fall. He was glad he'd remembered to bring his umbrella; he put it up and turned it against the wind and the beginnings of the rain. His car was only a hundred yards away and he was suddenly glad of that. He was surprised how tired he was after eight hours in the shop, even though he'd only taken over at two o'clock. He wasn't used to a full day's work any more, he told himself wryly. He swung his briefcase a little as he moved towards his car and home.

When it came, the attack was swift, effective and almost silent. These men knew their business, though in fact beating people up is by no means the intricate science they liked to pretend it was. They had a heavily gloved hand over the victim's mouth almost before he knew he was being attacked. His cheekbone was broken before he fell; the kicks upon his writhing body were delivered rapidly and clinically. Lockhart stooped over the prone figure in the alley, muttering a curse and an injunction to keep silent, but neither he nor his minions who had delivered the attack knew whether the victim was still conscious enough to hear them.

They were gone before anyone even realized there had been violence. Their car was three miles away on the road back to Brunton by the time a passing pedestrian heard the faint moans of their victim.

Clyde Northcott's interview for membership of Birch Fields Tennis Club had its humorous aspects. A theatre audience might have found it highly amusing, but there was no audience of any kind, and all of the people involved in the action were far too conscious of their positions and responsibilities to derive enjoyment from it at the time.

Clyde was dressed in a suit and tie. That was a novelty for a start. He usually wore sweaters and trousers for his plain-clothes CID work. Occasionally a jacket, if a visit to a particular place demanded it, but very rarely a tie. Few of the officers at Brunton nick had seen him wearing a tie since the mem-orable day a couple of years ago when he had featured as best man at the wedding of Percy Peach to Lucy Blake and set the bridesmaids aquiver with his presence. But he was feeling very stiff in suit and tie in the anteroom at the tennis club. He tried with scant success to look at ease as he waited his turn for interview and turned the pages of a tennis magazine he was not reading.

He still wasn't sure how he came to be here. At this moment, he was in fact quite sure that he didn't want to be here. It was mainly because of the steady insistence of Olive Crawshaw. Everyone told him that Mrs Crawshaw meant well and had his best interests at heart. That might be true. But all Clyde knew for certain was that Olive was not an easy woman to resist. He had tried, so he knew that. Mrs Crawshaw hadn't even acknowledged his resistance, let alone produced argu-ments against it. She was an irresistible force of nature. Tsunamis must be like her, Clyde felt; he hoped she would not leave similar disasters in her wake.

There were three people for interview and Clyde was the last on the list. He'd hoped to see the other two when they'd been before the committee, so that he could discover how they'd been treated and maybe pick up a few pointers for his own exchanges. But they did not come back to join him; it was as though they had disappeared from his life when they passed through the door at the end of the room and into the inner sanctum of the committee. He'd seen a film a month or two ago about people in Stalinist Russia who became non-persons and disappeared from the face of the earth without leaving any traces behind them. They must have felt much as he did as they waited for the decisions of Beria and the KGB. That was ridiculous, Clyde Northcott told himself firmly. This wasn't life and death. It just felt like it.

He couldn't hear anything from the room beyond the door, hard as he strained. There was a low hum of conversation, but not a single word could he distinguish. Once he heard what he thought might be laughter, but he couldn't be certain. His heightened imagination pictured something much more sinister. As each minute dragged past, he just wanted this business over and done with, wanted more than anything to be hurtling through the night on his Yamaha and feeling the cool, uncomplicated breeze against his face. Yet when a man with a cheerful face opened the door and called him in, he wished illogically that this confrontation could be postponed indefinitely.

The man said that he was the secretary. He led Clyde to the appointed chair and introduced each of the other four people behind the table. Clyde nodded a nervous acknowledgement to each of them in turn but registered not a single name or office as they were enunciated to him. He knew Olive Crawshaw. She sat at the chairman's right hand. Like the Son of God, some forgotten and unwelcome voice from Clyde's childhood reminded him. She gave him a bright smile, which he realized belatedly was meant to be encouraging. He grinned weakly back at her, but the chairman was already directing his first question at this last interviewee of the evening.

'I see from your application form that you are a police officer, Mr Northcott. We don't get many of them applying for membership of our club.'

Clyde said, 'I see.' There didn't seem to be much else to say. He could think of lots of reasons why policemen and policewomen wouldn't want to apply for membership of Birch Fields Tennis Club. Principally, because they wouldn't want to be sitting exactly where he was now, trying to find answers to all sorts of stupid questions. It didn't seem that it would be helpful to voice that thought at this moment. So he grinned weakly and said nothing more.

It was left to the chairman to say, 'Can you think why that would be?'

Clyde said, 'Not many officers play tennis. Not compared with football and cricket. And even golf, I think.' Percy Peach had been a damned good cricketer, it seemed. And, apparently, nowadays he was quite a good golfer. He'd never mentioned playing tennis. Clyde said desperately, 'We're getting a lot more women recruits nowadays. I imagine more of them play tennis.'

Olive Crawshaw said brightly, 'So you might prove to be an ambassador. The Pied Piper who leads in a whole phalanx of your colleagues behind you, Mr Northcott.'

The chairman did not seem to think that would be a welcome development. Arthur Swarbrick looked Clyde up and down and said, 'Why do you wish to become a member of Birch Fields, Mr Northcott?'

Clyde had rehearsed the answer to this: it was an obvious question. But what he had prepared deserted him at the critical moment. He said desperately, 'I used to play when I was a boy – well, a youth really. And I play football, but I don't really do any other sports. So I'm doing nothing in the summer as far as sports go. I sort of thought that . . .'

Olive Crawshaw came forcefully to his rescue as he faltered. 'Mr Northcott is a player of considerable talent and a young man of pleasing personality. He would be a valuable addition to our list of members.'

'You've seen him play, have you, Olive?' This was the secretary, presumably trying to be helpful.

He received a withering glance for his query. 'I haven't personally witnessed Mr Northcott's performance on the courts, but I have received excellent reports of it. He is far too modest to boast of his talents here, but I have reason to believe that he would be a considerable asset to the playing resources of the club, as well as a desirable addition to our membership, for the reasons I have already specified in sponsoring his application.'

There was a pause whilst the interview committee members consulted their copies of Clyde's application form. Then the chairman said, 'Birch Fields is an exclusive club. I make no apology for the use of that adjective. It means in my book that we have standards and that we maintain quality.' Swarbrick cleared his throat menacingly, as though daring anyone to challenge him, and addressed himself directly to Northcott. 'There has of late been a move to expand the social boundaries of our membership. You would be one of the implementations of this new policy.'

Clyde caught a stirring of discomfort in both Olive Crawshaw and the secretary. It was probably that which enabled him to find his voice and speak with conviction for the first time. 'Do you mean that I'm to be the bit of rough life that will demonstrate to the town how enlightened you have become?'

In the shocked silence, it was Olive Crawshaw who recovered first. She darted a venomous look at the chairman beside her and then said equably, 'Not at all, Mr Northcott. I'm sure I speak for the committee and the membership at large when I say that we welcome a relaxing of those social boundaries that have long been out of date. You may come from a very different background from that of most of our older members, but you will be all the more welcome for that. And you will be by no means isolated within the club by the nature of your family background. We are planning to recruit many other players from what would once have been called the working classes.'

The chairman seemed to have frozen, but there were stirrings of assent amongst his companions and even a muttered 'Hear! Hear!' from someone away to his left. Then the person on his immediate left spoke for the first time, raising an issue that was in the mind of everyone in the room but one which no one had cared to broach. Jason Fitton said quietly, 'Do you think your ethnic background would cause you any problems in this club?'

Northcott knew Fitton and his reputation, though he had never spoken to him face to face before. He was gathering confidence now from the divisions he sensed on the other side of the table. 'My ethnic background is no problem to me. My

colour might raise problems for others. I haven't so far seen
other black faces at Birch Fields.'

The issue that had been in every mind, including Clyde's,
was out in the open at last. Better to have it discussed here
and now, he thought, than in guarded tones in his absence.
No skin off his nose: he could still walk away from this,
whatever Mrs Crawshaw thought, if it pleased him to do so.
He thought it probably would.

The chairman said hastily, 'I'm sure there is no racism in
this club. I've never been aware of any.'

Those two weren't quite the same thing, as his fellow
committee members were aware. Olive Crawshaw took a deep
breath. 'We already have a considerable number of Asian
members, Mr Northcott. Since you raise the issue, I have to
admit that I think you will be the first black person to become
a member of our club. I think you are probably also the first
one to apply. My opinion – and my intention – is that you
will be the first of many.'

Clyde felt suddenly very calm. He could not have said why,
but he was aware now of all the information he thought had
passed him by during the introductions. 'I am grateful to Mr
Fitton for raising this issue. I would far rather it was discussed
openly than muttered about behind embarrassed hands.'

The secretary said, 'Doors that were previously shut to able
people like Mr Northcott are opening all over the country. We
wish Birch Fields to be a leader in matters like this. We do
not wish to give the impression of being dragged unwillingly
behind the rest of Brunton society.'

If they were making their first move in this direction in
2015, they were far from leaders in the area. But Clyde wasn't
looking for a fight. People soon decided you had a chip on
your shoulder if you chose to discuss colour at length. He
said, 'I'm glad we haven't skirted the matter, as happens so
often. In response to Mr Fitton's original question, I would
say that I do not anticipate any problems here deriving from
my colour. Backhand volleys might give me much more
trouble. And I have found the backhand smash totally
impossible.'

It was a welcome infusion of humour into a situation that

had become very taut. All the other members of the committee knew what the chairman's views on this were. Everyone knew that he had resisted efforts to broaden social recruitment and that it had only been the prospect of losing his position of eminence that had brought him to a reluctant acceptance of the new policy. Arthur Swarbrick had one final arrow in his quiver, which he now dispatched towards Clyde without prior warning. 'What did you do before you joined the police service, Mr Northcott?'

The man in isolation on the other side of the table took his time. He should have expected this, he thought. He was used to grilling people himself, and Percy Peach had taught him to produce his sharpest weapon when it was least expected. He said, 'I had various jobs. My longest period of employment was as an apprentice at the Mullard's electric factory.'

'And did you complete that apprenticeship?'

'I suspect you already know that I did not.'

'And why was this, Mr Northcott?'

Clyde shrugged his powerful shoulders. 'My mother would tell you that I got into bad company. I prefer to take responsibility for my own actions. I didn't work as hard as I should have done. I was very foolish. You don't get paid very much as an apprentice and my friends always seemed to have more money than I had. I discovered other ways of making money, which seemed at the time easier and more attractive. I was mistaken.'

Someone moved to alter this line of questioning, but Swarbrick held up his hand and smiled. He hadn't got his own way very often recently on the matter of recruitment to the club. This was an opportunity to show these stupid liberals that he was right and they were very wrong. The club needed recruits from the top drawer, and this big black man was certainly not top drawer. No one used that expression any more, but he knew what he meant by it. He wondered how strongly he could put his next point. Better be a little cautious, he decided: the bugger was a policeman and no doubt knew all about his rights. 'Were you involved with drugs at that time?'

Clyde felt very calm now. He didn't even feel any great

resentment against this old fogey. Swarbrick was a man of his time and a relic of that time: you didn't expect tolerance from men like him. He probably wasn't going to get into this tennis club now, but that didn't greatly matter, did it? He'd never quite understood why he was putting himself through tonight's experience. 'I was involved with illegal drugs, yes. For a very short period, I was even supplying them: I was not just a user but a small-time dealer. It was at that time that I first became seriously involved with the police.'

This was good, Swarbrick thought. He'd expected the man to be evasive, but he was serving his own head up on a plate. The chairman tried not to sound too truculent as he leaned forward and said, 'I think you should elucidate for us, Mr Northcott.' Then, in case the man did not understand, he said, 'Tell us all about this, please.'

Clyde enunciated every syllable distinctly as he said, 'I'm quite prepared to elucidate, Mr Swarbrick. I was a drug user myself for a time. I was never a heavy user and never in danger of becoming an addict. I said just now that I became seriously involved with the police and I should tell you how. I was questioned several times in connection with a murder that had taken place. I was completely innocent but for a time things looked very bad for me. I am in serious debt to the investigating officer in that case. He not only cleared my name but saw something in me that I had never seen in myself. Having established my innocence, he encouraged me to consider the police service as a career. I did so and have been fortunate since then to proceed to my present post.'

The words came easily to him, though he had never planned anything like this before he came here. It was the first time he had publicly stated his debt to Percy Peach; the DCI had firmly suppressed any efforts to do that at the station. There was a silence: perhaps his listeners wanted to be certain that he had finished his peroration. Then Olive Crawshaw said quietly, 'I think we should thank this candidate for being so frank with us. We much appreciate your honesty, Mr Northcott. Not everyone who seeks membership of Birch Fields is as honest as you have been tonight.' She glanced along the table to each side of her. 'Unless there are any further questions, I think we should now ask Mr Northcott to withdraw whilst we consider his application.'

Swarbrick seemed anxious to put further questions. But the secretary nodded and said quickly, 'If you would wait outside for a few minutes, Mr Northcott, we might be able to give you a decision tonight before we confirm it formally in writing within the next few days.'

As he sat on his own in the lounge, Clyde was surprised to find that his fingers were shaking slightly as he looked at them. It had been a strange business in there. He'd felt totally out of his depth at the beginning, marooned in an alien environment. Then, when first Fitton and then Swarbrick had offered him challenges, he had felt much more at home, much more determined to make his point than he had at the outset, when he'd scarcely cared what they thought of him.

He was surprised to find that there were still people playing tennis outside. He could hear the healthy thwack of ball on racket and the calls of the players. But the sun had already set and they wouldn't be able to play for much longer. He tried to visualize himself out there, playing a men's doubles perhaps, serving with all his might and dancing about at the net as he had done when he was still scarcely more than a boy.

They had good courts here. The two all-weather surfaces had crisp clear lines and an even, predictable bounce. He felt a pulse of enthusiasm for the game that he hadn't felt since he was sixteen and about to leave school. He'd come a long way since then: he wasn't the innocent, unthinking, gawky boy whom older men had said was 'promising' at tennis. It would be nice to come back to the game as a grown man and give it his best again. But probably he wouldn't be given the chance – not here, anyway. Those people who were in there discussing him knew all about his skeletons in the cupboard. They wouldn't want him because of his colour and his job, and the drugs business and his late-teens life would give them the excuses they needed to reject him.

'Mr Northcott?'

The secretary must have opened the door very quietly, because Clyde hadn't heard him. He was now shutting it equally carefully behind him before he turned to confront Clyde. 'I'm happy to tell you that the committee has accepted your application for membership of Birch Fields. You will receive the formal confirmation of that within the next few days, but I thought you would like to know immediately. May I be the first to offer my congratulations?'

They shook hands rather stiffly and then Clyde was away. He eased the Yamaha out of the car park and revved it very gently before moving away: a quiet exit was the least he could offer to Arthur Swarbrick, who he was quite sure had opposed his membership. The wind was cool upon his face, helping to control the unexpected exultation he felt. He'd stormed the citadel and triumphed. He had never thought it would mean so much to him.

Elaine was in the Bull's Head, the pub near her home where they had arranged to meet. 'Don't let the bastards grind you down!' had been her closing injunction to him as he'd left the station. He couldn't wait to give her his news.

He should have waited until he reached the table, but he saw her across the room and nodded at her with a great, stupid smile over the heads between them. She was on her feet by the time he reached the small table she had bagged for them. She threw her arms round his neck and kissed him hard upon the lips. Briefly, but on the lips. *Bloody hell, Clyde!*

FOUR

It was not a good beginning to a wet Thursday. DCI Peach had been summoned to the penthouse office of Chief Superintendent Thomas Bulstrode Tucker, Head of Brunton CID. It was pep-talk time.

'The Chief Constable is very pleased with my clear-up figures for serious crimes. Over the last six months for which statistics are available, they are apparently the best in the north of England.' Tucker clasped his hands on the table in front of him and tried unsuccessfully not to look smug.

Percy had seen the figures, though he hadn't anticipated that even Tommy Bloody Tucker would have the effrontery to claim the credit for himself. 'Best in the north-*west* of England, I believe, sir. East Yorkshire has even better figures than ours.'

Tucker waved a dismissive hand. 'Rural communities, Percy. Not strictly comparable with our urban hotbed, I always maintain.'

Peach didn't like the use of his first name. Any attempt at matiness from T.B. Tucker was usually a prelude to something unpleasant. 'Hotbeds are often useful to us, sir. It just depends whom we find in them.'

Tucker looked hard over the rimless spectacles he had recently adopted, wondering what to make of this statement. He decided that it was safest to ignore it. This was a time to be magnanimous. 'I am, as you are well aware, a fair man.' He tried to ignore his DCI's black eyebrows, which were rising in expressive arcs above the wide dark eyes. 'I am aware, as I hope any responsible senior policeman would be, that I have not achieved these figures alone. My success is not entirely due to my own efforts.'

He paused in expectation of assurances from his junior of his supreme excellence, but received only an irritating expression of total bafflement from Peach. He said with some irritation, 'I am saying that you have contributed to these excellent results, Peach. I would go so far as to say that I could not have achieved them without you.'

Percy was pleased to hear the return of his last name. He said sententiously, 'We are a team, sir. I work at the crimeface and confront the actual villains; you maintain your overview of the crime scene and bring to us a wider perspective.' You couldn't go wrong if you fed senior officers' own opinions back to them. That applied even when those opinions were meaningless bollocks, as Tommy Bloody Tucker's pronouncements invariably were.

Tucker stared at him suspiciously. As was often the case with Percy, he was sure that insolence was lurking, but he could not pin it down. 'I'm saying that you've done well, Peach.'

'Thank you, sir. I'll communicate your congratulations to the lads and lasses down below who have run the risks and produced the results.'

Tucker wasn't sure he wanted to go as far as that. People in the service should respect rank, he felt – especially his rank. He said gruffly, 'I'm offering you my congratulations, Peach. How far you choose to disseminate them is your own affair, but I would remind you of the need to maintain discipline in a society that seems increasingly to disregard it.' He waited for confirmation of this oft-repeated view, but found Percy staring at his ceiling. 'I don't want any slacking, Peach. I want standards to be maintained.'

'The price of freedom is eternal vigilance, sir.'

The look over the spectacles became a glare. 'That sounds like a quotation, Peach.' He spoke as if his DCI had produced the vilest obscenity.

'Might be Aristotle, sir,' Peach said cheerfully. 'Or might not.'

'Anyway, my instructions are that you should ensure that there is no slacking. I hope that is clear.'

'Eminently clear, sir. It gives me the chance to apprise you of our latest problem.'

'Problem, Peach?' Tucker asked heavily. He liked solutions, not problems.

'An ongoing problem, sir. Jason Fitton.'

'A prominent local businessman, Peach. An intelligent and well-educated man.'

'An intelligent and well-educated crook, sir. A man who covers his tracks well but who will eventually come to grief.'

'I am aware that he has at times been a suspect, but he has never been brought to court. He is a member of my Lodge.'

'That is not an automatic guarantee of integrity, sir.' Peach was studying the ceiling again, as if it was of surpassing interest to him.

Tucker resisted the impulse to look up there himself. 'He gives generously to the charities we support.'

'That does not surprise me, sir. You should take his money and deplore his morals.'

'Mr Fitton is a well-established and highly respected local employer. I would remind you that Fitton Metals is a sound and successful business.'

'It was when Jason's father ran it, sir. It is now no more than a front for far more dubious enterprises. Fitton owns most of the gambling outlets in our area, using dubious methods to maintain his monopoly. He also controls most of the brothels.'

'This is hearsay, Peach. Until you have concrete evidence, you would be well advised to—'

'Offers perks to policemen to encourage them to keep their mouths shut, sir. I don't suppose that he's made any suggestions to you at the Lodge, but—'

'Indeed he hasn't, Peach! And I tell you here and now that I resent the very suggestion that I would even consider—'

'Oh, indeed, sir. But some officers have in the past been tempted by the sexual gymnastics that are apparently on offer from Fitton's more experienced ladies of the night.'

'Peach, that is enough! I wish you to be aware that I have never been offered and have no desire to be offered any such favours!'

'No, sir. Of course not, sir. How fortunate are we who can get the full variety of sexual gymnastics in our own domestic environments.'

Peach fixed his attention on a new point of the ceiling, in the furthest corner of the room, and pictured Tommy Bloody Tucker exploring the wilder sections of the Kama Sutra with his wife, Brunhilde Barbara, nicknamed thus because of her Wagnerian physique and vocal volume. A slow smile slowly suffused the DCI's too-revealing features as the vision expanded and moved forward. Tucker looked at him with consternation and said rather desperately, 'If Jason Fitton is the danger you say he is, then of course we must keep our eye on him.'

'Yes, sir. I in the sleazier parts of the town, which his criminal empire dominates, and you in the more intimate exchanges of the Lodge.'

The glare became a glower. 'You should remember that no criminal charges have ever been brought against Mr Fitton. Proceed with discretion until you have real evidence, Peach. Innocent until proven guilty is still one of the pillars of our system.' Tucker jutted his chin in Churchillian mode and stared past Peach at some more acceptable world.

'And the price of freedom remains eternal vigilance, sir, as Aristotle may or may not have said. I shall remain vigilant wherever I see Mr Fitton's baleful hands at work.'

'I am sure you will find it very difficult to find the evidence you must have to pursue further action. And in the light of that—'

'You are quite right, sir. He makes it very difficult for us to find the evidence to bring him to court. There is a man in the intensive care ward of our hospital this morning as a direct result of Mr Fitton's orders, but I'm sure that as usual it will prove very difficult to trace the chain of command back to him.'

Chief Superintendent Tucker's eyes opened wide and focused hard upon his DCI. He was a copper, after all, though it was a long time since he had been an efficient or a likeable one. The last thing he wanted with his pension in sight was serious violence, maybe manslaughter. 'You must do what you have to do, of course. But proceed with caution.'

'I'll do that, sir.' For just a moment they were two law-enforcers in pursuit of a common enemy. Then the moment passed and Peach said, 'You wouldn't like to pursue this enquiry yourself, sir? In view of the seriousness of the incident and your intimate knowledge of our leading suspect?'

Tucker recoiled physically from the prospect of action. His body hit the back of his chair as he said, 'I never interfere

with my staff, as you know, Peach. I shall maintain my overview. And I don't know Mr Fitton anything like as well as
you seem to think I do.'

Best to distance yourself, if the man really was a villain.

Younis Hafeez had seen Clyde Northcott awaiting interview
at Birch Fields Tennis Club the previous evening. Interesting
that they were considering men like that. Hafeez had mixed
feelings about it.

It would take the heat off him in the club to an extent, he
supposed. Pakistanis were accepted here, as they were in most
other places in the town nowadays: with so many thousands
of them in positions of authority in Brunton and other northern
towns, you certainly couldn't ignore them. Asians were taking
over local government in many places, so the rest of the population had to pay attention to them. And men like Hafeez, who
had wealth and exercised power, commanded respect. Younis
knew better than most how respect followed in the wake of
power and money.

Birch Fields Tennis Club had been one of the last citadels
to fall, but there were three Pakistanis and a rather larger
number of Indians within its membership now – wealthy
Indians had always been tennis players. They were still resented
by some people, but that scarcely mattered any more: the tide
of public opinion was with them. A black man, who would
be so much more noticeable than them, wouldn't do any harm
to the standing of Asians in the tennis club, though. He would
divert what prejudice remained and make it easier for already
existing ethnic presences to establish themselves. Hafeez
thought he might even stand for the committee next year.

It would be easy enough to gain election if he chose the
right time and carried out the necessary preparatory work.
He'd get a hundred percent support from his fellow Pakistani
members; they'd harness the liberal section of the club which
he'd already identified and cultivated. That and the apathy that
usually attended the annual elections would see him home.
The hierarchy often had difficulty in persuading people to
stand for office in the club; there might not even be the need
for an election; he could wait to announce his candidacy until

the last day and simply make up the required number of nominees for the positions available. He knew how to manage these things: he'd taken over in other and more important places than tennis clubs.

He took out his keys and selected the key to the cleaners' room which he'd had cut three weeks ago. There was only one full-time cleaner, and she'd been glad to lend him her key for an hour for ten pounds. Hafeez had made sure that the bright new one which he now slid into the lock had been cut for him in half that time. The cleaner wouldn't split on him. She was rather in awe of him, and in any case she had far more to lose if her action was revealed.

There was never anyone in this room in the evenings. Hafeez installed himself in a chair by the window. There were all sorts of ways in which having a key to this room might be useful to him in the future. For now, this was sufficient. There was a small window that looked out on to the tennis courts; this was the nearest point in the clubhouse to them and you were within five yards of the wire fencing that surrounded the playing area and prevented balls from being lost. A point of vantage, where, if you positioned yourself sensibly, you could see without being seen. Seven o'clock on this bright summer evening was a good time to do this, Younis decided.

The women playing doubles were in their twenties, he decided after a few minutes of keen observation. They had very short white skirts and small, tight white pants beneath them. He was slightly below the level of the courts here: ideal for his purpose. He furiously cleaned the small pane of glass that was so vital to him when the women were at the net. They had tops without sleeves and he thought that one of them wasn't wearing a bra. But it was the lower end that interested him more. He'd scarcely seen more than an ankle when he was growing up, and the sight of racing calves and thighs and the glimpses of what lay above them still excited him, even after all the sexual experience he'd enjoyed over the last few years. He'd had girls recently, very young girls; their youth and their innocence had been most exhilarating. But he was keeping a low profile in that area, for the present.

It was much safer to interest yourself in the goods being displayed for you here. They were harlots, these English women, flashing their assets about for all to see. *Arsets*, more like. They didn't give a damn and they deserved whatever might happen to them, if they were going to flash their arses about like that for all to see. Well, for him to see, anyway. It gave him a thrill, as it always had, to know that they were unaware of his presence, that he was watching the movements of their flesh without them knowing it.

He had an erection now. The women had changed ends and there were new delights for him to see, new but equally brief pants. They didn't care as they stooped to pick up the balls at the back of the court, didn't even bend their knees in a show of modesty against prying eyes. Strumpets, they were, prancing about like that! But, then, only his dark eyes were prying, and they knew nothing about that.

He had a meeting in the middle of Brunton at eight. He must tear himself away from these erotic delights. He checked the sharp creases in the trousers of his expensive lightweight blue suit before he left the cleaners' room. No one saw him closing the door quietly behind him. The women were leaving the court as he came out of the club. They recognized the slim, good-looking Asian, though none of them had played with him, and called a cheerful greeting to him.

'Good evening, ladies!' he answered cheerfully as he passed them and moved towards his BMW. They had spoken with him enthusiastically, he thought. He sat for a moment behind the wheel of the big car before he started the engine. Shameless harlots. Deserved everything that was coming to them.

Peach knew from the first moment that he wasn't going to get anywhere.

He also knew that he had to play things exactly by the book. Jason Fitton was a man who knew all the rules, had expert and highly expensive lawyers, and would delight in turning the tables on him if given the slightest opportunity. None of these thoughts improved the DCI's spirits or temper.

Nor did the fact that an innocent pensioner who'd been badly injured was going to be unavenged. 'Daniel Grayson

had a night in intensive care. He is still under close observation in hospital.'

Fitton leaned back on the upright chair, contriving to look
at ease in a setting designed to make him feel exactly the
opposite. He smiled at the round face beneath the shining bald
head, well aware of the man's irritation. 'I'm sorry about that,
Chief Inspector Peach. One is always distressed to hear of
another's misfortune. Who is this man?'

'He was the manager of the betting shop in Darwen who
was brutally assaulted by your gorillas. I say "was" because
I don't think he'll ever work again.'

'That is sad – his situation, I mean. I don't know what you
mean by my "gorillas" and I utterly deny any connection with
the injury inflicted on this unfortunate man.' Jason sat back
again after delivering these words, even tipped his chair for a
moment on to its back legs to show how relaxed and unthreatened he felt. He looked with distaste around the interview
room, with its sage green walls and lack of windows. 'I came
here out of my sense of civic duty, because you asked me to
do that. I'm beginning to regret the public-spiritedness that
brought me to this place.'

Percy Peach regretted this meeting also. Fitton was only
here because you had to go through the diplomatic motions.
If, as a result of some later and greater crime, Fitton was
brought to justice, this violent assault might come home to
roost for him. It would be important in that event that he was
not able to say, 'Well, why did no one speak to me at the time
about this incident, if you thought I had any connection with
it?' You wasted your time now to cover yourself against hypothetical and frankly unlikely future events.

He stared hard at Jason Fitton's smug face, trying not to
reveal that he knew this was a contest he was going to lose.
'It will add to your sentence eventually, Mr Fitton. When
we arrest you and see you convicted of even greater and
even more vicious crimes, this one will be added to the
account.'

Fitton let a few long seconds elapse before he deigned to
reply. When you held all the important cards and your opponent
was playing a duff hand, it was a good tactic to take your time

and enjoy his discomfort. If an enemy lost his cool, he often did stupid things – like overplaying a duff hand. 'I think you had better be very careful about what you say here. I'm a fair man and a patient man, Chief Inspector. That's why I shouldn't like you to be accused of defamation of character.'

DS Northcott, who had said nothing so far whilst his leader silently seethed, now spoke as evenly as he could. 'The investigations in Rochdale and Rotherham have thrown up interesting information about other towns, including Brunton. There are a lot of people involved in the large-scale procurement of underage girls for the use of Asian and British middle-aged men.'

'I think you should leave this subject before you wander seriously out of your depth, DS Northcott.'

But for the first time Fitton had been a little disturbed. They had seen it in the momentary flutter of his eyelids. Northcott said, 'Names were mentioned. Yours was one of them, Mr Fitton. Enquiries are ongoing.'

Jason put his hands on the square table, pushed his chair back a little, prepared to rise. 'I do not have to stay here and listen to this.'

Peach was back in charge with even a hint of retreat in his adversary. 'Indeed you don't, Mr Fitton. Not today. Not even this week or this month. Perhaps not even this year. But the time will come.'

'I've had enough of this!' Fitton pushed himself up, but sank back when he could not rise elegantly. In this place, clumsiness seemed to him a confession of weakness.

'And when that time comes, your gorillas will turn into rats. Rats deserting a sinking ship. They'll be only too happy to put the blame on you for this and as many other crimes as they can, as they try to save their own miserable skins. I've seen it happen many times before.'

'I don't have to listen to this!' Fitton levered himself to his feet at last, stood staring down at Peach and Northcott. But he *had* listened, and the words would sing unwelcome in his head as he addressed himself to sleep that night.

It was Peach now who was unhurried as he stood up and said with formal irony, 'Thank you for coming in to the station to help us with our enquiries, Mr Fitton. I am unable say that the assistance you have given us is much appreciated.'

Fitton paused at the door of the small, square, claustrophobic room, trying to recover his normal smoothness and control. 'I expect I shall be seeing you in a different and more agreeable context, Mr Northcott, now that you have been accepted as a member at Birch Fields. Perhaps we might enjoy a game there together in the near future, Clyde.'

Long after he was gone, his use of Northcott's forename rang in the air like an insult.

Arthur Swarbrick's wife was not an optimist. She saw no cause for brightness in a glass half-full. The probability was that whatever was left in the glass was flat and needed to be thrown away.

She had reminded her husband throughout a successful business career of the people who were dangerous to him and she had been mainly right in her assessments. Or at least she claimed that she had been mainly right: like many people of her persuasion, she quoted her successes and conveniently forgot examples of when she had been wrong.

Shirley Swarbrick's sour view of life had been inhibited for a little while by her husband's retirement. They had given him a good party, an excellent meal and a cheerful send-off from the works where he had been MD. Shirley had been able to claim to him that all this was due to her steady efforts to warn him over the years against people who represented threats to his well-being. But then he was suddenly at home with her, in the house that she had had to herself for so many years, and despite her dire warnings about his advancing age, his health seemed good and his body much better for his age than she would have expected.

She insisted on giving him the sparse diet she had adopted for herself at home, and religiously administered his five-a-day ration of fruit and vegetables as though it was medicine that he must not miss. But she knew he ate and drank what he wanted when he was away from her, as he was increasingly, as a result of his chairman's duties at the tennis club. He ate the wrong things and he drank far too much, she told him repeatedly. Arthur nodded resignedly and ignored her cheerfully.

He was a typical man, she said. Their differing philosophies meant that she regarded that as a condemnation and he took it as a compliment.

Shirley decided quickly that there were compensations in the way the tennis club took over from his business in the proportion of the working day it occupied for Arthur Swarbrick. It meant that as his wife she could begin to warn him about situations and people there, very much as she had done when he was at work. He told her repeatedly that Birch Fields was a sports club not a factory, but that affected her attitude not one jot. 'You'll need to watch that Olive Crawshaw,' she told him with a tightening of her lips. 'She's not your type at all. She'll fill the places with blacks and yellows if she gets half a chance.'

Shirley was even more racist than Arthur, and as she spoke mainly within her own home, she had not learned to bridle her language as he had. 'You mustn't say things like that, love. They'll get you into trouble,' Arthur told her, knowing that she was not going to heed him. 'We have to move with the times, you know. Things aren't as they were when we were children.'

'More's the pity!' said Shirley darkly.

'You can't hold up progress, dear.'

'Progress!' She spat the word as if it were an obscenity. 'They'll take over your precious tennis club if you let them, just as they're taking over everything else.' Shirley didn't play tennis any more herself, but she was a social member of the club and used its facilities. This enabled her to observe the changing scene at Birch Fields and offer her pronouncements upon it. She regarded herself as the all-seeing spectator and informed commentator, the power behind the throne occupied by her husband.

'We accepted our first black man on Wednesday night,' said Arthur dolefully.

'Well, there you are, then,' said his wife, nodding her head at this triumphant conclusion to her argument.

'He's a policeman,' said Arthur, watching her closely from the corner of his eye. This could confuse her; she always said they should support the police as the last bastions of law and order and the representatives of righteousness in a decadent world.

Shirley frowned hard and said nothing for a few minutes. Then she muttered darkly, 'You can't rely on anything nowadays, can you? You watch your back, Arthur; that's all I'm saying.' She shook her expensively coiffured head. 'Other people don't think like you any more. They'll have you out as chairman if you give them half a chance. You just watch your back!'

'Do you really think so?' She had Arthur's full attention now, whereas previously he'd been half amused by her racist ramblings and thinking of other things. Perhaps, as she sat and drank her morning coffee and took her afternoon tea in the club lounge, she'd heard things that people wouldn't have voiced with him around.

Shirley was well aware that he was listening to her properly now. 'You need to watch that Fitton bloke, for all that he's white and British and educated. You know what he did to our daughter. And he'll have your job if you give him half a chance.'

He was surprised to hear it from her, but she was voicing one of his own deepest fears. Fitton was personable and educated, and he had money. It was an unwritten rule between him and Shirley that they didn't speak any more about the business with their daughter; they had an obscure feeling that it would make things worse if they spoke of it. But now she was confirming his fears that Jason would charm the members and slide into control if Arthur didn't take steps to avoid it. The man in charge had certain advantages, though. He'd better use them whilst he could.

His wife was into her conversational stride now. 'And there's that Asian bloke who always walks around in posh suits. Don't know his name. Don't want to.'

Arthur thought for a moment. 'Do you mean Younis Hafeez? He's keeping a low profile at the moment. There's a rumour that he was involved in the procurement of young girls for sex. The racket that people have been sent down for in other places.'

'Well, there you are, then.' Shirley delivered her favourite aphorism.

'But it's only a rumour and there's probably nothing in it. Don't you go voicing it around the club!' Arthur was suddenly full of apprehension. That good-looking, friendly Asian probably had a vicious side if you annoyed him.

Shirley Swarbrick nodded several times. 'You just watch your back down there, that's all!'

Arthur wished she didn't sound so much like an Old Testament prophet.

FIVE

Robert Walmsley was the managing director of Fitton Metals. That sounded a prestigious post. It had been exactly that at one time and on paper it still was. Robert was one of the few people who realized that he was much less important than he once had been.

Bob Walmsley had joined the firm thirty-seven years ago as a junior accountant and had worked his way upwards steadily. His efforts had been much appreciated and well rewarded by the founder of the firm, Derek Fitton. It had been Bob Walmsley who pointed out the potential offered by the steeply rising prices of scrap metal, and the opportunities that new technology was beginning to offer for the reclamation and re-use of various metals that would formerly have been mere scrap. There had been a splendid ten years when Fitton Metals had paid scrap prices and sold the re-treated products for handsome sums. It had grown from a small unit in a despised industry into the most prosperous firm in Brunton.

The man with his finger on the profit pulse had been Walmsley. Derek Fitton was a shrewd businessman who saw the national picture and knew how to strike a bargain with the industrial moguls he encountered. But it had been Walmsley who supplied him with the technical details and the forecasts of future prices which fixed the detail in the contracts he closed. Fourteen years ago, Derek Fitton had made Bob managing director, allotted him a considerable shareholding and told him that he was confident he was leaving the firm in safe hands when he retired.

Jason Fitton, Derek's son and successor as owner, had seemed a good employer during his first year. Bob Walmsley had told himself that he mustn't be too conservative; a certain amount of change was probably a good thing. You needed to be careful not to become too set in your ways. An infusion of new blood and new ideas might be just what the firm needed at this stage in its development. Jason was a personable and well-educated young man, who made a good impression on most of the staff with whom he came into contact.

But there weren't many members of staff, and as the years passed there were fewer still. Walmsley was the first man who was shrewd enough to realize that the firm was being allowed to freewheel. That was a polite word for it. Things got worse as the years passed; in his view, Fitton Metals was now being allowed to stagnate.

Bob heard rumours from elsewhere in the town and picked up the occasional fact that was more damning than rumour. The firm he had developed and grown to love was now being used as a respectable front for other and much darker enterprises. When he raised that thought with Jason Fitton, he was told in no uncertain terms that if he knew what was good for him, he would keep his mouth firmly shut.

Walmsley was clear-sighted about the facts of his situation. His shareholding wasn't worth as much as he might have hoped, but he had a lucrative salary and he hadn't too many years to go to retirement now. He wouldn't easily get another job if he lost this one: Fitton would see to that, even if redundancy in his fifties wasn't enough of a handicap in itself. As for the other and more emotional reasons he had to hate Fitton, they were surely irrelevant to the needs of the business and should be set aside from his judgements.

Robert Walmsley congratulated himself on one thing, at least: his appointment of a new PA two weeks earlier. There had been plenty of good candidates. Fitton Metals still looked prosperous, even healthy, on paper. Only one or two informed people like Walmsley knew that it needed an infusion of capital to service new processes and that it wasn't going to get that. The person he had appointed had seemed to be one of the very best candidates to become his new PA.

Anne Grice was an attractive woman of forty-four with good features in a heart-shaped face. She had dark, neat, short hair and wore a well-cut grey skirt and white blouse, and calf-length black boots. She also carried a general air of quiet authority. Bob had fancied, even at that first meeting, that she would not need to shriek at the junior secretarial staff who would also be part of her remit; they would accept the authority of this calm, experienced woman without question.

The major question in Walmsley's mind had been why she was planning to leave behind what seemed an even better post to take this one. He'd taken her briefly through her impressive curriculum vitae and then come swiftly to the point. 'You come here with a glowing reference from your present employer. He says that he would be very sorry to lose your services.'

'That is good to hear. Good for my ego. But I think that it is time for a change.'

'Forgive me for being ungallant, but I note from your application details that you are forty-four. You have at present an excellent salary and a satisfied employer. Why do you want to leave all that behind and come to Fitton Metals?'

'It's more convenient for me. Nearer to home.'

'But the money isn't any better than what you're earning in your present post – I'm afraid it might even be slightly less, if this year's bonus is as small as last year's.'

'It's adequate. Finance is not a problem for me. I need job satisfaction as much as money. You don't seem as if you'd be an ogre to work for, Mr Walmsley.'

It was a tiny shaft of humour and she'd given him a tiny smile to accompany it. She was very pretty when she smiled, but that hadn't swayed him. He was past the age for that, he'd told himself firmly. He wasn't convinced by her arguments for taking this post, but he couldn't press the matter further without becoming over-personal. She was divorced and perhaps she had a good settlement from that, but you couldn't pursue such things in an interview.

Anne Grice had seemed to have every qualification for the job, and her present employer in Preston had assured Bob over the phone that he would be very sorry to lose her. Walmsley had enquired if there was anything further about this post that she needed to ask him and been assured that there wasn't. She had researched the firm thoroughly before she applied. Another small, friendly smile lit up the rather serious face and convinced Bob that she would be easy to work with.

He'd told her that he had other candidates to see, that he

would let her know within three days what the decision was. He'd felt as she left that they both knew that she was going to be appointed.

Perhaps both of them had also known that Anne Grice had not revealed her full reasons for wanting to join him here.

Saturday afternoon. The courts at Birch Fields were very busy, as the days still stretched out and the season enjoyed a post-Wimbledon boom.

Clyde Northcott would have chosen a much less public occasion for his first appearance at the club, but he hadn't been given a choice. This game had been arranged for him. Olive Crawshaw was the directorial force behind his appearance in mid-afternoon, at the time of maximum exposure. 'You'll enjoy a good men's four,' she'd told him authoritatively. 'You blokes always do, I know. It's your favourite form of the game. You play mixed doubles when you have to, and most of you do it with good grace, but you tolerate us women rather than enjoy it. You're stronger than us and you're generally more competitive, though some of us do our best in that respect.'

Clyde couldn't imagine any man being more competitive than Olive, though he had more sense than to offer that thought. Nor did he attempt to resist the unstoppable tide of her plans for him. There was no sense starting his life at Birch Fields as a tennis Canute.

He realized quickly that Mrs Crawshaw had been more subtle and thoughtful in her arrangements than he had given her credit for. The three men he was playing with had been selected on the basis of character as well as skill. They seemed genuinely pleased to see him here and genuinely anxious to integrate him into the sporting ethos of the club. They treated him easily and naturally as an equal, when experience had taught him to expect at best a calculated reserve.

They were kind to his mistakes in their first game or two on court, as they would no doubt have been kind to the efforts of any new member. Clyde found himself more grateful than ever to Elaine Brockman and the reinitiation to tennis she had offered to him on the public courts in the park four days previously. He made mistakes, but far fewer than he would have done without that practise night, and not many more than the people he was playing with. He held his first service game, which he was sure he would never have done without Tuesday night's practise with Elaine. He managed to finish it with a cannonball ace down the centre line, which brought congratulations from partner and floundering opponent alike.

Clyde was pleased to find that Olive Crawshaw wasn't amongst those watching from outside the high metal fencing. She was in fact playing a women's doubles on the adjoining court, more than holding her own with companions to whom she was conceding twenty years and more. He was conscious between points in his own game of her darting about at the net, shouting 'mine' or 'yours' to her partner with the same certainty she had accorded to his application for membership, and congratulating and commiserating with friend and foe on the court.

Clyde would have thought she was completely unaware of him, had she not given him a surreptitious wink as they both stooped to collect balls at the back of their courts.

His game in the men's doubles was close. It demanded all his concentration, and as the set moved towards its climax he found himself more and more involved. He was pleased with a couple of winning volleys he made at the net, disgusted with himself when he dispatched an easy forehand well over the baseline. The other three men were equally involved in the contest, and Clyde became no more than another amateur player trying his best to ape the professionals.

There were spectators, of course, at this time on a Saturday. A host of eyes were trained upon this most noticeable of new members. Clyde's immaculate white shirt, shorts and socks made his colour even more striking than his height and his muscular physique, so that a growing number of members paused to watch the closely contested match on the club's premier court.

Most of them approved of what they saw. But there was one spectator who was not pleased. The chairman of the club, the man who had reluctantly accepted the inevitability of Northcott's membership only three days previously, was disturbed by this inescapable manifestation of the new man's presence.

Arthur Swarbrick watched for a few minutes with a face of stone, then disappeared into the clubhouse to reflect upon what he had been compelled to accept.

The following week, Anne Grice had been duly appointed as PA to Robert Walmsley at Fitton's Metals. After a week, Walmsley knew that she was as good as her previous experience and her references had said she would be. Bob was normally reserved and cautious, but after a fortnight he was prepared to reveal to her information he had previously regarded as confidential. A good PA inevitably gathered such confidences, he told himself. She even needed them, if she was to do her job properly.

It was in her third week in her new post that she sat for a moment in front of his desk clutching a file against her desirable but discreetly clothed bosom. Anne wasn't one for cleavage at work. Fashions had recently encouraged it, but in her view it wasn't efficient clothing for the wearer and it was likely to distract other people who worked around her. Anne was no frump. She looked attractive as she moved around the three offices where her word was already becoming law. As far as she was concerned, though, low necklines were for leisure wear, in other places and at other times.

Bob Walmsley wondered why his new PA had paused in her chair when he had finished dictating letters to her. For the first time since she had come here she looked a little uncertain. Perhaps she was wondering how to make the next move. He smiled at her and said, 'Was there something you wanted to raise with me, Anne?'

Mrs Grice responded immediately and without any further hesitation. 'I wanted to ask you a question. If you think it's impertinent, please tell me to go away and get on with my work.'

'I'm intrigued. Fire away, please – I shan't be offended, whatever it is you want to ask. You've already given me the right to refuse an answer, so I can't lose, can I?' Walmsley liked this intelligent, efficient, occasionally humorous woman.

He found that he already trusted her more than the woman she had replaced. That surprised him, when Mrs Grice had been less than three weeks in post, because over the last few years he had grown used to being quite secretive about anything concerning work.

She looked straight into his face as she said, 'I was wondering about the present state of the business. I've read through various files, as you invited me to do to ensure that I was suitably informed. Frankly, I don't like what I've seen.'

'And what exactly have you seen?'

'I've seen a business that's being starved of investment. Ten years ago you were ahead of the field, fifteen years ago even more so. The profits were healthy and the technology in use was bang up to date. I'm no engineering expert, but that doesn't seem to be the case today. We're still in profit, but for how much longer?'

'Have you spoken to anyone else about this?'

'No. I wouldn't do that without speaking to you first. Perhaps I'm drawing the wrong conclusions. I might be quite wrong.'

He gave her a grim smile. 'You're not wrong, Anne. You're absolutely right. I didn't think you'd work it out as quickly as this.'

Her wide mouth was rather thin-lipped as she nodded. 'I don't understand all the technical processes involved in reprocessing metals, but I can read balance sheets. The ones over the last five years make for grim reading if you're looking for progress.'

Bob Walmsley nodded. 'We used to spend generously on research and development, in the old days when Derek Fitton was in charge. And it paid off. We were ahead of the field, as you said. That was because we looked into all the latest American and Swedish technology and found out what worked and what didn't. Then we spent heavily on installing the best plant. It was all justified, because we recouped our investment and much more in profits. People in other, smaller businesses in the Midlands used to ask to come here and study how we were operating. That doesn't happen any more.'

'Why?'

Bob looked at her quizzically. 'I suspect you already know

that. The man in charge doesn't want to spend money. He has other priorities. Jason Fitton is a very different man from his father.'

The thin lips grimaced. 'And more's the pity, you almost said. Does no one ask the kind of questions I've been putting to you?'

'We're not a public company, with shareholders and meetings where they can question policy and the chairman. The whole country's been passing through a prolonged recession. Most people don't ask questions. Even the few who have reservations about policy seem to be content to keep their heads down and congratulate themselves on still being employed in trying times.'

'You sound frustrated. You sound as if you wished there were more people questioning what's going on.'

He looked at her steadily for a few seconds. 'Right now, Anne, I'm asking myself why you are concerning yourself with matters like this. I'm all in favour of people taking an interest in the business that pays their wages, but your concern is stretching beyond what would be normal for a PA.'

This time her smile was wide, seemingly untinged by any other concern than pleasure. She liked this man who was fourteen years older than her, who had already proved a considerate and generous employer. He had answered her questions fully, because he was a naturally honest man. A man of great integrity where business affairs were concerned, she had decided, after less than three weeks in his company. A man who shared all the reservations she had about Jason Fitton, the man who now controlled their destinies and those of numerous other people. She said, 'Thank you for being so frank, Mr Walmsley. I share your feelings about the present Mr Fitton.'

He should leave it at that, he thought. They'd been more frank with each other than was customary and probably wise for managing director and PA. Instead, he said, 'It's high time work was finished for the day. Do you fancy a quick drink in the White Hart?'

She smiled at him again; her dark brown eyes seemed in that moment to look right through him. 'I'm a divorced woman,

Mr Walmsley, as you clearly remember from the enquiries you made when I was appointed. Some people think that a divorced woman is desperate to leap into bed with any man who offers his services. As long as you don't put me in that category, I'm very willing to go for a drink.'

He tried not to show how nettled he was by her words. 'I was asking you for half an hour's conversation in a non-working context, Anne. I wasn't planning on starting an affair.'

'And in the light of that assurance, I'm very happy to go for a drink with you, Bob. I'm sure that I shall enjoy your company in a non-working environment.'

It was the first time Anne Grice had used his forename, denoting that she was dispensing with the formalities of their working relationship in this social context. She was daring enough to tease him a little, and her smile today was wide and genuine.

The relationship between Clyde Northcott and Elaine Brockman was proving itself eminently useful to both parties. At work, Elaine found the detective sergeant's advice soundly based and more useful than he knew. He spoke as if such things were obvious, but as a raw recruit who had come to the harsh reality of Brunton Police Station straight from the freedoms of university life, she was enormously grateful for his common sense and experience.

They were sitting in a corner of the canteen and she had just confessed to him that she was disturbed more than she had expected to be by the string of obscenities and scatological insults she had received that morning from a couple of the choicer representatives of Brunton's youth culture. 'It's depressing more than anything, I suppose. I was surprised by the violence of the delivery more than the stream of F and C words. They really managed to convince me that they'd rape me violently and bludgeon me and take great pleasure in both things if they had the opportunity. I hope I didn't let them see they were annoying me, but—'

'That's important. You must never let them see that they're getting to you, even when they are. You'll find that in time it becomes water off a duck's back – irritating more than disturbing.

Until that happens, you just have to behave as if you've heard it all before and it's merely tedious.'

'It's that all right. Even though I have heard it all before. There are plenty of unsavoury characters at universities, especially when they get a few drinks down them. It was the violence that was upsetting. I wouldn't want to be alone with some of those people – females as well as males.'

'They just go for whatever they think might be a weakness. The fact that you're pretty means that you get a sexual tirade from them.'

Elaine smiled wanly. 'You're suggesting I should regard it as a compliment?'

'You're a woman. They'll test you out in any way they can. I don't know how many times I've been called a black bastard and a black cunt in the last few years. Once you're a copper, you have to learn not to react. That's been a good thing for me. I'd have been on GBH charges if I'd been an ordinary citizen.'

She hadn't expected him to understand so thoroughly what she had regarded as a weakness; she'd been depressed by her morning, but she wouldn't have confessed that to anyone save him. She realized now how much she had come to rely on his advice and support at the station. Elsewhere, and pre-eminently in the exalted social echelons of Birch Fields Tennis Club, she was his mentor. In the mean streets of Brunton and in the sometimes even meaner confines of the Brunton nick's locker rooms, Elaine was a novice who needed to learn quickly. But at the tennis club she was a veteran at twenty-two. She had been a member since she was ten, when she had been welcomed on to the courts as a promising youngster who knew her manners and knew her place. She had passed through the rigours of adolescence and into womanhood with the club as one of her constants. Other considerations had ensured that she had remained 'promising' rather than the fully rounded sporting talent some had envisaged, but she remained a popular member of the club, known and liked by almost all its members.

It meant that she could give the newest recruit to the club, her colleague DS Northcott, experienced guidance in the nuances of tennis club membership, an area where Clyde was defiantly ignorant. 'I want to play tennis, not smarm my way around!' he announced to her with a vague but sturdy determination.

'I agree. You're not built for smarming. You haven't had the practice,' Elaine said with a very straight face.

'And I'm not going to start now!' His features set into an uncompromising ebony mask.

'No one's expecting you to do that, you great daft ha'p'orth.' One of her gran's expressions had jumped out when she least expected it. That was a sign of her affection for this big, awkward man who was so reluctant to dissimulate. She'd love to see what her beloved gran, who'd been born when there was scarcely a black face in Brunton and none of the Asian ones that were now so prominent, would make of Clyde Northcott. 'You enjoyed your game on Saturday, didn't you?'

'Well, yes, I did. Apart from the spectators and my failure to master the backhand smash. But that's what I want to do: play tennis. I'm not interested in all the rest.'

'But you've joined a club. You have to acknowledge that; you have to get to know people to get games. The tennis will follow. The two are interlinked.'

He knew she was right but he felt out of his depth. 'I've never been much of a joiner. No one's ever wanted me to join anything, for that matter. I suppose I'm like Groucho Marx – I don't want to join any club that would accept the likes of me.'

'Be a new experience for you, then, won't it? All part of the rich fabric of life and all that jazz.'

'I was never into jazz, either. People think you've got natural rhythm, just because you're black. I never had that. Perhaps it's because I've lived all my life in Lancashire.'

She grinned. 'Brunton's quite a long way from New Orleans, and not just geographically. But you're making my point for me: you need to embrace the new experience. And speaking of developing your rhythms and of joining in at the club, you should go to the summer ball at the weekend. Show your face, become a popular and active member of the club, get yourself lots of tennis matches.'

It isn't easy for a black man to blanch visibly. But Northcott blanched invisibly and comprehensively at this suggestion. 'I couldn't do that. I'm no dancer.'

'You don't have to be, with modern dancing. My dad says you just jig about and do your own thing. I wouldn't admit it to him, but he's right, really.'

'I'm much too big to jig about. I look stupid.'

'It's all in the mind, Clyde. You have to take these things on. If you keep a straight face, people think you know what you're doing – even think that you're an expert, if you remain po-faced for long enough.'

Northcott decided that it was time for a decisive rejection. 'You have to dress up and pretend you're enjoying yourself. I haven't got the gear and I couldn't possibly enjoy it.'

'You've got the gear, Clyde. It used to be evening dress for the summer ball, but they made it lounge suits to encourage a better attendance a year or two ago. I'll come with you, if you like.'

It was as low-key as she could make it, but the offer threw him into confusion. He'd been determined to reject any idea of attendance at the summer ball, even to ridicule it, but now this entrancing girl was offering to accompany him there. Bloody bleeding hell! What a dilemma to be on the pointed horns of. 'You don't really want to go. You're just being kind to the misfit.'

She shook her head resolutely. 'Time I joined in again, after being pretty much absent from club activities for the last thee years. Joining in things like the summer ball is part of being in a club, as I told you. Even when I have to go there with a daft new member who has two left feet and no sense of rhythm.'

'Last time I went to a disco I got myself into a punch-up. That was seven years ago, long before I became a copper.'

'I won't expect you to be in full terpsichorean practice, then. And please don't get yourself involved in a punch-up at Birch Fields: I have a reputation to keep up. They think I'm a respectable young lady there. I'd rather like them to keep that illusion.'

And so it was settled. Another function that DS Northcott would never have ventured anywhere near was now to be attended and endured.

SIX

Percy Peach was impatient. Not at the station, where people had grown used to that, but at home. He didn't like keeping secrets from his mother-in-law.

He had an unusual relationship with Lucy's mother. She was the only person in his world who understood how he had come by the initials D.C.S. That cricket-mad father who had christened his only son Denis Charles Scott Peach was now long gone. The seventy-one-year-old Agnes Blake was also a cricket fanatic and old enough to remember Denis Charles Scott Compton, the cavalier of English cricket in the drab post-war years. She felt that 'Percy' was an unworthy appendage accorded to her son-in-law by an alliteration-obsessed police service. She had a cuttings book of Percy's achievements as a dashing Lancashire League batsman in the local East Lancs cricket team. A photograph of Percy in perky blue cricket cap stood on her mantelpiece beside the older black-and-white one of her dead husband, pictured with sweater over his shoulder after taking a cluster of wickets in the Northern League.

Percy had wanted to tell Agnes about the baby as soon as he knew of it himself. But Lucy had wanted to wait until after the first scan. 'Let's get all the preliminary tests and checks done first.'

'But your mum's been desperate for grandchildren for so long. It seems cruel to keep this from her.'

'Things go wrong in the early stages. People have miscarriages.'

'Not you. You're prime breeding stock.'

'Thank you, kind sir, for that fulsome compliment. I feel as if I'm being paraded round the auction ring at the cattle market. You'll be poking me in the ribs with a walking stick next.'

'Not with a walking stick, my love. And not in the ribs.

But don't you think we should let Agnes know pronto? It will make her week. Correction: it will make her year.'

'I know all that. But it's early days. Let's get the preliminaries safely over before we tell her. She'd be heartbroken if we told her I was pregnant and then had to tell her a month later that it was all over.'

Percy knew that Lucy would be pretty heartbroken on her own account, whilst he would be trying to put a brave front on his own devastation. But he saw the logic of what she was saying, even though he felt like a small boy bursting with his secret each time he saw Agnes. But now, after much deliberation about whether or not to wait until after the first scan, Lucy was about to reveal the great news to her mother. They had saved it for a Saturday night and the news was to be the climax to her favourite meal.

Percy had insisted that mother and daughter should be alone with each other when the news was revealed, much as he would like to have seen Agnes's face at that moment. He sat in the lounge and listened to the shriek of delight from the septuagenarian in the kitchen as her daughter gave her the tremulous tidings. He was on his feet by the time Agnes Blake arrived in the room and flung herself into his arms.

'You did it, Percy! I knew you could!'

'It was nothing, Mrs B. Persistence told. It was almost a pleasure, at times. Difficult for me to keep up with young Lucy's incessant demands, of course, but—'

'Percy!' His wife's yell from the door compelled him to embrace his mother-in-law and give Lucy the most benevolent of beams over her shoulder.

When Agnes eventually divested herself of her son-in-law, she gazed up into his face exultantly and said, 'He might be a cricketer, Percy!'

'He might indeed, Mrs B.' Percy mimed an extravagant cover drive.

'He's got the genes, hasn't he? With my Bill as his grandfather and you as his dad. He could play for England.'

'Or he might be a girl,' said Lucy from the doorway. 'She might be a Wimbledon champion. Or a female prime minister – I expect women will be in charge, by then.'

Agnes considered this sobering possibility. 'Don't you know what it's going to be? They can tell quite early now on these scan things, can't they?'

'We haven't had a scan yet, Mum. And we don't want to know the sex in advance. We agreed on that. As long as it's healthy, we don't mind which it is, do we?' She took Percy's arm in a proprietorial manner and looked to him for confirmation.

He nodded. 'We don't want a girl with my looks and Lucy's brains, Mrs B. Anything else is acceptable.'

Agnes shrieked with laughter, as she almost always did at Percy's sallies. 'Oh, go on with you, Percy Peach! You don't look so bad, when you're scrubbed up a bit.'

'And your daughter's not the complete idiot he implied! Aren't you going to say that, Mum?' Lucy's amusement was a little forced.

'Of course you're not, love. But that's just Percy winding you up, isn't it? I thought you'd have been intelligent enough to see that.' Agnes looked to her son-in-law for confirmation, then burst into delighted laughter at his solemn nod.

They toasted Horace, as Percy and Lucy had been calling the not-yet-visible bump for the last few days, in the vintage port the father-to-be had purchased for the occasion. Agnes was cautious because she had to drive home, and Lucy took only the token sips appropriate to a dutifully pregnant citizen, which meant that Percy had to undertake the onerous task of celebrating for three. Agnes said eventually, 'I'm glad you've decided to wait for the birth to find whether it's boy or girl. I think that's nice, though I couldn't quite say why. I admire your self-control. The knowledge wasn't available in my day, but I don't think I'd have been able to resist finding out the sex if it had been me. He'll be a cricketer, though; you mark my words.'

Lucy grinned at her affectionately, enjoying her mother's unconcealed delight almost as much she had enjoyed Percy's original reaction. 'I told you, Mum, it might be a girl. And I still think she might be a tennis player. I wasn't bad at tennis, until I joined CID and Percy Peach put a stop to all that.'

Percy was spluttering into a denial, but Agnes was far more spontaneous and swift. 'It'll be a lad, our Lucy. And he'll be a cricketer. I can feel it in my bones.'

'He might do all kinds of things, Mum, as the new generation.' She glanced mischievously at Percy and then lit her mother's fuse. 'He might even be a golfer.'

'A GOLFER!' Agnes Blake shrieked in capitals, as she invariably did when the baleful exercise of golf was mentioned. 'No grandson of mine is going to be a GOLFER! Game for toffs and degenerates, GOLF is!'

Lucy shook her head soberly. 'You might just be right there, Mum. Percy's quite good at it, they tell me. But I'd hardly call him a toff.'

'He gave up cricket far too early and took up that stupid game!' muttered Agnes Blake darkly. She gave the man in question one of her rare scowls.

'Anno Domini, Mrs B.,' said Percy, shaking his head sadly. Then he added piously, 'And a sense of duty, of course. Someone has to keep an eye on the toffs and the degenerates at the North Lancs Golf Club.'

Agnes screeched her delight at that notion. 'Oh, go on with you, Percy Peach! You're a regular caution, you are!'

With which familiar observation, she bade them farewell and departed joyfully to convey her great tidings to the women in her village at the foot of Longridge Fell, who had known Lucy since she herself was a child.

The Saturday night when Lucy and Percy delivered their great news to Agnes was also the night of the Birch Fields Tennis Club's summer ball. The latest recruit to the club was in reluctant attendance. Clyde Northcott was still adamant that this was emphatically not his scene. The presence of Elaine Brockman was the enormous bonus that had been necessary to secure his presence here.

He was already regretting his concession, magnificent as his partner for the evening looked at his side. The emerald necklace she sported above her low-necked green dress must surely be costume jewellery; he was pretty sure that no one below the rank of duchess was allowed to possess real emeralds as large as that. But real emeralds couldn't possibly have made Elaine look prettier, in his not entirely unbiased view.

For her part, Elaine thought that it was splendid to see her man spruced up in a dark blue suit and a discreet lighter blue tie. She knew he would be uncomfortable in the early part of the evening, but he carried these clothes well, despite his reluctance to don them. He stood erect and impressive in his formal wear, not only the tallest man in the room but, in her view, the most impressive one. She had been proud to take him in to meet her parents when he had called to collect her. Her dad had been deadpan as usual, scrupulously polite, scrupulously the same as he had been with the other boyfriends she had visited upon him over the last few years. But her mother was easier to read and she had been impressed by Clyde. Understandably, in Elaine's view: the man's physical presence was something no woman could ignore.

She found it was so at the summer ball. Everyone in the room was conscious of Northcott's presence, even when he stood at the edge of the dance floor, talking quietly with her and one of the men with whom he had played tennis.

Only one man found it easy to ignore him.

The chairman of the club did not arrive until the dance was well under way. Most people had enjoyed a dance or two and a drink or two and were pleasantly relaxed by the time Arthur Swarbrick made his appearance. Everyone in the room knew him and he was received either enthusiastically or politely as he made his way around the edge of the floor and greeted his members at the greatest social occasion in the club's calendar. Elaine was conscious of his progress, aware that he had known her since she had joined the club at ten. He had seemed an old man to her then, a grandfatherly rather than a fatherly figure. She calculated now that he couldn't have been more than fifty then. She prepared her best smile for him.

Shirley Swarbrick greeted her by name, then smiled graciously as she was introduced to Clyde. She passed on swiftly to the next group at the side of the dance floor, making steady progress towards the table and chairs discreetly reserved for the chairman at the furthest point from the band. Her husband was a little behind her, delaying his progress deliberately by a few words to the adjoining group. Then he stood in front of them, and Elaine knew suddenly what he was about to do.

Arthur Swarbrick stood directly opposite her, produced a very deliberate and very mirthless smile, and said, 'Good evening, Elaine. It's good to see you back here.' He studiously avoided any acknowledgement of the tall, dark figure who stood dutifully and expectantly at her side. Then he switched off his smile and moved briskly on to the next group of people by the dance floor, as if the man who everyone in the room was aware of had not been present.

Elaine moved to follow him, but Clyde had his strong hand on her elbow in a flash. 'Leave it!' he commanded in an urgent whisper. Swarbrick moved on to rejoin his wife. Only those in the immediate vicinity were conscious of the very deliberate snub he had just administered.

Elaine Brockman was pink with fury. 'He can't be allowed to get away with that!' she hissed at her companion.

'He can and he will. It's much better left at that. It becomes bigger if you react to it. I have some experience of these things.'

A new voice spoke in Elaine's ear. 'He's right, love. Leave it, for now. He won't get away with it. I for one will take it up with Mr High and Mighty Swarbrick, and there might be others.' Olive Crawshaw had materialized mysteriously beside them; Elaine had not seen her previously during the evening. Olive said to the offended party, 'You're absolutely right, Clyde. Just carry on as if nothing had happened.'

'Nothing has,' said Northcott evenly. 'Nothing that I haven't experienced a hundred times before and dealt with.'

There was an immense dignity about him, Elaine thought. He was almost a figure larger than his mere self, though she wasn't at all sure what she meant by that. Pretentious nonsense, she could hear her late tutor at the university telling her, though she was sure of what she meant in her own mind, and that was something quite impressive. These reflections were brought to an abrupt end by Clyde seizing her hand and propelling her on to the dance floor, an action she had been convinced he would never take of his own volition.

Clyde didn't have to coordinate his actions with hers for this number: they were standing opposite each other and gyrating individually. And he managed a respectable attempt at what her father would have called 'twitching and twirling'. After five minutes of this, Elaine had recovered her equilibrium and some sense of perspective. Even, perhaps, her sense of humour. She said to Clyde, 'You danced well there. I think you must have a natural sense of rhythm. Something in the genes, perhaps.'

'Watch it, sprog. You're still on probation,' said Clyde, with a face as straight as hers.

She wasn't sure whether he meant as a police officer or as his girlfriend. Could she claim that status yet, or would that be assuming too much? The upshot of the Swarbrick incident was that the evening went well from there on. They relaxed with each other, danced as much as was necessary, and got on well with the friends she already had and the ones he was rapidly making. Elaine resolved to tell Arthur Swarbrick if she ever got the chance that his action had broken the ice agreeably for them.

Clyde even managed the last waltz, holding her with increasing confidence as they moved slowly around the crowded dance floor. He behaved like the perfect gentleman in the taxi afterwards and left her at the door of her home with the briefest chaste kiss on her forehead. She wasn't sure she wanted him to be such a gentleman, although she was sure that her dad would have thought it admirable. And she still wasn't quite sure that she was Clyde's girlfriend, even though she was quite sure now that she wanted to be.

There were other issues at the summer ball. Those with an interest in the control of the Birch Fields Tennis Club were watching each other closely on this key occasion in the club's social calendar.

Olive Crawshaw had already noted and condemned Arthur Swarbrick's conduct towards Clyde Northcott. She spent part of the evening wondering whether a private rebuke was enough, or whether she should prepare the ground for a formal complaint in committee against the respected chairman of the club.

Probably not, she thought. She joined in the dancing when she was invited on to the floor by her friends, but she also canvassed support discreetly amongst like-minded members against what was plainly racist conduct.

She deliberately ignored one man who would no doubt have given her his support. Olive had been one of the pioneers in the introduction of Asian members into the club, but she didn't trust Younis Hafeez. She didn't like the way he looked at women and she particularly deplored the way he looked at young girls. Olive was in charge of junior girls, and she had noticed Hafeez's presence beside the courts with a disturbing frequency when her girls were playing. He professed an interest in the development of young talent, but she noticed that he wasn't around when the boys were playing and that he took no interest in *their* progress. Olive Crawshaw knew better than to utter formal warnings against a man as powerful in the town and the tennis club as Hafeez, but she let it be known, whenever she could do so discreetly, that mothers and young women should not trust the man any further than they had to.

Younis Hafeez was aware by now that Mrs Crawshaw was one of his few enemies in the club. He had nothing tangible to go on, but he had noted her attitude towards him when her youngsters were around. She wasn't dangerous, in the greater scheme of things, because he had far more power than she had and next year he planned to have much more. She was a troublesome wasp, to be swatted away when the time was right. To switch his metaphors, he had bigger fish to fry tonight.

He took care to dance with the right people. He was a good dancer, in this decadent Western mode. He could twitch his face and flick out his arms and shift his feet with the most nimble and most degenerate of them. The women were flashing their thighs and twitching their buttocks in varying lengths of skirts and in high heels, but for tonight he pretended not to notice. He did his version of the perfect English gentleman, which he thought he had mastered over the years.

It was in fact a trifle smarmy, too universally affable to be genuine, but it was enough for most women. His smooth good looks were grafted on to his smooth good manners, and the combination sufficed for most of the passing and superficial contacts he had to make tonight. He was gathering votes for next year's elections. The process amused him: it was a relief from the darker concerns that had dominated much of his week.

The other man with an interest in the future domination of the club did not appear until late in the evening. Jason Fitton chose his moment carefully. He left the casino he owned in the centre of the town when business was at its briskest, then drove to Birch Fields to present himself at the summer ball at precisely ten thirty. He was immaculately dressed as usual, the only man in the place to be clad in a genuine Savile Row suit. His tailoring was important to him, as was his education and his money. The combination gave him confidence, made him feel that he could run rings round these northern yobs. When he was in this mood, he conveniently forgot that he was a native of Brunton himself.

He danced with various attractive women, choosing only those dances when he could display affability and graceful movement without losing dignity. Jason was a man intensely conscious of appearances. He had advanced in life by making the right public impressions, and he wasn't going to change now. How he behaved privately, and particularly in one-to-one situations, might be quite different. But his real self was not for public display. He might be a womanizer and all kinds of other things when it suited him, but on this public occasion he had decided to be a model of relaxed charm.

The summer ball became more boisterous as the hours passed and the drinks were downed and the decibel levels of conversation and music rose. Arthur Swarbrick had had enough by midnight, but he knew he must stay until the end, to safeguard his interests as well as to be on public display for his members. His wife was dispatched home with a neighbour at twelve, as the three of them had previously agreed. This wasn't really Shirley Swarbrick's scene any more and she had attended only to give loyal support to her husband, an impulse she had rather regretted after his public attempt to snub the new black member. Whatever you felt about black men, you couldn't do that nowadays. She would take him to task the next day over it: Arthur was his own worst enemy at times.

Arthur was aware of Jason Fitton and of Younis Hafeez in the last hectic hour of the ball. He had leisure to observe, because he did not dance himself in those last sixty minutes. He was an expert in the realities of club politics by now. He had worked to attain office; he had worked to gain the committee support that had made him chairman; he had worked to get the right people on the committee and sub-committees in the last few years to maintain and strengthen his position as chairman. He had grown used to spotting future rivals. He noted Fitton and Hafeez now as two men who might have ambitions towards his office. He noted Olive Crawshaw also as an enemy, but not as an aspirant to the chairmanship. She would never be a supporter of his, but neither would she be a rival for the highest office of all, as far as he could see. There was no woman in sight yet with aspirations to the chair; thank God for that at least, thought Arthur Swarbrick.

He was almost sorry when the summer ball was over. He had enjoyed the last hour, when he had been able to watch from the sidelines as others performed. It enhanced your feeling of power when you felt that you were an informed and advantaged spectator, watching others jockeying ineffectively for position. He mustn't allow himself to become complacent, but he felt secure as chairman for another year or two yet. Longer, if he played his cards right. He'd have to strike the right course between being the bastion of conservatism he had been until now and the enlightened elder statesman who could lead the club into new pastures and new prosperity. He knew he was the man to do that: it was merely a matter of convincing other, less clear-sighted people of his worth to Birch Fields.

The band packed their instruments into cars and departed swiftly after the one o'clock conclusion to the ball. A fleet of taxis picked up many of the participants. Some drove themselves and full quotas of passengers away, after noisy leave-takings and noisy injunctions to drive carefully. Assignations for future meetings and future games rang across the Tarmac from car to car as the park gradually emptied and silence dropped back beneath the stars.

One car remained at Birch Fields when all the other vehicles had gone at two o'clock. It was there even three hours later, as the first grey streaks of the new day crept slowly into the eastern sky.

It had the corpse of a dead man in the driving seat.

SEVEN

Clyde Northcott did not go to bed immediately when he paid off the taxi outside his flat. It was late, but he was preoccupied with many things. He sat in his armchair and reviewed the evening.

This wonderful girl seemed to be taking him quite seriously. He'd been on his best behaviour so far. When Elaine saw the worst of him, would the scales drop away from her eyes? Would she still need him, would she still want his company, when she was established in the police service and making the rapid progress expected of a graduate entry? What would her family think of him? What did they think of the little bit of him they had already seen? Would they forbid her to see him again, or at least to have any lasting association with him? How would that feisty girl react if they gave her injunctions like that?

It was surely impossible that the two of them could construct anything serious, with backgrounds as different as theirs were. She'd been a star at the local comprehensive and then gone on to a good university and got a good degree. That's what he'd been told at the station, though he wasn't even quite sure what exactly constituted a good degree. He'd been brought up in Bolton – they called it Greater Manchester now, but he never used that. If you were black, people automatically assumed Greater Manchester meant that you'd been reared in the violent criminal underworld of Moss Side, where even coppers feared to venture and the criminal barons held their violent sway.

Clyde couldn't remember anything of his dad, who'd departed when he was three and never returned. His mother had been good to him when she was around, in her slapdash, erratic way. She hadn't been much more than a kid herself when he was born, but he hadn't realized that at the time. He'd relied mostly on his gran, who'd usually been there when he got home from school – not that there'd been a lot of school in his later years. His gran was the one person he'd really loved. He'd like to be able to take Elaine to meet her now, he thought, but she'd died last year. It was the first time he had endured such bittersweet nostalgia. He seemed to have spent a lot of his life guarding against loving anyone other than his gran.

The years from sixteen to twenty-one, which Elaine had spent in the sixth form and at university, were his black years. He'd learned to fight, in all sorts of ways: he'd had to do that to survive. He'd used drugs and begun to deal in them. He'd been a suspect in a murder case, and if someone other than Percy Peach had been in charge of it, he might have been arrested, charged, perhaps even convicted. People of his background weren't usually given the benefit of the doubt. All this had made him in the end a better copper; he was certain of that now. Poachers turned gamekeepers knew more than others and could look after themselves, Percy Peach said. He wondered if Elaine knew that he'd been Percy's best man at his wedding to Lucy Blake. That must surely impress her; he must feed that fact in at the right moment, as Percy always did when he was interrogating people. But station gossip being what it was, she probably already knew.

But whilst he had been going through what some called the university of life and others just called a criminal phase, Elaine had been a pillar of rectitude. She came from a model middle-class family, who had no doubt watched over her education and her development as assiduously as virtuous and educated parents should do. Her mum and her dad had been polite, even friendly, tonight, but what would they think if they discovered the full details of his adolescence and his pre-police days? Apart from that, would they even consider any policeman a suitable companion for her? Elaine said they disapproved strongly of her choice of the police as a career, so they were hardly likely to approve a large black policeman as a consort for her.

Clyde wasn't sure exactly what a consort was, except that he knew Prince Albert had been one for Victoria. He had an obscure feeling that Elaine would have found the idea of himself as a consort quite hilarious. He liked the sound of her laughter; he decided that he would now go to bed on the thought of Elaine Brockman's laughter. It was always genuine and always generous. She liked him, even if she found him amusing. At ten past three, he put his head down, switched off the light and finally fell into a contented sleep.

His mobile phone wasn't far from his bedside, but it rang several times before his ears worked and his brain stirred into reluctant life. 'Clyde Northcott!' he snarled into the mouth-piece, as if his name was some sort of rebuke. The illuminated digits on the phone told him that it was seven fifty-five.

'We have a suspicious death.' Percy Peach's voice; Clyde struggled and managed to lift his head and shoulders from the bed. That was the equivalent of standing to attention when you were roused in your pit from the deep sleep of the just.

'You're almost an eyewitness.'

'What do you mean?' He scratched his head, feeling like Stan Laurel in those old pictures he had once watched with his gran. It was too early in the day for him to keep up with Percy's badinage.

'That posh tennis club you joined, when you decided to become upwardly mobile.'

'What about it?'

'That's where the murder was. I'm sure that's what this death will turn out to be.'

'I was there last night,' said Clyde dully.

'That's almost certainly when the poor bugger was killed. You're not offering me a confession, are you?'

'No, sir.'

'You pissed, DS Northcott?'

'No, sir.' Clyde tried hard to shake himself into life.

'Hangover, is it?'

'No, sir.' Clyde swung his feet on to the floor and felt almost human. 'Just lack of sleep. I was rather late to bed.'

'Dirty bugger.'

'No, sir.'

'Never mind.'

'Yes, sir.'

'PC Brockman isn't there with you, then?'

'No, sir.'

'Losing your touch, are you?'

'PC Brockman isn't here, sir. She's never been here.'

'Pity. Most women seem to like big tough buggers like you. Today might have been useful experience for her, as a graduate entry. We might have to let her tag along to learn from the expert and the hard bastard. Might even arrange for her to attend her first post-mortem examination, in due course.' New coppers were expected to throw up at the sights and smells of their first PM. It was one of the clichés of police life.

'Do you want me to join you, sir?'

'I suppose so. You'll be bugger all use, I expect. You've got some sort of hangover – probably drank too much when you didn't get our new graduate entry into your bed. I can tell that from the number of "sirs" you're sprinkling around.' Percy didn't like the acknowledgement of his rank to be too frequent. He said undue deference was a substitute for clear thinking. Only wankers like Tommy Bloody Tucker were keen to hear the perpetual iteration of their seniority.

'Is it a member of the tennis club who's been killed, sir?'

'You're expecting it to be, aren't you?'

'Yes. That would be logical, even if only statistically.'

'You're right. You're beginning to think at last. It was a prominent member of the club – a man you already know.'

Clyde's mind flashed back to the previous evening and to Arthur Swarbrick circling the room to greet his members at the summer ball. He could see the chairman now, being scrupulously polite and friendly to Elaine, whom he had known since she was a child, in order to set up the snub he was about to deliver to his new black member. A man who behaved like that made plenty of enemies. He wondered which one had seen fit to end his days. This case might not take long and he might have a leading role in finding the solution. He felt his first real excitement as he sat on the edge of the bed and sleep finally dropped away from him. 'Was it the chairman, sir?'

'You're "sirring" again. And no, it wasn't. You're our favoured inside source here, big man, so come up with the goods.'

'I've only just joined Birch Fields.' Clyde narrowly prevented himself from adding a defensive 'sir'. 'I don't know many important members. There was Younis Hafeez, I suppose. He was mounting a charm offensive during the busiest part of the evening.'

'It wasn't him.'

'Then I'm lost. You said it was someone I knew, But—'

'You knew this bugger, Clyde. It was Jason Fitton. I'll pick you up in fifteen minutes.'

The tennis courts were open at Birch Fields and a few people were playing. They had to walk much further than usual before they could begin. The whole of the car park was surrounded by the ribbons denoting a crime scene.

Peach and Northcott donned plastic footwear covers and took the designated path towards the point furthest from the clubhouse, where a square of high fencing provided the final privacy to Jason Fitton and the vehicle in which he had died. The Bentley gleamed in the bright morning sunlight. From any distance, the figure in the driving seat seemed just another manifestation of modern affluence. It was a tribute to Savile Row that even in death Fitton looked from the rear to be in tune with the quality of his vehicle.

Death compels a sort of respect, even in policemen who have seen it many times. Fitton was a known villain, whom Brunton CID and both of these men had been pursuing for years. Yet now he was inanimate and powerless before them; what remained of him was beginning the process of deterioration that would reduce to mere matter what last night had been human. What had been mortal and individual and flawed, with the potential for good or evil actions, was now but seventy kilograms of decaying matter. The abruptness and finality of the transition from life to death compels a moment's pause for thought even in policemen.

Jack Chadwick had been a policeman for many years. He was now a civilian in charge of the scene-of-crime team. He was as efficient as any man around in this office; before nine o'clock on a Sunday morning he had somehow managed to assemble the varied team of civilian specialists appropriate for this task. There were only two police officers present. Two constables in uniform, one male and one female, had drawn the short straws. They were stooping low as they moved around the car park, gathering with tweezers any detritus that might have even the most tenuous connection with what had happened to that still form in the Bentley.

The driver's door was wide open. The photographer was taking pictures of the corpse in situ from every angle he could contrive before it was removed for its inevitable dissection in the pathology laboratories. The immaculate material of the suit was largely creaseless and undefiled. But the cause of death was clear enough and the instrument of that death was still in place. Fitton's head was slumped forward, but the cord that had destroyed him by biting deep into his throat was still visible at the sides and rear of his neck. The loose ends, which had most surely been twisted and tightened, now hung limply at the back of his jacket where the killer had dropped them.

Jack Chadwick, who had known Peach for years, materialized silently at his side to answer the questions the DCI scarcely needed to speak. 'Someone directly behind him tightened that. He was garrotted. He didn't stand a chance. He raised his hands to that cord, but he didn't even get his fingers between cord and neck. I doubt the whole thing took more than thirty seconds.'

'Swift and efficient. A man?'

'Not necessarily. Anyone attacking from behind could have twisted the cord fiercely enough to do the job. No great strength is needed, once you have the advantage of surprise. And probably a real measure of hate to make you that ruthless, but that's speculation.'

Peach grinned ruefully. 'There are a lot of people around here with reason to hate Fitton. He'll be no loss to humanity. There'll be a few coppers glad to see him gone, Jack.'

'Including one DCI Peach.'

'No comment. You know the score as well as I do. This is still murder, the same as it would have been with an innocent old lady. The difference is that we'll find there are a lot more candidates for this one.'

Chadwick stared dispassionately at what had brought him here so early on a Sunday morning. 'The pathologist will give you something definite and official, when he's applied his rectal thermometer and whatever else he brings to prod with and when he's measured the progress of rigor. But I'd be amazed if this man did not die last night. Some time during the early hours of today, I'd say.'

Clyde Northcott spoke for the first time. 'The dance went on until one o'clock. I was here until then. Fitton came late, but he was still here at the end. My guess would be that he died in the hour after one. Someone was obviously waiting for him in his car.'

'Steady on!' said Peach with some enjoyment. He turned to Chadwick. 'These raw lads still make assumptions, Jack, the way they did in your time.'

'I seem to remember you being a rather raw young lad, in *my* time,' said Chadwick wryly. He liked the big black man who was so anxious to learn – not as much as the curvy, green-eyed young Lucy Blake whom he'd replaced as Percy's bagman, but that was for other, entirely unprofessional reasons. 'Percy means that you can't just assume that the victim was ambushed. These might have been people known to him, whom he invited willingly into his car. Or they might have been waiting here and given him no choice but to admit them – if they'd ordered him around at gunpoint, for example.'

Northcott nodded. 'You said "they". Do you think more than one person was involved in this killing?'

Chadwick grinned. 'Now you're asking the right questions, Clyde. Searching ones.'

'Obvious ones, more like,' said Percy sourly.

Chadwick said loftily, 'It's impossible to give you a definite answer on that. All we can be certain of is that someone has occupied the passenger seat of this vehicle quite recently. Possibly last night, but not certainly last night – it could have been earlier. It's possible that Jason Fitton was talking to someone beside him when someone in the rear seat threw that cord round his neck and killed him very swiftly. But it's equally possible that the person in the rear seat simply took his victim by surprise. The car was in darkness: it would have been perfectly possible to crouch down and conceal yourself as the unsuspecting victim approached, then spring into action once he had installed himself in the driving seat. Or Fitton might even have been accompanied to the car by someone friendly to him, someone quite innocent of this crime, who subsequently fled and who has not so far presented himself as a witness.'

'Or herself,' said Northcott dutifully.

'Or herself, indeed. We may never know the full facts of the matter.'

'We'll know,' said Peach with determination. 'We'll know everything that happened in this car. Everything we need to put someone away for this.'

Chadwick looked at the pair with affection. He'd known Percy Peach since he was a raw recruit. He'd put a few backs up, had Percy, then and now. But he got results. Honest results. And he was passionate about putting villains away. He lived his professional life to do that. 'We've dusted all the handles, but we haven't come up with any prints, except Fitton's. Whoever else was here last night wore gloves.'

'Which suggests premeditation on a summer's evening,' said Peach slowly. 'You wouldn't expect anyone to be wearing gloves.'

'I'm sure no one who'd been to the summer ball would have put gloves on,' said Northcott. He glanced across at the clubhouse and the now deserted dance floor. 'It was very hot in there. I was glad to get out.'

'That's the kind of observation I get from this bugger,' said Peach to Chadwick. 'He's really sharp-eyed when it comes to observation.' He turned back to Northcott. 'You said Fitton arrived late. At least you were aware of something other than PC Brockman's tits. Did you see Fitton having an argument with anyone?'

'No. He was rather like Hafeez. He seemed to be mounting some kind of charm offensive, particularly where the women were concerned.'

'Enough to make some jealous big-server follow him to his car and sling a cord round his neck, was it?'

'Not what I saw. He wasn't trying to get off with any particular woman. He was putting himself about to be charming, not offensive. It was a bit superficial, I suppose. I wasn't paying a lot of attention to him, but he seemed anxious to be pleasant to the men as well as the women. He certainly didn't lay hands on any women inappropriately, not whilst I was watching him.'

Peach looked at Chadwick and cast his eyes towards the heavens. 'That's the kind of language we have to use now, Jack. People don't grab a feel or goose women. They "touch them inappropriately".'

'Or men, sir. They can be touched inappropriately as well nowadays, if they're lucky,' Northcott pointed out. 'Or unlucky, of course, depending on your point of view.'

'This sod was unlucky,' said Peach, nodding towards the corpse in the vehicle. 'I'm sure you've heard quite a lot about Jason Fitton, Jack.'

Chadwick looked sympathetically at Northcott and nodded. 'From what I've heard of him, there'll be plenty of people rejoicing when they hear the news today. I'm sure if Fitton was doing anything offensive, it wouldn't have been on public display for you to see. You've questioned him with Percy here about his past villainies, so he'd be conscious of your presence in the place last night. He wouldn't miss you, would he? You're sort of . . . well, noticeable.'

Northcott grinned. 'I like that word, "noticeable". I must remember it. It's more acceptable than "You can't miss him; he's that great big black bastard", which is what I usually get.'

Peach sighed. 'I shall take the useless great lummox away now, Jack. You can see how standards are going down. I look forward to receiving your further observations along with the PM report in due course. When the pathologist finally deigns to turn up, that is.'

EIGHT

'Thank you for seeing us at such short notice, Mr Walmsley. I'm Detective Chief Inspector Peach and this is Detective Sergeant Northcott.' He rolled the ranks out like a man setting the sights on a rifle. 'Apologies again for coming here at Sunday lunchtime. We wouldn't do that if this wasn't an urgent matter.'

Peach was watching the man, even as he made the routine apologies. He looked a pillar of rectitude and what little they knew of him so far said that Robert Walmsley was just that. But you never knew what you might turn up if you kept an open mind. 'I'm sorry to say that we are the bearers of bad news, Mr Walmsley. We often are, I'm afraid. It's one of the penalties of working in CID.'

This man didn't look particularly penitent, despite the apologies, Bob Walmsley thought. Peach wasn't what he'd expected in a senior CID man. He was short and bald and round-faced, with a small toothbrush moustache which was as black as the fringe of hair he retained. He had an air of restless energy, accentuated by the fact that the big black man who accompanied him was so still. Both of them appeared to be watching him intently, though they could surely have nothing against him. Bob felt ridiculously defensive as he said, 'I think we'd better go into the dining room. We won't be disturbed there.'

They went into a silent, plainly infrequently used room at the front of the big detached house, where they sat on upright chairs on opposite sides of a large oak table. As near to a police interview room as you could get in a private house, Percy thought. He liked that: he wasn't a man given to putting people at ease, unless he sensed genuine distress. He wasn't anticipating real grief and the pain that accompanied it here. Robert Walmsley's relationship with the dead man, though of long standing, had been a working rather than a private one.

He looked as if he was in his late fifties and unlikely to give way easily to displays of emotion.

'There's no point in trying to wrap this up, Mr Walmsley. We've come here to tell you that your employer died suddenly last night.'

'Derek Fitton? There must be some mistake. He died some years ago.'

'That was your original employer. You present employer is – was – Jason Fitton.'

Walmsley had been realigning his chair so that it would be exactly opposite them. He slumped on to it heavily now, his face riven with shock. 'Young Mr Fitton? But I saw him a week ago. He was in good health then.'

'He was in good health twelve hours ago, Mr Walmsley. He's dead now. We're treating it as a suspicious death. Hence our presence here at this moment.'

Walmsley was silent for a second or two. Then he said dazedly, 'I was his managing director at Fitton Metals.'

'That's why we're here, sir. You are the senior man in his company. You're in a position to tell us all sorts of things about him.'

'I don't know him that well. I knew his father much better than I know Jason. I should say "knew", shouldn't I? This is all such a shock to me, you see.'

'I appreciate that. Why didn't you know him as well as you knew his father?'

He gulped a little, his prominent Adam's apple lurching visibly in his throat. 'Sorry. I've never had to think about that before. You must think me very stupid. I'm usually quicker than this; I suppose I'm in shock. Well, I suppose it helped that Derek Fitton and I were much nearer to each other in age. Derek was older than me, but not that much older. About ten years, I think – he died relatively young, you see. And we sort of developed the firm together. Fitton Metals was quite small when I first began work in the yard. Scrap metals of all kinds, but mainly steel, were all sorted in one place, in those days.' For a moment, his face brightened with the memories of those happy, busy, exciting times.

'So you had a close relationship with the original owner of the firm?'

'Very close. Mr Fitton was the entrepreneur who made the deals that took us forward and enabled us to grow. I flatter myself that I had the vision to see the possibilities of new technology. We took the opportunities to recycle what had been mere scrap into valuable, reusable materials. They were stirring times: we trebled our profits and almost doubled our workforce in five years. It was good for us and it was good for the town.'

Walmsley's face, which had been frozen with shock at their news, became animated and expressive as he recalled those best of days. Peach brought him abruptly back to the matter in hand. 'It's a family firm. You must have known Jason Fitton, even in those days.'

'I did, but not as a presence in the firm. He was away at school during our most rapid years of growth. His dad was really pleased to be able to send him to one of the best public schools. It meant in his own mind that he'd made it. Derek was delighted to be able to tell his friends that he'd sent his lad off to Eton, where the toffs and the politicians go.'

'And Jason took over the firm when his father died.' Peach was watching closely for some sort of reaction.

'He did, yes. There'd been talk of us becoming a limited company, with a proper board and shareholders. Derek Fitton was ready to take that on, but he died quite suddenly.'

'And his son ruled against it.'

'Yes. He said he might review the decision in a few years' time, but he wanted for the present to keep control in the family's hands.'

'Which meant *his* hands.'

'Yes. He was an only child. He had complete control.' Bob was trying to speak evenly, but a tinge of bitterness edged into the phrase.

Peach said quietly, 'You sound as if your relationship with the younger Mr Fitton was much more strained than that with the original owner.'

Bob Walmsley looked hard at him. He was no fool. On this bright Sunday morning, he wanted to pretend that things had been better than they really had between him and the man they had just told him had died in suspicious circumstances. But he knew that the business of these men was detection; they were going to find the true facts of the situation in the next few days. If they felt that he'd tried to deceive them, they would want to know the reason why. 'I suppose it was inevitable that we'd have a few problems. I'd enjoyed what, in retrospect, were certainly the best days of the firm. Growth is always exciting, and although Derek Fitton had done the best of all of us out of it, I had no complaints. I never thought when I came here that I'd end up as managing director, on a fat salary and with generous bonuses. Jason is – was – the new generation. It was inevitable that he would see things differently.'

'He wasn't as single-minded as his father, was he?'

This man Peach was leading him on, offering him chances to denigrate the dead man. Was he merely seeking information or setting some sort of trap? Bob wished he had more experience of this kind of questioning. He was used to interviewing candidates for jobs and putting them through the mill. It was a long time since he had been questioned himself; he wasn't used to feeling so uncertain. It was many years since he had needed to pick his way so carefully through what suddenly felt like some sort of minefield. 'No. Single-minded is quite a good word for it, I suppose. Fitton's Metals had been the be-all and end-all for his father – and for me, I suppose. Jason had wider interests, other concerns.'

Peach grinned unexpectedly, the round face creasing into a disc of pleasure. He turned his face for the first time away from Walmsley and towards his colleague. 'We know something about those other interests, don't we, DS Northcott?'

'We do indeed, sir. They've been a source of enduring interest to the Brunton CID section over the last few years.'

Walmsley said stiffly, 'I don't know anything about his other concerns. I confined myself to what I know and what I can control here.'

Peach's smile grew even wider, when that had not seemed possible. 'Very wise, sir, I'm sure. Whereas we were very interested in Jason Fitton's other businesses, in Brunton and in other parts of the north-west.'

'I know nothing about those.'

'Oh, come, Mr Walmsley, you're an intelligent man. Far too

intelligent not to have heard rumours at least of the money he was making away from Fitton's Metals.'

'I heard rumours, yes. It's impossible not to if you move amongst the local business community. I take care to gather as little knowledge as possible about Mr Fitton's other activities.' His lips set with a Puritan thinness.

He'd hesitated for a fraction of a second over his selection of the last word, and Peach was glad to show with another beam that he recognized the careful choice. 'You were very wise to have nothing at all to do with those "activities", Mr Walmsley. I should have wanted them at the longest arm's length I could contrive if I'd been in your shoes. But, of course, the man was your employer, so there were limits to how much ground you could put between you and him.'

Bob gave him a tight smile but held his peace. The less he said about his relationship with Jason Fitton the better. 'I didn't know and didn't wish to know about the other things that occupied Mr Fitton when he was not here.'

'How often was he here?'

'Not very often.'

This time Peach's smile was grim rather than benign. 'You'll need to do better than that, Mr Walmsley. We're investigating a serious crime. We need to enlarge our knowledge of the victim, and you are a man ideally placed to help us.'

'Not *ideally* placed. I didn't see as much of him as you might expect. We had no social contact at all and he has appeared at the works very infrequently in the last year.'

'How infrequently, Mr Walmsley?' Peach stressed the repeated word as if it were a taunt.

'Four or five times in the last six months. Certainly not more than half a dozen.'

'Was that his only form of communication?'

'He didn't do emails. We've spoken on the phone a few times. Usually when I've rung him to ask for decisions or support.'

'What kind of support?' Peach was on to the word like a terrier pouncing on a rat, making Walmsley regret immediately that he'd used it.

'Usually financial. The business continues to make money, but technology never stands still. You need investment and

modern plant if you are to stay ahead of the opposition.' Bob
heard himself repeating the phrases he had used many times
before. He wondered if they sounded as stale to his listeners
as they did in his own ears.

'And did Mr Fitton offer you this support that you felt
was needed?'

'A measure of it. As I have told you, my relationship was
nothing like as close as the one I had with his father, who
was in the works almost every day and was as devoted to its
progress as I am. Jason had other interests, other outlets for
his investment. I understood that.'

'Did you, Mr Walmsley? Or did you bitterly resent it? I think
that in your shoes I would have gone for bitter resentment.'

'We weren't at daggers drawn, as you seem to think we
were.' Bob wished he'd chosen a different metaphor. 'I'm
sorry. I'm still in shock about this. Jason Fitton made it quite
clear that he held the power and that he would make the
important decisions, and I accepted that. He was content to
leave the day-to-day direction of the firm in my hands, which
I suppose is a sort of compliment. I would have preferred the
more hands-on and committed approach I'd been used to from
his father, but at least I felt that Jason trusted me to know
and run the business without him at my elbow.'

'How many people are employed at Fitton's Metals?'

'About a hundred and thirty in all, including drivers and
ancillary staff. Not all of them are permanently on site.'

'Would you describe the late Jason Fitton as a good
employer?'

It sounded strange, that description of the man as 'late'.
Strange and very final. Bob should have felt exultant, but he
felt only a strange numbness. 'Not as good as his father. But
I think most people would say he was OK. We haven't had
to cope with redundancies, as many local firms have during
the recession.'

'You're not "most people", Mr Walmsley. You are the most
informed person available to us. Would your verdict on the
man be "OK"?'

'That's hardly fair. I was very close to Jason's father.'

Clyde Northcott spoke suddenly after a long, watchful silence.

'We're not asking you to be fair, Mr Walmsley. We're asking you to be informative. We need your help.'

'He wasn't the ideal employer, but I'm sure there have been worse.'

'There is no need for you to be coy in this matter, Mr Walmsley. DCI Peach has already indicated to you that we have been pursuing enquiries into Jason Fitton's other activities over the last few years, and particularly over the last few months. DCI Peach has been cautious in his language. I am prepared to speak off the record and to offer you my own opinion. I regarded Jason Fitton as a thoroughgoing villain who dealt in all sorts of mischief. There is no call for you to defend him or to obscure his faults. He has been transformed overnight from villain to victim. We need the fullest account of him you can give to us, warts and all.'

Bob Walmsley looked into the long, intent black face. 'You said you were treating this as a suspicious death. How did Mr Fitton die?'

Northcott glanced at Peach and received in return the most minimal of nods. 'He was strangled with a cord, Mr Walmsley. He was in the front seat of his car when the cord was thrown around his neck by person or persons unknown. He died very quickly. His death will be confirmed as murder before this day is out. That is pretty well all the knowledge we have at present. In return for that information, we expect your fullest cooperation in what will be a full-scale murder investigation.'

Bob looked from one to the other of the two very different but equally expectant faces. 'Thank you for telling me that. You confirm much of what has hitherto been mere speculation for me about my employer. I heard rumours that Mr Fitton had been involved recently with prostitution, and even that he might have been mixed up in some way in the recent procuring of underage girls for immoral purposes in Rotherham and Rochdale – and other towns round here as well, for all I know. I won't comment on that, not because I'm being uncooperative, but because I haven't the knowledge to do so. I've taken care to learn as little as I can of any activities of my employer outside Fitton's Metals. My working life is as managing director of that firm, and I am – I suppose I should now say *was* – concerned with my employer's activities only in so far as they affect this firm and my work in it.'

It was a long statement and he was breathing hard and a little unevenly at the end of it. Peach let the silence stretch in the quiet room, waiting to see if tension would make the man add anything to it. He said eventually, 'That sounds almost like a prepared statement, Mr Walmsley.'

The man on the other side of the table weighed the implications of that and spoke coolly. 'I'm not entirely surprised that you should say that. It is the first time that I have spoken to the police in this vein, but not the first time I have uttered these sentiments. I move amongst the business community in the town, and the activities of my employer have been the subject of lively and increasingly scurrilous enquiries over the last year or two. I have usually refused to comment. When forced to do so, because my questioners were either old friends or old customers, I have taken the same sort of attitude as I have just expressed to you. My concern is with the health of Fitton's Metals as a business and with the well-being of the people who work there. I have separated these other activities and interests of the owner of the firm as sharply as I can from his position as owner and employer here. If what I have just said to you sounds like a prepared statement, it is because I have uttered the gist of it many times before, though in more informal contexts.'

Peach nodded, reflecting on his words, apparently accepting the logic of what he had heard. 'You do not seem to be astonished by the news we have given you this morning.'

'I am shocked by what you tell me has happened to Jason Fitton, but not entirely surprised. I imagine he moved in dangerous circles.'

'Nor do you seem to be greatly distressed.'

Bob looked evenly into the dark, near-black eyes in the deceptively bland face. This man Peach was anything but bland, and he couldn't imagine that anyone around him had an easy life. 'I've indicated some of the difficulties of working for Jason. I'm upset by his death, especially if it's murder, as you say it is. No one should be allowed to get away with murder, and I hope you make an arrest quickly. But I'd be a hypocrite if I pretended that I was stricken with grief. I've never been accused of hypocrisy.'

'Thank you for your honesty. Did Mr Fitton have a PA at Fitton's Metals?'

'No. As I've indicated, he's rarely shown his face in the place over the last few years.'

Peach nodded. 'We shall need to speak to your own PA. She must have got to know something of him and whatever relationships he had in the place over the years. PAs do that, we find. They keep their fingers on the pulses of organizations.'

'They do indeed. But my present PA has only been in post for a short time. I can give you the address and phone number of my old one, who has now retired. She knew both Derek Fitton and Jason Fitton and saw much of the development of the firm over the years.' He'd almost said 'and the decline of the firm'. That wouldn't have been diplomatic; it was much wiser to say as little as possible.

Peach took the details and said, 'The man you've described to us is a man who must have made many enemies. We need you to give us your thoughts on this and hopefully one or two suggestions – in confidence, of course.'

Bob thought for a moment, then shook his head. 'I'm sure you're right, but those enemies wouldn't be at Fitton's Metals. Most people here aren't even aware of the concerns I have about the future, because it didn't seem politic to spread alarm and dissension, as the old army phrase has it. The older Mr Fitton used to use that phrase, but I never thought I'd be quoting him about his son's actions in the firm.'

Peach raised his impressive eyebrows. 'You can't think of anyone who wished him ill?'

'Not at Fitton's Metals, DCI Peach. I'm confident that you will find his killer elsewhere.' He saw them off. His unsmiling face at the front door was a reflection of the grave news they had brought to him.

NINE

Younis Hafeez had been inside the Brunton casino only once before. On that occasion he'd been in a party of five. He'd been going through the motions of social interplay, when the business of the day had already been concluded. After twenty minutes he had made his excuses and left. He wasn't a gambling man. He took risks, but only when he felt that the odds were stacked in his favour.

At one o'clock on the afternoon of Sunday the ninth of August, almost twelve hours after Jason Fitton had died, Hafeez moved into the manager's office at the casino to meet the man he had summoned to see him here. Although this was an alien environment, Younis took care to look as thoroughly at home as if he was used to visiting it daily. 'Inscrutable' was a cliché word. Hafeez was inscrutable, though his features were much more mobile than the term usually implied. People could not read his thoughts, because he was chameleon-like, adapting his visage and its expressions to whatever he thought was appropriate for his purpose.

Jim Forrester, the man he had come here to see, was shrewd, unscrupulous and well informed, and he was operating on his own ground: Hafeez had arranged to meet him in his office at a time when the casino would be deserted. Yet Jim Forrester had no idea what Hafeez was about. The Pakistani told him soon enough, but in the exchanges that followed Forrester had no idea what was real, what was bluff and how far the man could implement his threats if he was denied.

Hafeez glanced round Forrester's office, noted the picture of three smiling children on the desk, Forrester's token of innocence in the dubious world in which he operated. He sat down in front of the desk before he was invited to do so. 'Your employer died last night.'

'Yes, I heard that.'

The radio announcement at noon hadn't given a name; it

had just stated that the body of a man had been discovered at Birch Fields Tennis Club and that the death was being treated as suspicious. But Hafeez had expected Forrester to know that the corpse was Fitton's. News travels fast on the criminal grapevine. There is always a copper or one of the many civilians the police service now employs who will let things slip, accidentally on purpose, if you make it worth his while. The police have their informers; they don't care to publicize the fact that the traffic is two-way.

'You must be wondering what's going to happen to you.'

Forrester had been wondering that for the last two hours, but he said only, 'We'll be taken care of. Mr Fitton was a good employer and this is a profitable place.'

'That's why I'm here.' Hafeez released his first smile. 'This is a profitable place. That's why I am taking it over. And there are other and very different profitable places in the Fitton Empire. My colleagues and I are interested in all of them. I'm here to tell you that your future will be safe as long as you assist us to make a smooth transfer, and then replicate the loyal service you gave to Mr Fitton.'

'How do I know that I can trust you?'

'You don't.' Hafeez was quite unsmiling now, staring into the man's face with a calm lack of emotion which was more chilling than anger would have been. 'You don't have any option in this matter, Mr Forrester. My colleagues and I will be taking over this and the other concerns of Mr Fitton. Including the brothels and the betting shops and certain other enterprises that are scarcely off the ground as yet.'

He meant the procurement of underage girls. And boys, in lesser numbers. And their transfer to other parts of the country, where they would be abused and raped by other men – rich, mainly middle-aged men – who would pay well for their squalid pleasures. Forrester knew something of these things, but he'd had no involvement himself and didn't wish to have any. He'd managed to keep them at arm's length, though you couldn't work as a right-hand man for Fitton without hearing something of this lucrative branch of his activities.

Forester glanced at the photograph of his children on his desk, then quickly back into the brown, unsmiling face opposite him. He knew in that moment that Hafeez was reading his thoughts, but he had no idea whether he was despising him or not. 'I might want out.'

'I see. That might not be possible, Mr Forrester.'

'I know nothing of your organization. I can in no way—'

'You know a lot about Jason Fitton and his various enterprises. We shall be taking these over and we shall require your silence. If you are working for us, which I am offering you the opportunity to do, we shall be assured of that silence. If you do not accept our generous offer of continuing employment, others steps might be necessary.' Hafeez's voice was quiet, but he articulated the words very clearly, which made his message only more sinister.

Jim Forrester swallowed hard. He was being offered an ultimatum. Either he continued the work he had been doing or he would be quietly disposed of, with his body perhaps never discovered. Hafeez might be bluffing – even in this dark, increasingly gangsterish world into which Fitton had plunged him, people didn't kill unless they had to. There was always a risk with murder, even with people like him whom few people would miss. But he wouldn't like to test that theory with Hafeez. This unexpected visitor looked like a man who would be utterly ruthless.

Forrester licked his lips and said, 'I know about this place and the other casinos and something about the betting shops and the other gambling outlets. I haven't much knowledge of the other things you've mentioned. If you think I am competent to do so, I am happy to accept your offer to carry on the work I've been doing. Assuming, of course, that you obtain control of Mr Fitton's enterprises, as you anticipate you are going to do.'

It was the nearest he could get to a moment of defiance, and it felt rather pathetic even as he delivered it. Hafeez looked at him steadily for a moment; only his narrow brown eyes showed the cruelty that the rest of his features were masking. Then he gave a small smile and said, 'You have made a wise decision, Mr Forrester.'

Both of them knew in that moment that there had been no decision at all. The man on whom Fitton had relied here was accepting the inevitable. Jim tried to sound happy as he said, 'I shall open up as usual tonight. I shall continue the normal operating routines unless I receive other directions from you.'

'That will be in order. There is no reason why this should not be a productive working relationship for both of us. There may be certain changes to implement in due course, but you will receive adequate notice of these.'

Forrester hoped this sinister visitor would go now. That would at least allow him to collect his thoughts. His mind was still reeling from the impact of this meeting. He had been wondering for the last two hours what the outcome of Fitton's death would be for him, but this baleful arrival in the office where he was used to reigning supreme had unnerved him completely. Hafeez did not rise but continued to sit and look at him, as if wondering just how long he would tolerate this survival from a less efficient era. Jim found the silence so oppressive that he asked eventually, 'How did Mr Fitton die?'

He thought Hafeez would deny all knowledge of what the police had already said was a suspicious death. Perhaps he thought that any confession of ignorance would be a kind of weakness. He said, 'He was at the tennis club dance last night.'

'Yes. He went there from here.' It was a pathetic attempt from Jim to reclaim some sort of status.

'I was there myself.' It sounded as if he was trumping the card that Forrester had played.

'Was there some sort of argument?'

Hafeez gave him again that mirthless, condescending smile. 'I don't know. I wasn't involved in his death myself. You should remember that and reiterate it, should anyone speak to you about the matter.'

'Yes. I'll do that.'

'I think Fitton was killed after the dance was all over, after the rest of us had left the place. His body was found in the car park this morning. The police have the matter in hand.'

Younis Hafeez stood up at last. Perhaps he had been waiting for the questions about Fitton's death. For an instant he stood looking down at Forrester, who struggled clumsily to his feet. 'I shall be in touch. I look forward to rewarding what I am sure will be your loyal service to your new employers.'

Jim Forrester sat for a long time in his silent office after his new employer had gone. He looked at the photograph of his children on his desk, then picked it up and put it away in the deepest drawer.

Clyde Northcott had never seen Olive Crawshaw look even slightly disconcerted. Admittedly, he hadn't known her for very long, but she had seemed as constant and irrepressible to him as Niagara Falls. In introducing him to the tennis club, persuading him to apply for membership, and securing that membership for him in the face of opposition, she had been totally certain and totally inexorable. The psychologists would no doubt have something to say about the way water dominated his images, for he now decided that her inevitability and her predictability recalled to him pictures he had seen of the Severn bore, carrying all before it as it moved swiftly upriver.

On this Sunday afternoon and in the presence of Percy Peach, he saw her for the first time looking uncertain. On her own territory, too, where you would have least expected it. Her house was a modern semi-detached, less grand and less individual than Clyde had expected. Forces of nature shouldn't live in conventional places like this. The garden was exactly what he would have expected. Geraniums and lobelia filled the beds at each side of the lawn. Along the front of the house was a bed of deep pink, perfectly formed hybrid tea roses, which bloomed in profusion and grew to an absolutely uniform height – as if they wouldn't dare to do otherwise, Clyde thought wryly. A small, very legible sign informed anyone who wished to know that the name of this impressive bloomer was Wendy Cussons. Clyde took a deep breath and rang the bell.

Peach was less inhibited by Mrs Crawshaw than Clyde had been from the moment he met her. This would be a good contest, Northcott thought. Peach in pursuit of facts was more than a match for anyone, including even the formidable Olive.

She took them through to a comfortable living room, where a man who looked ten years older than her sat reading the *Sunday Times*. 'Do you mind if Eric stays?' she asked. 'It will save me repeating everything you've said after you've gone. We could pitch him into the conservatory, but there's nothing I'm going to say that I wouldn't want him to hear. And he won't interrupt us: he's very well trained in that respect.'

'I have no objection to that,' said Percy, taking in the pair with the first of his all-embracing smiles. 'You might even be helpful to us, Mr Crawshaw, if you are able to enlarge on anything your wife tells us.'

'I doubt that,' said her husband. 'Olive's knowledge and opinions tend to be comprehensive. There is rarely much to be added when she reaches a conclusion. And my own memory isn't what it was.' He spoke with no apparent irony, but with a kind of resigned affection. It didn't seem the sort of marital relationship that Northcott or even Peach had encountered much before, moving as they usually did amongst the more dubious couplings of Brunton society.

'Your phone call told us that you wished to speak to me about the death at the tennis club. A suspicious death, the radio informed us at lunchtime.'

'Highly suspicious. Do you know who it was who died?'

'Indeed I don't.' She spoke as if the possession of such knowledge would be highly unseemly for someone of her integrity. 'I am looking to you for enlightenment, Detective Chief Inspector.' Edith Evans as Lady Bracknell, Peach thought. He'd seen the old film, but Northcott was too young and innocent for such things as cucumber sandwiches and the English establishment.

'And you shall have it. The victim was Jason Fitton.'

'I see.'

She seemed at a loss for words, which Peach had already decided must be a rare experience for her. 'You were expecting it to be someone else?'

'I have really no grounds for thinking it would be anyone. But I am only human.' She spoke as if confessing a moral weakness. 'A natural curiosity has overtaken us since we heard the news bulletin. I am not exactly surprised that you now tell me the victim was Jason Fitton – I presume that we are speaking of a victim of murder or manslaughter. I confess that I had rather favoured the notion of Arthur Swarbrick as the dead man myself. But Eric is of a commendably more open mind. He had not committed himself.'

Her husband smiled. 'She flatters me, Mr Peach; she does that when it suits her.' He grinned at his wife affectionately. 'I shan't speculate. I don't have the necessary knowledge of the tennis club membership and wives to do so.'

'Partners, Eric. You need to say "partners" these days, to be at all comprehensive.' Olive corrected him with a fond smile.

Peach had watched the husband-and-wife exchange as closely as he observed everything when he made a business visit to someone's house. He had no idea yet what would prove to be relevant to this crime. Olive Crawshaw was a suspect until proved innocent, and the state of her marriage might well be important. People under stress of any kind often behave out of character. This marriage appeared unusual but perfectly sound, with an intelligent older man becoming a little vague and prepared to concede the initiative. He looked at the woman now and said, 'Why did you think the victim would prove to be Arthur Swarbrick?'

Olive took her time. How she presented herself might be important if she was to allay suspicion. That thought excited her and adrenalin surged through her veins. 'Good question, DCI Peach. I'm not sure I can give you a very convincing answer.' She glanced for a moment at the very serious Clyde Northcott. 'Mr Swarbrick and I have had certain contretemps in the last few weeks. We've known each other and opposed each other for years; we have very different views of the world, but I needn't go into that here. Suffice it to say that we've never been bosom pals and we've argued regularly over tennis club policy for quite a long time now. We understand each other, but that doesn't mean we'll ever become friends. We've had two or three open clashes over the last few weeks, however.'

'Then you had better tell us about them.'

'Is this relevant? You've just told me that Arthur Swarbrick isn't the victim. I'm thankful for that, though in view of what I've just said you may find it surprising.'

'No, I don't find it surprising, Mrs Crawshaw. I should find it much more surprising if you were disappointed that he wasn't last night's victim. I don't expect a few differences over the policy of a sports club to make women wish to see their opponents killed. However, Mr Swarbrick will be investigated, as will everyone else who was in attendance last night, until we can clear them from suspicion or extract a confession from someone else.'

'Including me?'

'Including you, Mrs Crawshaw.'

She smiled at him, showing that she was neither apprehensive nor intimidated. 'That's really rather exciting, don't you think, Eric?'

Her husband smiled rather apprehensively.

'This isn't a game, Mrs Crawshaw, exciting or not. Tell us about Arthur Swarbrick and your most recent disagreements with him.'

She looked at Northcott. 'You sergeant can tell you about the most recent ones.'

'I want to hear it from you, not from him, Mrs Crawshaw.'

Olive felt for the first time at a disadvantage. She didn't know whether Clyde had told his chief about his interview and Swarbrick's opposition to his membership, or about last night's more openly insulting behaviour towards the club's newest member. 'Arthur Swarbrick is conservative in most things. In everything, as far as I can see. He'll maintain vehemently that he isn't a racist or a bastion of privilege, but as far as I'm concerned he is both.'

'I imagine from what you've said so far that you head up the opposition in the club. You are probably what he would call a dangerous leftie, or at least a liberal do-gooder, who is anxious to see all standards and traditions disappear.'

She pursed her lips and then nodded. 'You put it rather trenchantly, DCI Peach. But that's probably a fair summary.'

'So Mr Swarbrick opposed my colleague's application for membership of Birch Hills?'

'I think it's fair to break the confidentiality I should normally accord to discussions in committee, in view of the crime you're investigating. Yes, Arthur opposed Clyde's membership, as it was predictable that he would do. That was despite the fact that the general committee of the club had agreed that we should make every effort to broaden the social spectrum of our membership and cast our net much more widely.'

'But your chairman opposed this policy?'

'It was predictable. He opposed Asian membership fifteen years or so ago. That is a battle that has long since been fought and won. Or fought and lost, in Arthur's case. You can see how tardy, even prejudiced, we've been at Birch Hills when I tell you that Clyde is our first black member.'

She looked directly at Clyde, who smiled nervously. This was the wrong way round, he thought: it was supposed to be the interviewees who were nervous and embarrassed when you conducted interviews. He said, 'Mrs Crawshaw encouraged me to apply for membership of the club and I am sure she was instrumental in securing my acceptance. I am not sure that I would have pursued membership without her . . . her encouragement.'

Olive grinned delightedly. 'Without my pitchforking you in and giving you no option, you mean?'

Clyde gave a rather sickly smile. 'You supported me throughout. You also arranged for me to meet and play with friendly members for my first game. I shall always be grateful for that, at least.'

'Elaine Brockman and I supported you, you mean. You've got a gem there, Clyde, and if you're as sensible, as I believe you are, you'll hold on to her. I've known her since she was ten. She's bright as well as pretty.' She glanced impishly at Peach. 'Too bright to become a policewoman, in her dad's view.'

Peach said unsmilingly, 'We don't have policewomen any more, Mrs Crawshaw. They're all police officers now. That's the result of campaigning by liberal do-gooders, I suppose. PC Brockman is graduate entry. Be ordering us all around in a few years, I expect.'

'It's good to find a senior policeman so open to new ideas.'

Peach smiled graciously. 'I deduce from your attitude that Mr Swarbrick annoyed you last night, Mrs Crawshaw.'

She looked at him, then at Northcott. The immediate shake of the head told her that he had not informed his chief of Swarbrick's attempt to humiliate him publicly. This man Peach seemed able to divine all sorts of things that she hadn't expected him to know. 'It was a small thing really, but designed to be very wounding. Arthur was touring the edge of the floor, doing his gracious chairman's act of welcoming members and their guests at our summer ball. It's old-fashioned and to me it reeks of elitism, but he likes to do it and most people seem to appreciate it. A Brunton version of the local aristocrat at the hunt ball, if you like – Arthur would certainly have revelled in that role.'

'And did my sergeant disturb the even tenor of this traditional circuit? He has a tendency to do that, does DS Northcott; he's what's technically known in police jargon as a hard bastard. All right for simple, rough-cut souls like me, but a little crude for Birch Fields Tennis Club.'

'Clyde behaved impeccably. He showed grace in the face of blatant ill manners.'

'That doesn't sound much like him,' said Percy doubtfully.

'It is exactly like him, as far as I am concerned. I have not known Mr Northcott for as long as you have, but I am prepared to back my judgement in the matter.'

'There's really no need for all this!' said Clyde, by this time highly embarrassed by the spectacle of these two formidable adversaries picking over his corpse. 'It was a trifling incident which was over in a few seconds. Most people didn't even notice it.'

'If that is so, it is because you chose not to take offence. You rose above Swarbrick's petty snobbery and dismissed it as the futile nonsense it was.'

'DS Northcott is good at rising above things. He has the build for it,' said Peach. 'Would you now tell us exactly what happened, please?'

Olive Crawshaw sighed. 'When the chairman arrived at Clyde and Elaine Brockman in his peregrination, he stopped and made a great fuss of Elaine, whom he has known, as I have, since she joined the club as a child. That was fine. Miss Brockman has been away at university for three years and has made very few appearances at the club during that time. Arthur very properly welcomed her back. But he then pointedly ignored her partner for the evening, whom he should have welcomed cordially as his newest member. Clyde was waiting to be greeted, but he was left standing like a muffin beside the girl of whom Arthur had just made such a fuss.'

'"Standing like a muffin",' said Peach slowly, as if making a mental note of the phrase. 'He's also good at that, is DS Northcott.'

Olive gave him a thunderous look, which left Percy quite unabashed. 'Clyde conducted himself with admirable restraint. I was proud of him.' She spoke of the huge black man as if he were a favourite pupil of twelve rather than the most formidable DS in Brunton's CID section. 'He showed himself to be the bigger man in what could have been a very embarrassing situation. He refused to take offence.'

Clyde said rather desperately, 'It wasn't very embarrassing for me. I'm used to much worse than that. It's like water off a duck's back to me. I think we should move on.'

To his relief, Mrs Crawshaw nodded. 'We should do just that, with a major crime to be investigated.' She darted another disapproving look at Peach, who responded with the blandest of his smiles. 'I shall have a word with Arthur Swarbrick about it when the opportunity arises.'

'Now that you have found that he is still with us in this world, when you thought he had been thrust out of it.' Peach nodded. 'Did you see Jason Fitton during the evening?'

'Yes. Not until around eleven, I think. He arrived late but made sure that everyone knew he was around, once he was in the room.'

Peach nodded. 'This is good. You don't seem to have missed much of what happened last night.'

'I was on my own at the ball. Eric attends other social events, but he says that the formal ball at the tennis club is not his scene.' She glanced briefly at her husband, who nodded his agreement. 'I danced a few times, when asked. I'm an old-fashioned person. I don't ask men to dance unless a ladies' invitation or excuse-me is announced. They don't have many of those nowadays. I was free to observe the passing scene for most of the evening.'

'Which now makes you an expert witness, as far as we're concerned. Did you see anything worthy of note in Mr Fitton's behaviour?'

'No. He circulated quite widely, making himself as agreeable as possible, in a superficial sort of way.'

'You didn't like Mr Fitton, did you?'

'Is that relevant? Or is it an intrusion into my private opinions?'

'It's highly relevant, as the man is at this moment being cut up in the pathology lab for the purposes of finding his killer.'

Peach saw Eric Crawshaw flinch away to his left, but his wife gave no such evidence of weakness. 'You're quite right, of course,' she conceded. Then she gathered her thoughts for what she planned to say. 'Derek Fitton was a great benefactor of this place. He built up Fitton's Metals, bringing prosperity and employment to the town. He used his wealth to help a number of local charities, without ostentation or publicity. I didn't approve of his sending his son to Eton, simply because I don't approve of private education. I don't think the state system will improve whilst the rich and the influential can buy out of it.' She breathed deeply, then turned reluctantly away from what was plainly a hobby horse. 'But that was his business. I got to know Derek Fitton quite well. I admired him and I was saddened by his early death.'

'But his son was a different kettle of fish?'

She winced at the cliché, then added to it with gusto. 'A different kettle of *stinking* fish, you might say. I don't know the details of how he made his money and I don't wish to know them. But I think he was a malignant influence in our town, whereas his father had been a benevolent one.'

'Brunton CID section would agree with you wholeheartedly on both counts. We had been investigating Jason Fitton for some while at the time of his death.'

'But not arresting him. Not putting a stop to his baleful activities.'

'You need evidence to put a man in court, Mrs Crawshaw. I'm sure that you would agree that is a good thing. But it makes it difficult to bring charges against clever men. Most of the major criminals nowadays are clever men. I'm told that clever people in criminology departments at universities are busy compiling PhD theses on the subject. Meanwhile, we poor devils at the crimeface work very hard to assemble the evidence to charge men like Fitton. It's a fact of life we have to live with.'

Olive nodded. 'Which we liberal do-gooders have forced upon you.'

Peach smiled at her. 'It might surprise you to know that I agree with most of the restrictions now placed upon the police. Please treat that as confidential and don't broadcast it amongst my colleagues: I have a reputation to maintain.'

Olive returned his smile.

Northcott could see what he considered the unlikeliest of agreements between these two people who had had the greatest effect upon his recent activities. He said, 'I was aware of Fitton's presence last night. He was one of the few people there whom I already knew – in a quite different context, of course. I didn't see him do anything suspicious or have any significant disagreements with anyone at the ball.'

'As you have already informed me earlier in the day, DS Northcott. But you had distractions, viz. the multiple attractions of PC Brockman. I'm sure Mrs Crawshaw was able to be much more single-minded and observant.'

Olive smiled. 'I confirm what Clyde has just said. Fitton knew what I thought of him and he barely acknowledged me, but I'd say he was anxious to avoid any sort of conflict last night. In my opinion, he was showing himself at the biggest social function at Birch Fields because people he considered important were there. People with money and influence in the town, whose support he needed for his future plans.'

Peach nodded thoughtfully. 'Clients of his, would you say, Mrs Crawshaw? I don't mean at Fitton's Metals, but in his other and more dubious enterprises.'

There was quite a pause whilst she considered this. 'You're probably right. I wouldn't like to speculate about who those clients might be.'

'I see. Well, that's quite understandable. You have an enquiring mind, but you don't have the information that we have assembled over the years. Was Younis Hafeez at the summer ball?'

Peach had seemed quite relaxed with Olive Crawshaw. He had even seemed to be enjoying her company. But this last

question was fired at her like a pistol shot. She stared hard at
him, recognizing his aggression. 'He was there, yes. I didn't
see him in conversation with Jason Fitton. That does not mean,
of course, that no such conversation took place. I am neither
omnipresent nor all-hearing.'

'He had an association with Fitton that interests us. That's
why I ask about him.'

'You mean he's another wrong'un, as we call them in
Lancashire? You don't surprise me. I don't know Hafeez well,
but I wouldn't trust him as far as I could throw him. That's
just from what I've seen of him around the tennis club. I used
to be in charge of the youngsters – boys and girls from ten to
fourteen – and I didn't like the interest he took and the way
he used to watch those kids.'

'How is he with older women? Women in their twenties,
say?'

'Older women should be able to look after themselves, in
my opinion.'

'But not all women are as resourceful as you.' Peach caught
a smile at that thought on the face of Eric Crawshaw, away
to his left, but kept his gaze on the face of his wife.

'I suppose you're right. It's surprising how naive some
women can be where men are concerned, even at the age of
thirty or forty. I'm sure Younis Hafeez would be dangerous.
He's good-looking, I suppose, in a slightly sinister sort of way:
you can never quite tell what he is thinking. He has a nice
olive skin and he can be quite charming when he puts his
mind to it. I've seen him in action once or twice.'

'Thank you for being so frank. Everything you have said
here will be treated as confidential, as you would expect. Did
you see anything last night or are you aware of any previous
happening that would suggest who killed Jason Fitton? Again,
any speculation will go no further than this room.'

Olive gave the matter due thought. It was rather exciting,
this game of cat and mouse with a real detective; it helped
that the body of a man she had despised was at the centre
of things. 'No. I'm sure there were several people there who
either feared or hated Fitton, but I can't give you any further
pointers.'

'Did you leave before the end of the ball, Mrs Crawshaw?'

'No. I stayed to the end. I removed the hand of a harmless lecher from my right buttock during the final stages of the last waltz. Then I drove myself home.'

'And your husband will no doubt be able to confirm that for us.'

Olive's face filled with outrage. 'You're treating me as a suspect, aren't you?'

'These are the questions members of our team will be asking other people who were there last night. It's routine. We proceed by elimination.'

'But I get the big cheese who's in charge. I'm treated as a major suspect, despite my complete cooperation in answering your questions.'

Clyde said hastily, 'I'm sure you should take that as a compliment, Mrs Crawshaw.'

She gave Peach a baleful glare, then said tersely, 'I must have been back here by about one thirty. Eric will be able to confirm that for you.'

Three faces turned expectantly towards the man in the corner of the room. He stared blatantly at them, then said, 'I don't think I can do that, dear. I was fast asleep when you came in, and you were kind enough not to disturb me.'

Clyde couldn't be absolutely sure, but he though there might be a tiny hint of mischief in Eric Crawshaw's tone. His features were as open and innocent as those of a child.

Peach said with more open relish, 'Perhaps there is someone else who could confirm to us what time you left Birch Fields, Mrs Crawshaw?'

'I don't think there is. Most people were in couples at the close of the dance. I slunk away on my own, as you would expect.'

'I can't imagine you slinking anywhere, Mrs Crawshaw. It's just a pity that no one can confirm your movements at that time to us. Ah well, just routine, as I said.'

Clyde made sure they were in the car and out of sight as well as earshot before he said, 'You quite enjoyed that, didn't you?'

'I suppose I did. We're not seeing anyone else today, so we

had time to indulge ourselves with La Crawshaw. Nice to move amidst the educated gentry, as opposed to the crude yobs we usually have to pit our wits against. Or against whom we have to pit our wits, as Olive would no doubt prefer me to put it.'

Grammar was a mystery to Clyde and he was content that it should remain so. 'I'm surprised she was so tolerant with you.'

'Product of state education, you see, Clyde. Not a shirt-lifting public schoolboy like Jason Fitton. People make allowances for deserving lads like me.'

'Interesting that she should be so suspicious on her own account of Fitton and Hafeez. We have all sorts of knowledge that she doesn't possess, but she has them down as villains.'

'Interesting also that she had the wrong victim in mind. We must have a good look at this Arthur Swarbrick, chairman and bigot.'

'He seems a routine sort of racist to me, after my two meetings with him. I wouldn't have put my money on him to be either a murderer or a murder victim.'

Peach watched the Tarmac racing beneath their wheels for a moment, then said with one of his more impish smiles, 'It might just be Olive's attempt to divert us, of course, guessing at the wrong victim. Quite clever, if it was.'

Clyde rose immediately to the bait, shocked by this suggestion about his sponsor and supporter at Birch Fields. 'You can't possibly consider Olive Crawshaw to be a serious candidate for murder.'

'Why not? She spoke with real passion when she described her feelings about Jason Fitton. And she hasn't got an alibi. We don't even know what time she got home last night. Eric denied her that. He seemed a little odd at that moment. I wonder what she's saying to him now.'

'Olive didn't kill Fitton.'

'She has the intelligence and the coolness to plan it and get away with it. I like her, but I've liked a couple of other murderers too, over the years. Olive Crawshaw had motive, opportunity and capacity. First rule of detection: don't rule out anyone with those three until you have the full facts to do so.'

Peach stared at the road ahead with a thoughtful smile.

In the house they had left, Olive Crawshaw was serving her husband a cup of tea. 'I thought you did very well, Eric,' she said tenderly. 'It's a while since you had to talk with policemen, isn't it?'

TEN

Anne Grice was dealing with a situation she had never encountered before. But very few PAs would have had to tackle anything like this, she consoled herself. She was a methodical person who preferred to avoid surprises. She could think on her feet when it was necessary, but she preferred to avoid that. The whole of her training and experience had reinforced these qualities in her: a PA should be calm and organized, especially when chaos reigned around her. Sometimes even your direct employer could be drawn into the maelstrom, but even then you should remain calm; it was part of the service you offered him.

Bob Walmsley wasn't panicking, but he was disturbed. That was understandable, with the owner of the firm meeting sudden death over the weekend. The place was full of speculation. People wanted to know how Jason Fitton had died and who was involved. They also had more personal anxieties. What was going to happen to Fitton's Metals now that its absentee owner had met a violent end? More pertinently, what was going to happen to his employees and to their jobs? Anne knew well enough that an uncertain future was the greatest of all sources of alarm and anxiety.

So many people came into her office during the first hour of the working day that she had the greatest trouble in insulating the managing director from the excitement outside. That was one of her functions as a PA, but she had never had more difficulty in exercising it. She needed some compromise if she was not to lose out against the chaos. At ten o'clock she buzzed her boss. 'Mr Walmsley, there are all sorts of speculation out here and on the floor of the works. Rumour is feeding upon uncertainty, as you would expect. Could I bring in a few senior people to see you? Maybe you will be able to offer them some form of reassurance.'

Bob forced himself to be calm. 'Yes, I think that would be

an excellent move, Anne. I'm waiting for a couple of people to ring me back. Could you bring in a small delegation at half past ten? I might have something a little more definite to report by then.'

She assembled the group carefully. The sales director, who had endured two difficult years. The research and development chief, who had been frustrated recently by declining funds. The shop steward from the factory floor, who would be able to report to the skilled and semi-skilled workers that nothing was going to happen immediately. The senior driver, who was due to take a delivery out at eleven o'clock and was wondering what he should tell the recipients about future supplies. And she herself, who would represent the office staff and report back to them calmly upon the meeting with the managing director.

She arranged for five chairs to be set in front of Walmsley's desk and led her little posse in when she was given the signal to do so at exactly ten thirty. The boss looked harassed, as they would have expected. Anne glanced along the line of chairs and saw that no one was certain as to who should speak. She took the initiative and delivered the formal statement she had planned. 'We were all very sorry to hear of Mr Fitton's death. I am a recent arrival, but the other people here knew our owner for a long time. We are both shocked and sorry to hear of his death. It may seem insensitive to raise these matters so promptly, but we are also concerned about what is going to happen next. Most of the people who work here, male or female, have families to consider, so we hope you will not think it insensitive if we ask you to keep us informed of developments and of present thinking about the firm's position.'

There was a muttering of approval from the four people who had come with her into the managing director's office. She'd said the right things, been diplomatic without disguising the real reasons why they were here, thought Bob Walmsley. She was an intelligent and highly capable woman, Anne Grice, as he'd decided within a week of appointing her.

'Thank you for those sentiments. There are a couple of people here who can go back to the time when Jason's father controlled the firm and was much more in evidence than Jason chose to be of recent years. I understand your concerns and I am doing what I can to allay them. Most of you will know that Jason Fitton had no children. It seems likely that owner-ship and control of the firm will pass to Derek Fitton's two great-nieces in Leeds, one of whom was Jason's god-daughter. I am awaiting a phone call from Mr Fitton's solicitors which I anticipate will confirm that. As the older people here will recall and I have just mentioned, Mr Derek Fitton was much more hands-on in his control than his son chose to be. I cannot think that the new owners are going to wish to take a more active part in the running of the firm. They would, in my view, be foolish to do so, given the expertise and special knowledge possessed by its workers, not least in this room. I am sorry that I cannot offer you anything more definite than this, but you now know as much as I do at this moment.'

It was a nicely turned little speech, Anne thought, with just the right infusion of flattery at the end, which was probably genuine rather than mere smarm. Bob really did appreciate the qualities of the people who worked for him and he knew his workforce well. She voiced the question she had heard circulating around the works before she brought her group in here. 'Is there any news yet on how Mr Fitton died? The radio and television said it was being treated as a suspicious death.'

'The chief investigating officer came to see me yesterday. I wasn't able to help him much, but I suppose he thought that as the senior employee in the firm I might be able to provide useful information. It seems that Mr Fitton died after the summer ball at Birch Fields Tennis Club on Saturday night. I was not at the dance myself, but I think the police are treating his death as murder or manslaughter; they certainly spoke of him as a victim.'

Even in this small group, there was the tiny frisson of excitement that mention of the greatest crime of all invariably rouses. Anne Grice thought at first that there were no questions from her little group, as people clutched their files and prepared to go back and report to their juniors. But David Browne, the man in charge of research and development, had not moved at all. He was a thin, intense man with thick horn-rimmed glasses which he had not changed for years and a receding hairline that made him look older than he was. He now said abruptly, 'Do you think there will be an increase in the funds allotted to research and development, Mr Walmsley? Our budget has been pared to a minimum and the firm is going to suffer for that in the coming years unless it is restored. I think you agree with me on this.'

Walmsley handled this unexpected and rather premature bid for funds and special consideration rather well. He smiled affectionately at Browne, reducing the tension that his plea had aroused amongst the others. 'I do agree, David, and I shall be putting the case for increased research funding as soon as the opportunity arises. But the answer to your question can only be that I do not know as yet. As soon as I learn more, I promise that you will all share that knowledge. Perhaps we could agree now to meet at the same time on Thursday morning, when I shall bring you up to date with whatever developments take place in the next three days. If you cannot be here yourself, please delegate someone else to attend. Meanwhile, I look to senior people like you to bring as much calm as you can into what is a distressing situation for all of us.'

He was still sitting at his desk when Anne came back into the room to see what he next required on this most extraordinary of Monday mornings. 'Could you bring me in the latest auditors' report on the state of the business and the latest detailed profit and loss figures, Anne? I need to be precisely informed when I speak to the new owners in an hour or so.'

He was certain to be that, thought Anne, as she extracted the relevant papers. Bob was of the old school: he preferred to be able to refer to papers in front of him rather than reading things on a computer screen. He felt more confident that way, he said. He was a good man, her new boss, as well as competent. He was quite sincere when he said he wanted to safeguard the futures of all the people who worked here.

She took in the files and he asked her to sit down, because he wanted to dictate letters to alleviate the anxieties of important customers and trading partners. He looked a little drawn and tired, but quite calm. He flicked through the profit and loss accounts, then gave her the first smile she had seen from him in two hours. He leaned back, making a conscious effort to relax in his leather chair.

He looked her full in the face and said slowly, 'Life is going to be a little more straightforward for us, from now on.'

Shirley Swarbrick let the CID officers into the house. She'd studied them closely as they arrived and introduced themselves. There were two of them: a big black detective sergeant who rather frightened her and a detective chief inspector who bounced in as if he couldn't wait to get moving. Well, at least they'd sent the man in charge of the case, even if he didn't look very impressive. The senior man was what was appropriate, in view of her husband's standing and his position as chairman of the tennis club.

'Mr Swarbrick will see you in the living room,' she announced magisterially. 'I'm sure that you will have no objection to my presence.'

'We need to see him alone, I'm afraid. If you would like to provide us with a cup of tea or coffee, that would be much appreciated.'

'But I might be able to contribute bits of information that my husband has omitted. He tends to overlook things which a woman notices.'

'Does he, indeed? Well, in that case we shall need to probe his memory. And we may even need to see you alone at a later date, Mrs Swarbrick, depending on how things go. People recall things differently, you see. They even contradict each other on occasions, and that is usually of great interest to us. That's one of the main reasons we like to speak to people separately.'

Arthur Swarbrick had appeared in the hall halfway though this. He resolved the matter by saying, 'In that case I think it would be best if we spoke in my study, gentlemen.' He led them into a small room at the front of the house and shut the door comprehensively behind them. 'Women!' he said, and cast his eyes to heaven, as if hoping that the single word would establish a significant male bond between three very different men.

Peach sat down unhurriedly in the chair indicated to him

and said briskly, 'I'm Detective Chief Inspector Peach. You already know Detective Sergeant Northcott.'

'I do indeed.' Swarbrick masked any antipathy behind a mask of affability. 'Bad business, this. Bad for the tennis club.'

'And bad for you as the chairman of it, I expect. Won't help recruitment, will it – a murder on the premises?'

'A murder, Chief Inspector? You're convinced Jason's death was that, then?'

'We are, Mr Swarbrick. The official confirmation will take a little time, but we have to get on with things, make an arrest as quickly as we can. That's why we're here this morning – not to make an arrest, unless you care to make a confession, but to press forward our enquiries.'

Arthur volunteered a rather uncertain laugh. The mention of a confession seemed to call for that. He found that the two men who sat with him scarcely smiled. Instead, Peach said, 'You have a senior position at Birch Fields. You have been around for a long time. You are no doubt well equipped to tell us more than anyone else can about what goes on there.'

'I'm not sure about that.' Arthur, who'd been determined to be urbane and in control of events before they came, already felt uneasy. 'I don't play as much as I used to, and there are no doubt younger members who—'

'Our team is busy speaking to some of them at this very moment, Mr Swarbrick. In particular, to those who attended the summer ball on Saturday night. We ourselves have already spoken with Mrs Crawshaw, as well as with the managing director of Fitton's Metals.'

Peach sat back and looked with satisfaction at his shining toecaps for a moment, giving Swarbrick the impression that they already knew many significant facts and that he had better be very careful about what he said this morning. Arthur said nervously, 'It's a mystery to me how this could happen at Birch Fields.'

'Is it really, sir? Well, less of a mystery than it is to us at the moment, no doubt, because we have no knowledge of the club and what goes on there.'

Arthur tried to lighten things a little. 'That's not entirely true, is it, Chief Inspector? Your sergeant here has recently become a member of our club. He was present, indeed, on Saturday evening, along with one of our lady playing members, who I understand is now a member of your staff.'

'DS Northcott is indeed now a member at Birch Fields. I didn't even know he played tennis until quite recently. Dark horse, isn't he?'

Peach beamed affably at Swarbrick, who had hoped for a ridiculous moment that this was an allusion to the colour of Northcott's skin. He said uneasily, 'I haven't had the chance to get to know Clyde well, as yet.'

'Really? Well, I expect you will be making every effort to get to know him better during the coming weeks. Assuming that you are not under arrest and held in custody during that time, of course.' Peach nodded thoughtfully at that possibility, ignoring another awkward laugh from Swarbrick. 'I understand from Mrs Crawshaw that you welcomed DS Northcott as your newest member on Saturday night.'

Arthur had been wishing bitterly before they came that he had not snubbed Northcott so decisively at the ball. He was even more embarrassed to find the man now in front of him, watching his every move and assisting in the investigation of a murder. 'Yes. I didn't have as much time for conversation as I would have liked. I had to get round as many of my members as I could. It was no more than a formal greeting.'

'Or non-greeting, as the case might be.' Peach nodded happily. 'Well, it doesn't seem to have any bearing on what happened later. DS Northcott hasn't reported any suspicious behaviour on your part.'

'I should hope not.' The third of Arthur's nervous laughs sounded loud in the small, quiet room. They had become progressively more desperate.

'Jason Fitton died in the car park at Birch Fields, probably, but not certainly, in the hour after the dance was concluded – that is, between one and two a.m. yesterday. You saw him during the evening?'

The man made a simple fact sound like an accusation, Arthur thought. 'I did, as did lots of other people.'

'Did you speak to him during your original round of greetings?

The one in which you spoke to PC Brockman and ignored DS Northcott?'

Arthur almost contested this. But the man he had insulted was sitting watchfully in front of him, though he had said not a word as yet. He decided just in time that it was better to ignore it. 'No. Jason did not arrive until later in the evening. At around half past ten, I think. I hadn't seen him before then.'

'That tallies with what other people have told us, which must be reassuring for you. Did you speak to him in public?'

'No. I didn't speak to him in private either, since that is what your question seems to imply. The dancing was getting pretty hectic by that time in the evening. I think I nodded to him across the room at one point.'

'Did you see him having any sort of altercation with anyone else who was there?'

'No. But I have to emphasize that I scarcely saw him.'

'Do you, indeed? Would you say that you knew Jason Fitton well?'

'No, not well. I knew his father quite well, when he was alive. He wasn't a tennis player, but he ran a scrap metal business and I ran a joinery business in the town, so we were business acquaintances. Derek's firm grew very successfully during the years in which I knew him; the two of us remained friends as well as business colleagues.'

Peach sensed that Swarbrick was happier to talk about dead father than newly dead son. 'But you didn't like Jason as much as you liked his father.'

Arthur made himself take his time. This man Peach was getting to him; he couldn't afford that. 'I didn't. I felt I'd never really got to know Jason. He was away at school, of course, and then he spent time in London. He didn't really appear much in Brunton until his father died and he inherited the firm.'

'That is more than twelve years ago. I'd have thought you'd have now known him quite well, especially as he's a member of your tennis club.'

Arthur liked the idea that the tennis club was his personal fiefdom, which Peach seemed to be accepting. But he had to distance himself from Jason Fitton. 'Not a very active member, as I said. He can play reasonably, but he seems to use our social facilities as much as our playing ones. And I was never as close to him business-wise as I'd been to his father. Over recent years, I've seen his managing director, Bob Walmsley, much more often than I've seen Jason.'

'Business-wise, yes.' Peach weighed the word with some distaste. 'Some of Jason's business interests were highly dubious, were they not?'

'I've heard rumours to that effect. I cannot enlighten you further.'

'I see. This is one of the areas where we could probably enlighten you, Mr Swarbrick, but I cannot do so until we have enough evidence to go public. Meanwhile, Jason Fitton is a murder victim and our job is to find out who killed him.'

'From what you say, he's no loss to our town. Perhaps you won't be as determined as usual to find who it was who disposed of him.'

For a moment, he had let real venom creep into his tone. Peach noted it and let the man's words hang for a moment in the room. They could hear movements from his wife at the back of the house, but the tea or coffee that he had suggested earlier did not arrive. He said quietly, 'We shall find Fitton's killer and put him in court, Mr Swarbrick. Who else did you see speaking with him on Saturday night?'

'Younis Hafeez.' The name came too promptly upon the heels of the question to sound spontaneous. Hafeez was a man whom Swarbrick detested, but he should not have let that become so apparent. 'I say that only because it's the picture I have of Fitton at the ball. He was talking to Hafeez when I first saw that he was there. I suppose the image has stayed with me since I heard that Fitton was dead.'

'Were the two of them arguing?'

He would have liked to say yes. He would have liked indeed to say that they had almost been at each other's throats and that a couple of hours later one of them had been murdered. But these men were talking to others, patiently and accurately unravelling the events of Saturday night. They'd expose him if he lied, and come back to ask him why. 'They were too far away for me to be certain whether there was any dispute. They were on the other side of the dance floor and there was a lot of noise and laughter, so I could not be at all certain how amiable their exchanges were.'

'So you didn't detect any sign of a dispute between them?'

'No. That doesn't mean that there wasn't one. Just that I didn't see anything. I was preoccupied with other concerns.'

Clyde Northcott, who had kept only a watching brief until now, said, 'Was Mrs Swarbrick with you throughout the evening, Arthur?'

Swarbrick felt a sense of outrage at the use of his forename by this black policeman. But Northcott was a member of the tennis club now, and thus entitled to such familiarity. 'No. She'd only come to the ball because of my position as chairman of the club. She departed with some neighbours of ours at twelve o'clock. I felt I had to stay until the close, because of my position.'

'And when did you leave, Arthur?'

Again that use of his forename. Northcott's tone was neutral, even friendly, but he was taking the piss. Nor did Arthur like the direction of his questions. 'I didn't need to hurry, because I knew Shirley was safely at home and in bed. I thanked the band for their efforts, then watched them put away their instruments and depart. Most of the members and guests had gone by then, though a few of them were still laughing and shouting to each other across the car park.

'Why did you stay so long, Arthur? I should have thought that you'd be anxious to be away, being on your own by this time.'

'I didn't think like that. I suppose that being chairman for years now has brought a certain proprietorial quality to my actions. It seemed natural to me to take my time and see most people off the premises. It probably seems silly to you, but I feel a sense of responsibility about things like the annual ball. You want to see it go well and when it's all over you want to see everyone depart home safely.'

There was a short silence. Then Peach, with one of his more innocent smiles, said, 'Of course, another explanation would be that you waited your chance to dispatch your sworn enemy Jason Fitton from this world.'

'That's outrageous!'

'It is, isn't it? But it's the way we simple souls are taught to think, you see. We coppers are always looking for the black side of human nature. I suppose that's because we come up against it so often.' Percy beamed his satisfaction at this philosophical observation. 'We'd better have your reaction to my outrageous suggestion, I think.'

'I certainly didn't do any such thing. Fitton's death has nothing to do with me.'

But you didn't reject my description of him as your sworn enemy, Percy noted silently. He stopped smiling and barked, 'Where and when did you last see Jason Fitton, Mr Swarbrick?'

'During the dance. Fitton was on the other side of the floor from me, and he was talking to someone, not dancing. It was somewhere near the end, but not right at the end. I don't think he danced the last waltz.'

'Thank you, sir. That's commendably precise.' *And carefully prepared*, Peach thought. *You expected to be asked just those questions*. 'What time did you leave the club?'

'I couldn't be precise about that. It was probably about one thirty. It's only ten minutes from here by car, but I made myself a cup of tea at home and was still in bed by two. I didn't disturb Shirley, who was sleeping soundly by this time.'

You're telling me that no one can confirm your story before I can point that out to you. Percy wanted to ask him if he and Shirley slept together, but that would be an unjustified intrusion. He might be back to ask it later in the week, if this innocent-looking man turned out to be a prime suspect. Tommy Bloody Tucker always wanted a prime suspect, irrespective of whether the evidence warranted it or not. He was still looking straight at his man as he said, 'Why didn't you like Jason Fitton, Mr Swarbrick?'

He looked as if he was going to deny it, but then shrugged his shoulders rather too elaborately. 'No particular reason. We had different temperaments, I suppose. I'd known his father well and liked him; I suppose I expected Derek's son to be from the same mould. But he wasn't. He was a maverick: he was prepared to deal with anyone and to consider anything that would make him money.'

Peach nodded slowly, without taking his eyes off Swarbrick's face. He was sixty-two: they'd checked that before they came here. He looked all of that and more now. He still had a plentiful crop of grey hair, but his face was also grey and the lines on it seemed to have deepened during their interview. There was nothing surprising in that: most people did not confront violent death more than once in their lives, whether first-hand or more distantly. 'Who do you think killed him, Mr Swarbrick?'

'I don't know, Detective Chief Inspector Peach. That's your job rather than mine, surely.'

'My job, yes.' Peach paused for a moment, as if the matter needed thought. 'But with the help of the public, of course. With the help of all good and responsible citizens. In this case, you are the citizen who knows most about the people who were at Birch Fields Tennis Club on Saturday night. I need hardly point out that there is a high probability that one of them was responsible for this killing. I'd like your thoughts on who might have committed this grave crime. Feel free to speculate: this will go no further, unless, of course, it proves fruitful, in which case your helpful contribution to our enquiries will be acknowledged.'

'I'm sure Jason had many enemies. You've hinted at some of his illegal activities. He was a rich man from them, but I imagine he must have made quite a few enemies.'

'Some of whom were no doubt at your summer ball on Saturday night.'

'I suppose that is so. Olive Crawshaw didn't like him any more than I did. And Olive's opinions are quite different from mine. I suppose that just shows what a wide range of enemies Jason must have had. I can't see Olive as a killer, though.' He sat back, even smiled a little, as if anxious to emphasize how fair-minded he was.

Peach said unsmilingly, 'Whereas we have to consider everyone, until we know otherwise. Who else, Mr Swarbrick?'

Arthur had left the man he most wanted to implicate until last, so that he might preserve the impression of neutrality. 'You'll have to consider Younis Hafeez, I suppose. Is it racist to say that I wouldn't trust that man very far?'

'Not if it's an accurate statement of your feelings. That's what we need from you at this point.'

'I think Hafeez has had business dealings with Fitton, but you will know more about that than I would.'

'Indeed we do, Mr Swarbrick. Why do you think he might have killed Fitton?'

'I think he's a man capable of murder, that's all. I've no real evidence to offer you.'

Peach nodded, waited a few seconds to see if Swarbrick would add to that thought, then stood up. 'Please ring this number immediately if you have further thoughts or discover significant facts when you speak to people at the tennis club.'

They had travelled some distance in the car before Peach said, 'Swarbrick disliked Jason Fitton much more than he's so far admitted to us. I wonder why.'

'I was wondering exactly the same thing, sir,' said Clyde Northcott gnomically.

ELEVEN

T he PM report was available by Monday afternoon. So were the initial findings of the forensic team, who were still examining the dead man's car and clothes with the thoroughness permitted by modern machinery and techniques.

Peach brought in DC Brendan Murphy and PC Elaine Brockman to examine the findings with him and Northcott. Clyde was dubious about involving Elaine. 'She's not even CID and we're not inviting the rest of the murder team in. It will cause talk around the station. People will think she's getting special treatment. It will make things difficult for her with the rest of the uniforms.'

'She's graduate entry, isn't she? Those buggers are supposed to get the widest possible experience in the shortest possible time, so that they can order us all around in a few years. PC Brockman needs to learn to look after herself. And she's got the local hard bastard to look out for her, if push comes to shove. Tell them Tommy Bloody Tucker authorized it, if they ask any questions. Anyway, she's a long-standing member of the tennis club where this crime took place. Her knowledge of previous local shenanigans might be invaluable to us, seeing as you seem to have learned so bloody little about the place.'

And so it was that a rather wide-eyed and determinedly silent Elaine Brockman joined the three experienced CID men to dissect these latest findings. She was given a photocopy of the sheet that the others were holding and found herself glad of the opportunity to look down at the words of the reports. It wasn't long since she'd used the technique in small groups at university, studying the print in front of her intently so as to avoid catching the tutor's eye and being asked for her opinions. It was the first time she'd ever been in any sort of contact with Percy Peach, and his fearsome reputation made him more threatening than any tutor had ever been.

There were no new revelations about the murder weapon.

The thin cord that had been ruthlessly tightened around the dead man's neck gave them nothing. The victim had no doubt raised his hands to it as it killed him, but had not even succeeded in getting his fingers between cord and neck in his brief struggle to maintain his life. That struggle had been as hopeless as it was brief. It had lasted only seconds and there was nothing beneath the corpse's nails that could help them. He had not laid hands on his enemy, not torn hair or flesh or skin from whoever had dispatched him so ruthlessly.

The cord itself, the murder weapon, was equally unrevealing. It was a hundred and twenty-four centimetres, or just over four feet in length. The two ends had been twisted savagely and swiftly to kill Jason Fitton, but whoever had done that had worn leather gloves. With the leverage possible for someone attacking an unsuspecting victim from the rear, no great strength had been necessary in the killer. A woman – even a child – could have done this. The cord was obtainable anywhere. There were examples of it in the maintenance rooms at the tennis club, amongst the spare nets and the fencing wire and the paint tins, but the cord could just as easily have been brought in from outside, because it was freely available in any hardware shop.

The car gave them little more. The Bentley was regularly valeted. It had last been cleaned on the Tuesday before Fitton died. That was annoying, because it left four full days between valeting and death, time for a variety of passengers to have occupied every seat in the car. Fitton had driven to Manchester on Wednesday and to Leeds on Friday for business meetings; as yet it had proved impossible to establish whom he had met on either of these expeditions. No one knew whether he had carried passengers with him in the front or rear of the car. Fibres and head hair collected from the front passenger seat of the Bentley showed that at least two and probably three people had occupied it since it had last been cleaned.

Particular attention had been paid to the rear seat on the off side of the vehicle, since that was almost certainly where the killer had sat as the cord was tightened around the victim's neck. But again all that had become clear was that at least two people had sat there between Wednesday and Saturday.

These might or might not have included the killer: it was possible that if he had been aware of forensics and clad himself accordingly, he might have executed the crime without leaving enough of himself behind to be identified. Or herself, of course: policemen always think and speak of males, since nine-tenths of violent crimes are committed by men. There was nothing helpful in the footwell in front of that seat where the killer had sat, indicating again that he had been careful and methodical. Or perhaps simply lucky in his choice of footwear and the nature of its soles; you couldn't afford to exclude even the unlikely, at this stage.

Hairs and fibres had been carefully isolated and stored by the forensic team, as part of the routine in these circumstances. They might eventually provide DNA matches with samples taken from someone arrested for this crime, but that was hypothetical and very distant. It could not be conclusive in itself, since more than one person had occupied the relevant seats in the Bentley in the days before the murder.

Younis Hafeez arranged to see the CID on his own working patch. You didn't want people like that defiling your home, and he had things there that were completely private and needed to remain so. He'd been expecting the call, of course. Indeed, it had taken rather longer than he had expected to arrive. That had made him nervous, or as near to nervous as he ever came.

Peach looked up at the block of offices as Northcott parked the police Mondeo. A large, undistinguished block. Expensive, possibly even impressive in an overbearing sort of way, but without a scrap of architectural merit. Functional but characterless. Some of these places were different inside; they could be quite agreeable to work in or live in. It was nevertheless surprising two minutes later to find that Hafeez's office was so pleasant.

The lift took them swiftly and silently to the top floor, where Hafeez's section occupied a third of the space. The anteroom where his PA operated was generous in size, but modest compared with the spacious suite with long windows on two sides that Hafeez himself occupied. 'Please take a seat, Detective

Chief Inspector Peach. I've been expecting you.' He gestured towards the low, wide, ridiculously soft and comfortable armchair beneath the west-facing window. 'And you too, Clyde.' He smiled into the uncompromising dark face of his fellow member at Birch Fields, greeting him as if he were an old friend rather than a recent enemy. 'It's nice to feel under these distressing circumstances that there is a fellow tennis player involved in the search for a killer.'

'You know that murder is involved, then?' said Peach. He spoke as aggressively as he could, but it was difficult whilst sitting on the very edge of this too-comfortable chair, feeling like a pea on a drum, one of his dead mother's favourite similes.

Hafeez gave him a condescending smile, relaxing above him in a higher and less accommodating chair with his back to the light, reversing the positions Peach liked to establish between questioner and questioned. 'Foul play is suspected, the bulletins tell me. I always take police information seriously.'

'If you took police warnings seriously, we might be speaking in a different place, or perhaps not speaking at all.'

Younis Hafeez's smile diminished, but did not disappear. He was on his own ground and he had the advantage. He planned to retain it. 'I shouldn't need to remind you that no charges have ever been brought against me, Chief Inspector. That is because there was no substance at all in the spurious accusations which some spiteful people chose to make against me. I am only sorry that the police, and in particular the CID section at Brunton, chose to listen to squalid rumour and engage in interrogations that could only embarrass them. I'm sure that your Chief Superintendent Tucker would now support that view. Thank heavens that there is still such a thing as an enlightened senior policeman.'

'We thank heaven each day for Chief Superintendent Tucker. His name is rarely off our lips,' said Percy grimly. He looked round the spacious office, with its thick carpets, lavishly expensive furnishings and almost total absence of the normal business accoutrements such as a computer and filings cabinets. 'We are not here to investigate the trafficking in underage girls and their enforced prostitution, which still interest us, but the very specific crime of murder. I hope that will be a relief for you.'

'Since I am not involved in either of those totally reprehensible crimes, it will be a matter of total indifference to me, Mr Peach.' He turned elaborately and graciously towards the man who sat alongside Peach in a matching low chair. 'And Clyde, of course. I wouldn't like Clyde to feel left out. Tea? Coffee? Biscuits and cakes? Something stronger perhaps? I shall not indulge myself, but I wish to offer whatever will emphasize to you how welcome you are here.' He uncrossed his immaculately trousered legs and raised a hand, as though ready to click his fingers and summon whatever delights they chose.

Peach was already irritated by this elaborate, mannered charade. But he knew that was the intention, so he maintained coolness and control as he said, 'Refreshments will not be necessary, Mr Hafeez. Mr Jason Fitton was a business associate of yours, wasn't he?'

Younis maintained the carapace of oily charm which all three of them knew was but a pretence. 'I knew the man. We were hardly business associates. I have no use for scrap metal, even in its recycled forms.'

'That was not the business I was referring to, as you know. He was involved in procuring underage girls and a smaller number of boys for their use and abuse by young and middle-aged men, the vast majority of whom were Asian. It's a vile but highly lucrative trade, and you are one of the men who have made it so. You were paying Fitton, and he was happy to accept your money. You were one of his better clients, with ready and seemingly bottomless funds and no doubt many customers eager to sample the goods you offered.'

Hafeez frowned a little. The crinkling of his forehead was more than usually noticeable, for his olive-skinned face was abnormally smooth and unlined. He shook his head sadly and said, 'I have no knowledge of such things. I suspect that you are merely seeking to distress me. Or, more charitably, that you have confused me with someone else. People tell me that white people often do that with Asians. I find that insulting, but I refuse to take offence, because I recognize that you have a difficult job to do, DCI Peach. No doubt your resources are also strained: everyone in the public services seems to complain about that nowadays. Often it seems to me merely an excuse for sloppiness and poor service.'

'You spoke to Jason Fitton on Saturday night, not long before he died.'

'How sinister you make things sound! I suppose that is one of the senior policeman's skills. Yes, I spoke to him. We are members of what I believe to be the town's premier sporting club and the summer ball is its biggest social occasion of the year. Of course we spoke to each other! We know each other well from our business dealings and we both relax by playing tennis at Birch Fields. It would have been unnatural if I had not spoken to Jason on Saturday night. And despite the foul and unwarranted accusations you have just made about girls of school age, I do not indulge in unnatural copulations, Detective Chief Inspector.'

'What was the subject of your final conversation with Jason Fitton?'

'I cannot remember. Perhaps your team, who seem to be questioning everyone who was present at the summer ball, will be able to enlighten us. It was something and nothing, something quite trivial – probably no more than a polite social exchange. Had it been more significant than that, I should have remembered it.'

His tone was mocking, but his command of English was more complete and his delivery more precise than that of many native Brunton residents. He had moved into the area about ten years earlier, but Peach had no record of where he had been before that. Perhaps he had spent all or most of his life in Britain. 'I can accept that you exchanged only meaningless pleasantries in public. But I was enquiring about your final conversation with our murder victim. The one you had in the car park when other people had departed, perhaps.'

'The one we had immediately before his death, you mean?' Younis produced his most taunting smile and passed it leisurely over first Peach and then Northcott. 'I'm sorry to disappoint you, but no such conversation took place.'

Northcott found himself wanting to hit the man's smiling,

eminently civilized face, much more than he ever wanted to
hit the scum who flung the vilest obscenities and racial abuse
into his face in the interview rooms at the station. He said
tersely, 'When did you last see Jason Fitton?'

'At approximately twelve minutes to one on Saturday night,
shortly before the band struck up the last waltz, which I believe
is customary on these occasions.'

Clyde made an elaborate business of recording this, as if
he anticipated a triumphant rebuttal of it at some later stage
in the investigation. He looked round at this strange business
accommodation, which, apart from the desk and the leather
chair behind it many feet away at the other end of the room,
might have been a spacious sitting room in a penthouse flat.
'How do you make your money, Mr Hafeez?'

'Younis, please. We're members of the same tennis club
now, aren't we? I hope we shall be able to play against each
other in the near future, Clyde. Or even partner each other,
perhaps. Yes, I think I should enjoy that. In the meantime,
how I make my money is my own concern. Perhaps I inherited
it: that is probably the best solution for you to adopt, if you
are curious. I don't propose to offer you any further information, and the English law is on my side. It is an admirable
institution, much respected by us former colonials. I expect
you feel the same, Clyde.'

'We have information that you paid very large sums to Jason
Fitton over the last year.'

'Have you indeed? I should be glad to have the name of
your source. Such information is highly confidential, even if
it is correct – which in this case it isn't.'

Peach volunteered his first smile since the beginning of the
meeting. 'You know perfectly well that we don't reveal our
sources. We have access to Fitton's bank accounts, information
that would not normally be available to us. Even banks have
to defer to murder, Mr Hafeez. Sooner or later, you will have to
account for the three hundred and forty thousand pounds you
have paid over the last year into one of those accounts. Nothing
tangible seems to have changed hands. The natural assumption
is that the money is for services rendered. There are underage
girls being questioned in Oxford and in Birmingham at this

moment. The Vice Squad is assembling evidence which will eventually put people behind bars for a very long time. It would be of great benefit to Brunton if you were one of those people.'

Hafeez had hitherto been blandly inscrutable, but the mention of Oxford flashed real fear for an instant into those infuriating olive features. It passed almost before it had registered, but Peach noted it and was elated. 'Other people in other places are assembling the evidence that will eventually put you away. Our concern this afternoon is something much more specific. We are concerned with the murder of Jason Fitton.'

Hafeez shrugged his slim shoulders unhurriedly beneath the thin, smooth fabric of his expensive suit. 'What possible reason could I have to harm a man who you have just claimed was a business associate and a friend?'

'Neither of us mentioned the word "friend", Mr Hafeez. And we have an excellent motive for murder in your case. We hear that you are already attempting to take over his business empire.'

Younis was unnerved by that. He hadn't expected them to know about his visits to the casino and elsewhere, about his bid to take over the prostitution and money-lending rackets that had been the basis of Fitton's empire. Not yet anyway. Their underworld grapevine must be almost as efficient as his. And he'd no idea yet where the leak might be: he didn't know Fitton's employees as he knew his own. He did his best to refute the suggestion by saying formally, 'I assure you again that I have no connection with or interest in scrap metals or their recycling. Why on earth should I be interested in Fitton's business?'

'You wouldn't be interested in anything as honest and straightforward as that. It's his darker and more lucrative activities that would attract you, as all of us here know.'

Hafeez was shaken, not just by the fact that Peach knew this but by his earlier remarks about Oxford and Birmingham. They'd arrested others already for the girls who'd gone there and he'd thought that his own actions had been well enough disguised for him to pass unnoticed. But if that investigation was still ongoing, they might yet come for him. The urbane condescension with which he had treated the earlier part of the interview had left him now. He said carefully, 'How I make money and how I do business are my own concerns, not yours, as I told Clyde earlier. I did not kill Jason Fitton. I did not speak to him again after twelve forty-eight on Saturday night.'

'I see. When did you leave Birch Fields, Mr Hafeez?'

'Immediately after the dance concluded. I had no reason to stay around.'

'And were you accompanied?'

'No. I came to the ball on my own. I left on my own.'

'A pity, that, from your point of view. But quite welcome for us, in your case. It keeps you in the frame, doesn't it?'

'I note your attempt at police harassment. I'm sure Chief Superintendent Tucker wouldn't approve of it.'

Peach beamed his approval of this mention of Tommy Bloody Tucker, who behind closed doors was a resolute racist, one of a vanishing breed of senior police officer. 'Chief Superintendent Tucker surprises us all the time, Mr Hafeez. He would positively astound us if he gave you his support. In the meantime, if you cannot furnish us with an alibi for the time of this death, it might help your cause if you could suggest who else might possibly have killed Jason Fitton.'

Younis took his time. They were surely going to leave him soon and he'd be able to set about finding out who'd leaked the news of his approach for Fitton's empire. 'Olive Crawshaw might have killed him, I should think. That bitch was no friend of Jason's.'

'Have you anything beyond that which makes you believe she is implicated?'

He hadn't really expected them to take him seriously when he'd mentioned the Crawshaw woman. Perhaps they had stuff on her that he didn't know about. 'She didn't like Jason any more than she likes me. She's a venomous bitch.'

'Or perhaps she just has good taste in men. Anyone else you'd like to suggest?'

There was a chance here to implicate or at least sully the name of a man who stood in the way of his ambitions at Birch

Fields. 'Arthur Swarbrick. He was around at the end. He acts as if he owns the place. He hated Jason Fitton.'

'Hated? A strong word, Mr Hafeez. Tell us why you used it.'

'I don't know Swarbrick well, but I'll stick by that word. I've heard one or two things he's said, and I've seen the way he used to look at Jason.'

Peach stood up. Northcott followed suit, then stepped forward a pace so that he loomed above and disconcertingly close to Hafeez, who recoiled a step and looked nervously towards Peach. The DCI smiled again, 'No need to be afraid, Mr Hafeez. He's a hard bastard, DS Northcott, but he's quite tame, unless he has a real reason to attack. If that happens, I'm happy to release him and watch the carnage. Perhaps later in the week, eh?'

Clyde was still seething when they reached the car. 'He's well capable of murder, that bugger!' he snarled.

'Indeed he is. But that doesn't necessarily mean he did this one, does it? And Mr Hafeez gave us a couple of useful pointers, whether he meant to or not.'

TWELVE

Murder has its compensations, even for those tasked with finding the killer. The DCI had briefed his murder team each morning, but had otherwise hardly been in the station. It was a whole five days since he had been forced into direct contact with Chief Superintendent Thomas Bulstrode Tucker.

In an imperfect world, all good things inevitably come to an end. Thus it was that Peach's first task after his briefing on Tuesday morning was to answer a summons to Tommy Bloody Tucker's penthouse office on the top floor of the new police headquarters in Brunton. On a cloudy August morning, he plodded up the two flights of stairs with depression settling heavily around his shoulders.

Tucker had his opening salvo carefully loaded. 'We spoke of Jason Fitton on Thursday last. I told you he was a respected member of my Lodge and you said that you suspected him of serious criminal activity – a suspicion you admitted you were unable to support with hard evidence. He has now been murdered, Peach.' On which impressive pronouncement, Tucker glared accusingly over his rimless spectacles at his hapless junior.

'I'm well aware of that, sir,' Percy replied. 'I was detached from connubial bliss at an early hour on Sunday morning to contemplate his mortal remains in the car park at Birch Fields Tennis Club. At a time when more fortunate mortals were preparing for Sunday golf.'

Tucker's glare became a glower. He'd enjoyed his Sunday morning golf – very nearly broken a hundred, which was a rarity for this prince amongst hackers. 'I've read the post-mortem report and the details from our forensic team.'

Percy resisted the temptation to congratulate him upon his industry. 'And what are your conclusions, sir, as you bring your vast experience to bear upon this latest violent outrage in our community?'

Tucker seized upon the phrase: it was much easier than offering original thought. 'A violent outrage is exactly what this is, you know, Peach. I'm glad to see that you at least acknowledge that things are getting more and more violent under your command.'

'Technically your command, sir, as you often remind me when there is kudos to be enjoyed. As you also frequently assert, sir, we live in an increasingly violent society. I can surely not be held personally responsible for the violence exhibited in the nation as a whole.'

'I don't want excuses, Peach! I want results.'

'Yes, sir. In view of this urgency, perhaps you would like to take charge of the investigation yourself. I'm sure that it would be salutary for the lads and lasses struggling at the crimeface to observe and measure your personal impact.'

Tucker was aghast at this radical suggestion. 'You know that it is my policy never to interfere directly with my staff during the execution of their duties.'

'But there is no substitute for experience, sir, as you have frequently reminded me.'

'And my experience will be devoted to ensuring that this investigation is pursued with proper diligence.' He paused to savour the word and apparently found it worthy of repetition. 'Diligence, Peach! I hope you hear me!'

'I hear you indeed, sir.' Percy picked up his chief's banner and ran with it. 'Murder most foul has been committed and its perpetrator must be brought to justice. Even if the victim was a villain of the first order and the town will be better off without him, his death must be diligently avenged. Otherwise anarchy that way lies!'

'Villain of the first order? Jason Fitton was a member of my Lodge.'

'But we know from previous experience that the two things are not mutually exclusive, sir.' Peach noted the puzzlement on T.B. Tucker's face and took heart from it. 'There are plenty of villains even in an exclusive tennis club, sir – probably even more than in your Lodge.' He savoured this concession for a moment. 'We have already interviewed some of the leading contenders, including one who proposes to take over

Fitton's evil empire. Did he garrotte Fitton in order to seize control of prostitution and loan-sharking and gambling in the town? That is what we are asking ourselves. Well, strictly speaking, DS Northcott and I are asking. We haven't communicated our thoughts to the team as yet, because I was apprised of your wish to see me this morning.'

Tucker wished the man wouldn't use words like 'apprised'. It wasn't seemly in a DCI. You should be a chief constable before you indulged yourself with words such as that. He decided something more basic was necessary. 'I don't want you pissing about, Peach. I want you pursuing this case with all your bloody might.'

'All my bloody might, sir.' Percy weighed the phrase as if committing it to memory. 'I think that is being applied, sir. Would you care to hear my frank appraisal of the present state of the investigation?'

There he went again. 'Appraisal' – definitely not seemly for a DCI. 'I hope you've not been pratting about, that's all.'

'I don't think I've pratted for a single moment since I heard about this crime on Sunday morning, sir. I have to report that we are still adding to our list of suspects. We are not near to an arrest.'

'That is emphatically not what I wanted to hear, Peach! We need results. We need to maintain our position at the head of clear-up rates in the north-west.' Tucker jutted his jaw like John Wayne preparing to liberate Burma.

'We saw the man who is manoeuvring to take over Fitton's more dubious business interests yesterday afternoon, sir. He is to my mind a leading suspect in the case.'

Tucker liked that phrase 'more dubious'. It seemed to cover you either way. If the man proved not to be guilty, you could always back down and maintain that you'd always considered him one of the town's benefactors. 'You'd better tell me who is this mysterious person whose name you have so far withheld.'

Peach held it back a moment longer. 'He's Asian, sir.'

'Ah. A promising suspect. You do well to be suspicious, Peach.'

'Thank you, sir. A very smooth Asian. A very sinister one also. He goes by the name of Younis Hafeez.'

Tucker blanched. Percy found it a pleasing phenomenon: he could have watched it for much longer. 'You must proceed with great caution, Peach.'

'And why would that be, sir?' The black eyebrows arched impossibly high beneath the shining bald head.

'Mr Hafeez is a prominent local citizen. A representative of our immigrant community. I should not need to remind you that you must tread very carefully here.'

Tucker's racial bias operated as usual only against the lower sections of Brunton society. 'Prominent indeed, sir. And rich. How do you think he makes his money?'

'I don't know, Peach. That is not our business.'

'That was exactly his attitude, sir. I find it strange that you support it. I think how the man makes his money is very much our business. I do not think you will wish to find yourself in Younis Hafeez's corner in the months to come, whether or not he murdered Jason Fitton.'

'You must take great care not to offend our Asian community, Peach. I have noted before that you are rather insensitive in this area.'

And you are the most bloated hypocrite I have met in almost twenty years of policing, thought Percy. *Which is saying quite a lot, because I've encountered quite a few, most of them in senior ranks.* 'Hafeez is a villain, sir. You can take my word for that. He's involved in large-scale trafficking in underage girls, the filthiest and most widespread scandal of the last couple of years. He covers his traces well and he uses others to do his dirty work. In my view, however, we'll have him in court and behind bars within the next year. But what we have to decide more immediately is whether he killed Jason Fitton. My own view, which I shall not pass on to others, is that I hope he did and that we can pin it on him. The town would then be rid of two major villains – Fitton and Hafeez – through one criminal act.'

Tucker blanched again. 'You will indeed not express that view outside this room. You are fortunate that I take a liberal view and allow as much rope as I do, Peach. These are two prominent local businessmen and their wealth must surely have benefited the town. One has been murdered and must be avenged. The other is a prominent member of our Asian community; any investigation of his movements needs to be handled with great care and sensitivity. Do I make myself clear?'

'Eminently clear, sir. Care and sensitivity are two of my most notable qualities.'

'I don't want anyone accusing us of racism, Peach.'

'I see, sir. Perhaps you should bring your own sensitivity directly to bear on the case.'

'That will not be necessary, Peach. I trust you to forge ahead and solve this. But tread very carefully.'

'I see, sir. Forge ahead and tread carefully. A difficult balance to strike. Perhaps I should bring your attention to another tennis club possibility. The chairman. Born and bred in Brunton and as near white as we can produce. No racial card to be played against us by Arthur Swarbrick.'

T.B. Tucker had no blanches left. He said wearily, 'He's another well-known and influential local figure, Peach.'

'Yes, sir. Unfortunately, that doesn't exempt him from suspicion. On the night of the summer ball, he was around the tennis club in the hour between one and two, after most people had left. He has no witness to when he eventually left the club or arrived home. And he was no friend of Fitton's. He's admitted to his dislike of our victim, and I have a feeling that dislike may prove to be much deeper than he has so far admitted. I am pursuing further enquiries, but I shall try to tread carefully whilst forging ahead.'

Tucker sighed heavily. 'Have you no possibilities from the normal criminal world?'

Percy considered this for three long seconds. Then he said, 'There's a woman, sir.'

'Ah!' The face brightened behind the rimless glasses. 'This could well be a woman, you know. No huge strength was required to tighten that cord.'

'Yes, sir. That's why I mentioned that we have at least one female suspect.'

Tucker attempted to lighten things. 'Not a prominent local businessman this time!'

'No, sir. Her gender would make that difficult. You probably don't know the lady. She's been a member of the tennis club for many years. I believe she was instrumental in securing DS Northcott's recent acceptance to membership at Birch Fields.'

Tucker leant forward and jutted his jaw. 'This sounds altogether more promising.'

'The lady's name is Olive Crawshaw.'

'I know her, Peach!' Tucker was animated by one of his rare eureka moments. 'She's a schoolteacher.'

'Indeed she is, sir. A senior and distinguished one. That does not automatically make her more of a suspect, does it?'

'She taught my niece. Bit of a harridan, as far as I remember.'

Percy considered this description and decided not to reject it. The formidable Olive might herself have accepted it, coming from Tommy Bloody Tucker. 'She admits to a dislike of the deceased and she has as yet no alibi for the time of his death.'

'Well, there you are, then. Proceed with expedition. I'm very happy to have been able to give you a pointer.'

Percy thought that even T.B. Tucker couldn't be serious about that, but there was no sign of levity in that noble visage. He stood up on this cue, but felt he could not leave without a parting shot. 'Of course, it's early days and we're still turning up suspects, sir. It's still possible there could have been someone in that car park who had no connection with the tennis club.'

He left the room with Tucker restored to his familiar state of bafflement.

Anne Grice looked up and down the considerable length of Clyde Northcott and gave him a welcoming smile. She was less certain about the bouncy little man with the round face and the bald head who had introduced him: this was not her image of a detective chief inspector. But it takes all sorts, as any senior PA quickly learns from the panoply of human life that passes before her during any week.

'I'm afraid Mr Walmsley is in Yorkshire today, talking to the new owners of Fitton's Metals. He's very busy following the death of our previous owner, as I'm sure you will appreciate.' She glanced down at her desk diary. 'He may be back this afternoon. Perhaps if you care to make an appointment for tomorrow morning, I could—'

'We're quite busy ourselves, Mrs Grice. But you may be able to tell us what we need to know. We'll speak to your very busy employer as and when it becomes necessary.'

'I'll give you whatever help I can, of course. I can't imagine that it will be much. I didn't know Mr Fitton. I haven't worked here very long.'

She was nervous; Peach sensed it. It might be significant.

'Yes, I realize that. I noticed it from a study of the list of employees that you were kind enough to email to us.'

Anne flicked aside a strand of dark hair and turned her brown eyes on to the round, innocent-seeming face. 'I've only been here for a few weeks. I've got to know our managing director quite well, as you'd expect, since I was appointed as his PA, but I never had the opportunity to meet Jason Fitton.'

It was the second time she had told him that and she'd used the victim's full name this time. No more than nervousness, perhaps, but nervousness always interested CID men. 'Why did you come here, Mrs Grice?'

'That is my own business, surely.'

He gave her a wide, understanding smile. 'It certainly is. It may be ours as well – ninety per cent of the facts we pick up this week will prove to be irrelevant, but we've no idea two days after a murder which ten per cent might be pure gold.'

'I can assure you that my reasons for taking this post had nothing to do with the crime you are investigating.'

'You can indeed assure me of that. If you choose to go no further, DS Northcott will simply record that you refused to answer the question.' The large black face beside him gave a small, affirmative smile to support that.

She looked from one to the other and gave them no answering smile. She was good at her job and was used to being highly respected. This felt almost like bullying, and Peach's smile made the moment not lighter but more annoying. 'I felt I was getting into a rut in my previous post. I fancied a new challenge with a different firm. I made the right decision. Mr Walmsley is both an efficient and understanding employer.'

'Which your previous boss wasn't?'

'I didn't say that.'

'Indeed you didn't. That is why I asked the question.'

He was trying to nettle her. Both of them knew it. She kept calm and produced a rather elaborate sigh to show that she didn't appreciate her time being wasted like this. She spoke like one instructing a troublesome child. 'My previous employer was fine and we'd had a good working relationship for eight years. I was driving ten miles to Preston each day, whereas this office is within two miles of my home. I fancied a new challenge with a bigger firm, in a more convenient place.'

'So you came here without any increase in salary.'

She hadn't thought that he would know that, still less that he would quote it at her. The English will talk about all sorts of intimate things, but money is usually out of bounds. Policemen were not social beings. Even as she thought that, her normal fairness and balance told her that they probably couldn't afford to be when they spent most of their time speaking with liars. 'Money wasn't the most important consideration. And with a bigger firm, the profit bonuses may well be more generous.'

'I see. Despite the fact that Fitton's Metals has been standing still and not paying any real bonuses for the last three years? I should have thought someone as efficient as you obviously are would have investigated that before you took the job here.'

'We are in a recession. Most businesses are suffering.'

'You are a Brunton resident. Are you sure that you didn't know Jason Fitton?'

Another sigh, another suggestion that her patience was being sorely tried. 'I knew *of* him, obviously. My previous firm even had occasional dealings with Fitton's Metals. But I didn't know the man personally.'

'But you knew all about him?'

She was torn between her natural inclination to show her efficiency and her wish to distance herself as far as possible from the man's death. 'I knew that he wasn't as well liked as his father had been when he was running the firm. All kinds of people passed through my office to see my boss in Preston;

one picks up bits of gossip, whether one wishes to or not. I kept whatever I heard to myself, as a good PA should.'

'As a good PA should, indeed. And I have no doubt that you are a very good PA, Mrs Grice. But to us you are not a good PA but a valuable source of information. So what impression did you form of the man who is now our murder victim?'

She considered her position for a moment, then spoke very carefully. 'If I am being treated as a source of information, can I be assured that what I say will go no further? It would obviously be quite wrong in normal circumstances for the managing director's PA to be offering her opinions on the owner of the firm.'

'Who is now the late owner. Hence our request. All information we receive is treated as strictly confidential, Mrs Grice. It will only ever become public if it passes out of our hands and becomes part of a court case. I cannot think that the impression you formed of Jason Fitton, a man you claim never to have met, will become that.'

Anne didn't like the use of that word 'claim' but decided it was better ignored. This man Peach was quite confrontational enough, without further encouragement. 'Jason Fitton wasn't the man his father was. That's what I heard. His father had built the firm up from scratch and was well respected, both by the other firms he dealt with and by the people he employed in increasing numbers as the business grew. Jason didn't sound either as reliable an employer or as pleasant a man as his father had been.'

'Yet you chose to come here and work for him. Presumably you didn't know when you did so that he was going to die within a few weeks.'

He'd used another insulting word: that 'presumably'. He was openly trying to rattle her. Well, he wouldn't succeed. 'I'd also heard that he didn't take much part in the operation of the firm. I came here to work for Mr Walmsley, not Jason Fitton.'

'Seems an unnecessary risk, though. Especially if you were as happy in your previous post as you have claimed. Mr Fitton was operating other businesses as well as Fitton's Metals. Much less reputable businesses. What do you know about them?'

'Almost nothing. I've heard rumours, as I told you, from people who passed in and out of my office in Preston. And people said things to me when they heard I was coming here. Things about prostitution and gambling, and even about these recent scandals where underage girls in Rotherham and Rochdale have been procured for middle-aged men.'

Peach pursed his lips, as elaborately and conventionally as she had previously sighed. 'Yet you still chose to come and work here.'

'I've already explained that. And rumour feeds on rumour and becomes vastly exaggerated. I don't believe in conspiracy theories.'

'Neither do I, Mrs Grice. Not until they are substantiated by convincing evidence, as I anticipate some of the rumours you heard will be in the next few months. Did you know Mr Walmsley before you came to work here?'

The question came swift as an arrow and out of the blue, when she'd been considering the dire things she knew about Jason Fitton. Anne made herself take her time. 'I knew of him. There is something of a grapevine amongst PAs and other secretarial staff. The names of the ones who are moody or who throw tantrums or are in any other way unreasonable are circulated more widely than they realize. I knew I would be working for the managing director if I came here: the post was advertised as his personal PA. So naturally I spoke to some of my contacts here before I even applied for the post. What I heard was good. I am happy to say that my experience over the last few weeks has confirmed that. Mr Walmsley is not only fair but very considerate. Normally, I like to keep my work and my private life strictly separate, but think I could say that we are almost personal friends.'

'Almost.' Peach frowned a little at the thought.

She was used to him now, so that she didn't accept the bait. 'Everyone in the firm is endeavouring to make the transition to new ownership as smooth as possible. Mr Walmsley and I are working hard on that. He is the man who makes the decisions and shapes policy, but I think I can say that I have been his conduit to the rest of the staff at this anxious time.'

'His conduit.' Peach nodded. He had this annoying tactic

of picking on particular words in what she'd said and weighing them out loud, as if he wished to cast doubts upon her integrity.

He paused for a few seconds, then smiled at her and nodded to Northcott, who said, 'For the record, you'd better tell us where you were between one and three a.m. on Sunday morning, Mrs Grice.'

She felt that she'd won a small victory when Peach had passed the questioning to his junior. She would treat as absurd any notion that she might have been involved in this strange death. 'Not killing the owner of the company that pays my wages. I was safely tucked up in bed, Detective Sergeant Northcott.'

'Alone?'

There was a moment of tension whilst she grinned at the two serious faces before her. 'Alone, I'm afraid. This is an imperfect world.'

Peach offered nothing in the police Mondeo as they drove away from the factory site. Clyde eventually ventured, 'You gave her quite a going-over. I didn't expect that.'

'Neither did I, Clyde, when we went there. But we're still clutching at straws in this, and she suddenly seemed one of the more worthwhile straws.'

'She's divorced, isn't she? She seemed very fond of Bob Walmsley. Do you think there's something going on between them? Do you think she knew him before she came here? Is that why she applied for her present post?'

'What a lot of questions, DS Northcott! Good habit to acquire, mind you. And we do get the occasional bonus in CID work. I went in there expecting nothing and discovered an interesting woman.'

THIRTEEN

Olive Crawshaw wished that it wasn't the long summer holiday and that she was busy at school. She needed things to divert her thoughts from what had happened to Jason Fitton after the tennis club's summer ball.

Physical activity might be the answer. She went to the club to play tennis that Tuesday afternoon. For over an hour, she was involved in a competitive doubles match with three players who were twenty years younger than her. She more than held her own in the rallies and lasted three sets without too much difficulty; indeed, she was pleased to see the rather overweight young woman on the other side of the net chasing vainly after one of her cross-court backhands. Whilst they played, she was totally involved in the physical challenges of racing about the court and playing the shots to the best of her ability.

When the game was over, introspection set in again. She had tea and cakes with the people she had played with, but she was more than usually silent during their chat and laughter over the teacups. Eventually, she excused herself, explaining that she needed to ensure that there were court reservations for the juniors she controlled within the club, and slipped upstairs to the club's offices.

She found her old opponent Arthur Swarbrick there and for once she was glad to see him. They had a common interest now, rather than the issues of club policy that normally divided the ultra-conservative chairman and the most forward-looking member of his committee. Olive was characteristically direct. 'Did the police come to see you about Jason Fitton?'

'Yes.'

'Me too. I didn't enjoy it.'

Arthur managed a reassuring smile. 'I shouldn't worry. They're questioning everyone who was there on Saturday night.'

'Not everyone is getting the top brass, though. Mostly it's

just the PC Plods, asking routine questions and recording routine answers from all and sundry. I got the top brass. DCI Peach and his bagman – I think that's what they call it, isn't it? It was a pleasant surprise to find that it was Clyde Northcott, who is now a member of the club despite your opposition.' That barb came out before she could still her tongue; she immediately regretted it.

'I had the same pair. Your black man didn't seem to be exactly on our side.'

'He has a job to do and he's getting on with it. Clyde will be a perfectly acceptable member of our club. For the moment, you'll have to accept my word for that.' She directed a sour smile at the papers on his desk rather than at Swarbrick: they were fellow sufferers today, not opponents. 'I didn't like that man Peach.'

Swarbrick nodded, happy to accept a rare agreement with this woman who was normally a thorn in his flesh. 'He got under my skin too.'

'It's his job to do that, I suppose. But he did seem to enjoy it.'

'He did indeed. I'm quite relieved to discover that you had the same feeling about him. I thought it might be just me he didn't like.'

'I don't think we should take it personally. I've been thinking about it. I reckon Peach likes to annoy people because when they're knocked off balance they reveal more than they would do otherwise. We might not like him, but I think he's a clever little bugger.'

A forthright word from Olive Crawshaw, who usually expressed herself quite trenchantly without the use of expletives. Arthur's concern disguised a flash of personal hope as he said, 'They can't suspect you, surely?'

Olive gave him a rueful smile. 'In television series the cops always say they suspect everyone who hasn't got an alibi. Peach made it quite clear to me that I didn't have one.'

'Me too. I suppose they have to ask about these things, but he seemed inordinately pleased when I had to tell him that I was here well after the dance ended and went home alone.'

'But Shirley was with you, wasn't she? I saw you dancing together earlier in the evening.'

'She went home early and was asleep when I got in. Now I wish she'd stayed.'

'I'm sure you do.' Olive thought mischievously that it must seem very contrived to the police, sending your wife home early and being left to your own devices. Arthur must surely be more of a suspect than she was. She said, 'They found out quite a lot about me, when I look back on those twenty minutes. They quickly established that I disliked Jason Fitton – well, much more than disliked him.'

'I shouldn't worry too much about that. I got the impression that they hadn't much time for the man themselves – but they have to investigate his murder, of course. They found out that I didn't like him either, Olive.' *But they didn't discover just how deeply I hated him or why*. He kept that thought to himself.

Olive actually knew all about the reasons for his hatred of the dead man, but chose not to raise them here. 'Who do you think killed him, Arthur?'

'I don't know. Perhaps it's best not to speculate, Olive.'

They were both using first names now: that hadn't happened for a while. It was surprising how a common threat could pull people together. Olive Crawshaw said, 'I'll pop in and see you later in the week, if you're here.'

'I expect I shall be.' They smiled bleakly at each other as she left.

Bob Walmsley kept his automatic welcoming smile on his face as his PA showed in the CID men later that afternoon. 'I'm happy to give you whatever help I can. That goes without saying, though I don't think I shall be able to add much to what I told you two days ago. I hope this won't take very long. I have only just got back from my visit to Leeds to meet the new owners of Fitton's Metals. Things are pretty hectic here at present, as I'm sure you can appreciate.'

Peach sat down beside Northcott in the chairs that had been set ready for them and looked hard at the managing director. 'You could have saved us a lot of time if you had been more honest with us on Sunday, Mr Walmsley.'

'I can't think what you mean by that. If there are any omissions, I am at your disposal for as long as it takes.'

'You hated Jason Fitton.'

It was blank and uncompromising and it made Bob Walmsley fearful. 'I didn't like him. I didn't like what he was doing to this firm. I didn't disguise that to you. I admired Jason's father and I thought his son was on his way to ruining this firm. The firm I have grown to love, if that is not too sentimental a word. I thought he was jeopardizing the livelihood of people who have worked here for many years.'

'You had a more personal reason to dislike him. Your wife's brother.'

Bob wondered how to react to this. 'It's personal, as you say. That's why I didn't mention it to you on Sunday. I didn't think you would find out about it.' He looked suddenly older than his fifty-eight years.

'All kinds of things come out in a murder investigation, Mr Walmsley. When people conceal them, it makes people like us think they may be significant.'

'This isn't, because it has no bearing on this death. I didn't kill Jason Fitton.'

'I think you'd better tell us all about it, in case there are any details that we don't yet know.'

Peach had put the onus on him. Bob didn't dare give him anything but the truth, because he didn't know exactly how much this dark-eyed man with the black fringe of hair around the bald head already knew. 'Gerald, my brother-in-law, had a small gents' outfitter's business in Blackpool. It was a modest earner but it occupied a wonderful corner site, which Fitton wanted for one of his betting shops. I think Gerald would have sold if Jason had made a reasonable offer, but he offered a sum that was quite derisory.'

'How long ago was this?'

'Twelve years. Fitton was gradually establishing his monopoly of betting outlets: we didn't know then how evil he was or what things he would resort to.' He stopped for a moment to look at the two expectant faces in front of them. He turned his head a little, finding it easier to speak to Northcott's more sympathetic face than to the unrelenting

Peach. 'Gerald turned down the offer and told Jason to get lost. It was a mistake. He had Fitton's heavies in the shop the next day. They dislocated one of his fingers as a little token of what might come next if he didn't cooperate. But what really upset him was that they said their next action would focus on his kids. He had two boys aged ten and twelve at the time, and his visitors pointed out what soft targets they would be. Gerald sold out for practically nothing to Jason Fitton the next day.'

'What became of him after that?'

The question was studiously neutral. Bob couldn't be certain what they knew. He didn't want to tell them this, simply because it increased his own motive for this murder they hadn't yet solved. 'He couldn't find another job, not a permanent one. He seemed to lose reliability as he became more depressed. He committed suicide five years after Fitton had closed down his business.'

'Did you raise this with Fitton?

'I tried to, on one of his rare visits here. He said Gerald was a melancholic and a loser, and that a death five years after he'd taken over the shop couldn't possibly be laid at his door. He also implied that my own employment here would be at stake if I pursued the matter further, or was even stupid enough to raise it again.'

Peach smiled grimly. 'I think I'd have wanted to kill the man if he'd treated me and mine like that.'

'I did want to kill him. But I had more sense than to do it. Someone else relieved me of the temptation on Saturday night.'

'Of course they did, Mr Walmsley. But we have to explore all possibilities as conscientious coppers, don't we, DS Northcott?'

'Indeed we do, sir. We didn't ask you this when we were merely gathering information about the firm on Sunday, Mr Walmsley. Where were you between the hours of one and three a.m. on Sunday morning?'

Bob had known that this was going to come. He gave the big black man with the notebook in his hand a little smile, trying to show how unthreatened he was by the question. 'I was at home and in bed, Detective Sergeant. Sound asleep, as far as I can remember.'

Clyde took what seemed a long time to make a note of that, feeling the tension building in the room. 'So no doubt your wife will be able to confirm that for us?'

Bob hesitated for a moment. He had known this question must follow the other one and he'd prepared what he wanted to say. But he was suddenly tempted to change that. Deborah would support him if he asked her to: she was an instinctively loyal wife. But the police machine was very efficient when it was on full throttle. They might know exactly where she had been. If he lied now, that might damn him further in their eyes. 'Unfortunately, she cannot do that. Deborah was away that night. She visited her mother, who is in her early eighties, on Saturday. She intended to come home in the evening, but she rang me to say that her mother had a chill and that she was staying the night.'

'Is there any other person who can attest that you were not at Birch Fields Tennis Club on Saturday night?'

He hesitated a moment, so that both men glanced sharply at him. 'No, I'm afraid there isn't. Of course, if I'd been out killing Fitton, instead of innocently tucked up at home, I think I'd have made sure I had an alibi.'

Peach was back in like an eager terrier. 'Would you, indeed? You're thinking like an experienced criminal, then. But I expect that's just because you're an intelligent man and can put yourself in our position. How would you describe your relationship with Anne Grice?'

The question came like a shot and Bob was stunned by its arrival. He took his time to answer it. When it came, his reply was as measured as the question had been abrupt. 'She is a very efficient PA. I am happy with the appointment. Indeed, I have congratulated myself several times on it during the last two days. Mrs Grice has worked admirably in the chaos that has inevitably followed this unexpected death. Jason Fitton was forty-six and we expected him to be around for the foreseeable future.'

'So you've worked happily together. Does the relationship extend further than that?'

Walmsley smiled patronizingly. 'I'm a happily married man, Mr Peach.'

'Would Mrs Walmsley agree? We sometimes find that long-term partners have quite different perspectives.'

'Deborah would certainly confirm it. We haven't seen much of each other in the last few days, for obvious reasons, but we trust each other absolutely.'

'Forgive me, but we coppers see rather a lot of the seamier side of life. Many men do not see a happy marriage as a reason to be monogamous. So could you now be quite clear about your relationship with Mrs Grice, please?'

Walmsley looked at him steadily across his desk. 'I could say that I regard your question as impertinent and refuse to enlarge any further upon the matter.'

'You could indeed, sir, and you would be entirely within your rights to do so. We should then simply log that you had refused to clarify the matter. We would have that on record as we proceed to explore other strands of this complex investigation.' Peach looked as if that would be entirely to his satisfaction.

'I have come to rely heavily on my PA in a very short time. The main reason is that she has proved even more efficient than I anticipated she would when I appointed her. As a result, I have trusted her with more and more details of the firm's business and with my thoughts on our senior employees. You probably know that she is a divorced woman who lives alone and is devoted to her work. She has given freely and generously of her time since she came here. I think it would be fair to describe us now as friends as well as working colleagues.'

'I see. That is very interesting.' It was almost the expression Anne Grice had used in answer to the same question earlier in the day. Almost as if that is what they had agreed between them to say. Peach volunteered a wide, innocent smile. 'Well, that's good, then. A man in your position needs as many friends as he can get.'

On that enigmatic and rather threatening note, he rose to go. Then, as Walmsley relaxed, he said, 'Why do you think Mrs Grice chose to come here? To a similar post and with a negligible rise in salary.'

It was Bob's turn to smile. 'I've no idea, Chief Inspector.

I'm just happy that she did. Perhaps you should ask her yourself.'

'Oh, we already have, Mr Walmsley. We spoke to her at some length this morning.'

'Yes. She told me about that, as you would expect. I'm surprised you thought it was worth the trouble, when she has been here for such a short time.'

'So was I, to be frank. We didn't intend it when we came here. But you would be surprised to know how much we learned from her.'

Bob said evenly, 'I'm sure she strove to be helpful, as is her habit.'

'Not about why she came here. She gave us a few reasons, but they were scarcely more convincing than yours. Incidentally, she says she was tucked up in bed and enjoying her beauty sleep at the time the owner of your firm died, just as you were. But perhaps you already know that. Have you had any further thoughts on who might have committed this crime?'

'Not really. I'm sure you now know much more about it than when we spoke on Sunday. Jason was killed by someone who was at that tennis club ball, I should think. Or some enemy from that murky underworld where he'd been making his real money over the last few years.'

'Or even some combination of the two.' Peach looked hard at Walmsley, wondering how much he knew about Younis Hafeez, who would qualify on both counts.

He got no reaction. Instead, Bob Walmsley said, 'I suppose you've considered the possibility of a contract killer? I'm sure plenty of Jason's enemies had the funds to employ a man to do that.'

'Including the managing director who thought Fitton was ruining his own firm.' Peach gazed thoughtfully at the ceiling for a moment. 'We hope fervently that this wasn't a contract killer. They're professionals, you see: they leave very little of themselves behind at the crime scene. People who aren't habitual killers usually leave much more of themselves in what we call the "exchange" of the crime scene. Goodbye for the present, sir. I'm sure we shall be in contact again before the end of the week.'

Bob Walmsley waited until they were well off the premises before he called in his PA. 'They're on to you, Anne. You'd better tell me exactly what they asked you this morning and what you said to them.' She shut the door and they sat down together, as good friends should.

Everyone in the small village at the foot of Longridge Fell knew now that Lucy Blake, who had married the policeman, was pregnant and that Agnes Blake, long-time resident and respected widow, was destined to become a grandmother. If all went well, that is: the older women in the village who were Agnes's contemporaries added that phrase like a mantra, as if it could insure them against medical disasters.

At six o'clock on a warm August evening, the Ribble Valley was at its best. For once Percy was not in a hurry and he drove slowly to savour the scenery. The great mound of Pendle Hill had the western sun bathing its slopes and did not look threatening on a night like this. It took darker days and darker skies to set people talking of the Pendle Witches and the hangings at Lancaster. He drove through Whalley with its ancient abbey and out towards the village of Mitton, where the three rivers met. He intoned as he drove the old rhyme which came back to him from school:

'Ribble, Hodder, Calder and rain,

All meet together in Mitton's domain.'

Then on past the green-topped towers of Stonyhurst College, where Gerard Manley Hopkins had penned much more complex and disturbing verses. 'Glory be to God for dappled things,' Percy said quietly, and put his hand on Lucy's knee.

'I'm not dappled,' she said, a little uncertainly. 'Though that might be the next thing that pregnancy brings, I suppose.'

'It's a voyage of discovery,' said Percy sententiously.

'It's a voyage of aches and pains and vomiting,' Lucy corrected him.

'The nights are drawing in,' said Percy irrelevantly.

They were too. The sun was invisible now, though they could see it gilding the woods and the hills away to their right, towards Whitewell and the glories of the Trough of Bowland.

This is the area the Queen had once said was her favourite part of Britain. Percy hadn't much time for royalty or the establishment in general, but he thought that in this matter his monarch had shown excellent taste. As they ran through the valley along the long flank of Longridge Fell, the sun emerged again, dipping away towards the sea on the Fylde coast twenty miles to the west. Percy was pleased that he had taken his time. Things in his life were dropping into perspective. For the first time since he had seen it, the image of that garrotted corpse in the car park became less vivid in his mind.

'I had to let my belt out another notch this morning to get into the trousers I wear at work,' said Lucy gloomily as they ran into the outskirts of her home village. 'It's not fair that you should put on weight all round. I'm sure I've put an inch on my bottom as well as what's been added to my belly.'

'And every inch is much appreciated.' Percy smiled benignly and gave her the low growl with which he prefaced sexual advances.

'Not by me it isn't. And please keep both hands on the wheel,' said Lucy firmly.

Her mother had the lights switched on and the electric fire on low when they arrived. The old cottage looked very cheerful. The scent from the kitchen was highly promising as Percy delivered the bottle he had brought into his favourite septuagenarian's hands. 'The temperature's dropping quickly in the evenings now,' said Agnes. 'Let me know if you want the heating turned up.'

'I don't need to be treated as an invalid,' said Lucy discourteously.

'What news of my grandchild?' Agnes couldn't delay any longer the question she had been planning to ask all day.

'We've had our first scan.' Lucy had planned to delay this, but she couldn't hold out against the eagerness on her mother's face. She reached into the handbag and brought out the picture which showed a tiny curled thing, which even at this early stage you could recognize as a child, or what was going to be a child.

Agnes stared at it in wonderment and joy and gave a little gasp of pleasure. There was a long pause before she said, 'We

didn't have these things in my day.' And then, still gazing at
the tiny foetus after another pause, 'How on earth can these
abortion people say that isn't a human life?'

'Let's not get on to that, Mum. I happen to agree with you,
but some of my colleagues would say that was anti-feminist.
Let's just say that everything seems to be going fine with
Horace at the moment.'

'It's a boy?'

'It's still too early to tell, Mum. We don't want to know
until the baby arrives. But we have to call it something, so
Percy came up with Horace. Apparently after some cartoon
character that he remembers and I don't.'

Percy beamed his satisfaction at such invention. 'Hungry
Horace, Mrs B. Lucy has to eat for two, you see. But things
are going well, apart from a couple of weeks of morning sickness, which I've managed to cope with quite well.'

Agnes rolled around on her sofa and cackled inordinately.
'You're a regular caution, you are, Percy Peach, and no
mistake!' It was her favourite description of her favourite man.

She was over seventy now, but her culinary skills had only
sharpened with the years. Roast beef and Yorkshire pudding
and three vegetables midweek. Percy poured the wine and
savoured the food, raised his glass to his hostess and said,
'You're spoiling us, Mrs B. Us and Hungry Horace.' He nudged
Lucy's stomach appreciatively.

After apple pie and custard, they sat in front of the fire in
the low-ceilinged lounge. They were warm, well fed and sopor-
ific. Lucy couldn't drink at present, Percy was driving and had
consumed his ration, and Agnes wasn't a drinker and claimed
she had already had enough to make her silly. No one fancied an
intellectual challenge, so they sat and exchanged harmless
gossip about the villagers who were Agnes's neighbours. Lucy
was particularly interested in a man she had called 'uncle' in
her childhood, who had seemed a pillar of the community and
the local church, until he had caused a local scandal and much
excitement in the village by leaving his wife to set up house
with a younger woman four years ago.

'He's back home from the other side of Yorkshire,' said
Agnes, as though the man had returned from the furthest realm

of Hades. 'Enid's taken him in, but I don't know whether it will last.'

'You never do with men, do you?' said Percy sanctimoniously. 'But at least his wife is displaying the spirit of Christian forgiveness. I only wish my own wife would show more of that.'

Agnes ignored her daughter's outrage at this. 'You're a proper caution, Percy Peach, and no mistake. I just hope Hector's back for good – he doesn't seem a bad man, to me – just a daft one. They seem all right together, but you can never tell what goes on behind closed doors, can you? Appearances can be deceptive.'

'Indeed they can, Mrs B. And now I must drive your daughter carefully home and tuck her safely up in bed for the night. You've no idea of the noises she makes in the morning, but I don't broadcast it at the station.'

Lucy was too tired to come back at him. It was good to leave on the sound of her mother's laughter and to know that the three of them had enjoyed a happy evening together. He had his compensations, Percy. Not many sons-in-law took such pains to amuse their wives' mothers.

He was genuinely solicitous about her welfare, sometimes too much so for her taste. 'I'm quite all right, you know,' she said later as they prepared for bed. 'Don't fuss. I don't need cosseting.'

'Pity. I enjoy the odd cosset. But in that case, your bum looks big in that!' he said daringly as she disrobed.

'I told you, I'm putting on weight, and not just on my belly,' Lucy disrobed to bra and pants and surveyed her rear dolefully over her shoulder in the mirror.

'The more of that bottom the better,' said Percy with conviction. 'You can't have too much of a good thing.' He waited until she was installed on her back in the double bed, then kissed her naked belly gently, his nightly compliment to Horace.

She was asleep quickly, but it took him a while longer, thinking of the evening that was gone. She was a wise old bird, Agnes Blake. She compensated for her lack of formal education with common sense and her vast experience of life.

It was almost a watchword for the CID, what she'd said: you never knew what went on behind closed doors. And appearances could certainly be deceptive. They were probably particularly so in the case of Jason Fitton's death.

FOURTEEN

Younis Hafeez was keeping his eye on the police investigation into his enemy's death. He had his spies abroad and he knew on Wednesday morning that there had been as yet no police talk of an arrest.

That was satisfactory, as far as it went. Meanwhile, he needed to get on with his takeover of Fitton's lucrative businesses. The police had said they knew of his intentions, but if he proceeded with caution, he could still take control. Prostitution and gambling were sure-fire ways of making money and would remain so for the foreseeable future. Loan-sharking had experienced bad publicity of late; it was subject to more scrutiny and was thus less profitable. But he'd take that over too, because it came with the Fitton package. He was going to be the biggest and most powerful man in this area, and it wouldn't do for people to think you couldn't handle everything your predecessor had taken on. The police hadn't managed to control Fitton, and they wouldn't control him.

He'd worked out the finances long before Fitton had been killed, and he reckoned he could manage it. It would be tight, for a few months, because there were a lot of people to sweeten before the profits began to accumulate. But he could do it and he *would* do it. He'd cut out the middleman. Fitton had been that in the most profitable business of all. Procuring young girls and young boys for middle-aged men with fat wallets and perverted tastes brought in unbelievable money.

The market was still there and probably growing, despite the recent arrests and exposures in Rotherham and Rochdale, in Derby and Oxford. He knew two of the men in the Oxford gang who had been sent down for upwards of twelve years for preying on vulnerable teenagers. That must be a warning to him. He was safe, so far, but he needed to be cautious in the next few months. Procuring youngsters was high-risk, but high profit. He would need to be more careful than that playboy Fitton had been, but he had the knowledge and the contacts to do this. He was sure that he could cover his tracks and outfox the dull-witted police teams, who had always previously been one step behind him in the contest.

Like many major criminals, Younis Hafeez was vain about his intelligence. And like many people on both sides of the law, a touch of megalomania set in as his powers grew.

He had his own hardmen – mostly Asian and all efficient and ruthless. But he'd need more as he expanded into Fitton's territory, and he'd need men who knew this ground and had been used to controlling the people on it. It was always better to frighten people into submission than to use violence, because violence brought attention you did not wish to attract to your activities. But you needed a judicious amount of violence, *pour encourager les autres*. Word got round and people deferred to you when they knew you had the power to enforce your decisions.

Hafeez had a distaste for the men he used for these things. You needed muscle, yet at the same time you despised it. These men were necessary tools, but he didn't want them coming to the penthouse office where he had met the police on Monday and where he entertained the affluent men who were his clients in his various other enterprises. If he was going to use the men whom Fitton had used, he would see them elsewhere, in the buildings he was going to take over from the dead man.

He was back in the Brunton casino, installed now in what had been Jason Fitton's office there, dealing with two of the hardmen who had been Fitton's muscle. He was going to take them on: word got around and it was good for morale lower down the organization for people to know that they could keep their jobs if they were good enough. But he would put them through the mill a little first. That was both his habit and his pleasure.

Abe Lockhart and his companion shuffled into the room and shut the door carefully behind them. They wanted to assess this new presence in their lives, who could cast them aside or take them on to new things, but they were not used to looking people directly in the eye. The sly sideways glance suited them much better: they were more used to looking down at the boots they sometimes used to enforce their commissions than to studying people's faces. Nor did they like bloody Pakis. But this one had money and power. They had better pretend they respected him and whatever it was he stood for.

Hafeez didn't disguise his dislike as he looked at them across Fitton's desk. These brutes were like Macbeth's murderers: in the catalogue they went for men, but they were dogs really – necessary but vile. That was one of the good things about an English education: it enabled you to see things for what they were. And one of the other good things about England was the law, and the latitude it allowed to clever men like him.

He said very precisely, with his diction emphasizing their different worlds, 'It seems the two of you are now unemployed.'

Lockhart spoke for the pair of them, as he normally did. 'We was hoping you might take us on, like. We was very sorry to hear about Mr Fitton.'

'Were you really? Well, the man was your meal ticket, I suppose. I'm taking over here now.'

'Yes, Mr Forrester told us that. He said you might find a use for us.'

'Did he? Very generous of him, considering that I haven't yet decided whether I shall have a use for *him*, let alone people like you. I can get bruisers very cheaply, Mr Lockhart. Can you give me any reason why I should employ you rather than others?'

'We're efficient, Mr Hafeez.' He'd memorized the name before he came in here, but he still hesitated over it. 'We're good at what we do. Mr Fitton never had any complaints. We're also discreet. We keep our lips zipped tight about whatever we are asked to do.'

'That's the minimum requirement. Anyone in my organization who breathes a word of what they have done or been ordered to do is out. *Down* and out, in fact: there are plenty of other heavies who would be happy to break your legs before they took your places.'

Lockhart gave a weak smile; he'd offered all he could think of offering. Words weren't his strength, and still less the strength of his companion. He looked sideways at that powerful, limited presence, then back at Hafeez with a grim expectancy. 'We're in your hands, sir.'

'Then you have some grasp of reality. I require men like you, because not all the people I have to deal with recognize reason when they see it. I need men like you to make them see the error of their ways.' Then, in case scum like this did not comprehend understatement, he added, 'I need people to draw blood and break limbs. Sometimes to do worse than that. Are you up to the task? Are you skilled in violence?'

'We're up for it, sir. And you'll find we're very reliable.'

'You'd better be. You'll get the same retainer you were on before, with extra for any special jobs I may wish you to undertake. You're on trial; this will be a probationary period.'

They wouldn't know what that last phrase meant, but he was happy to leave men like this feeling ignorant and inade-quate. And it didn't really mean anything. Men who lived by violence were always on trial, always as good or as bad as the last brutality they had applied. They stood in front of him waiting to be dismissed: he had never invited them to sit. He couldn't be gracious to thugs like this, even now, when it would cost him nothing and mean nothing. 'You'll get orders in due course. Now get out.'

Olive Crawshaw was feeling the strain. Four months ago, the doctor had told her that her husband had early-stage Alzheimer's disease. She'd asked the GP if he was sure of that, because she'd noticed only an increasing tendency to forgetfulness in Eric. Things had moved rapidly since then. He was safe enough at the moment, but she'd need to get someone in to watch over him at some point during the next school year. That wouldn't be easy, because he was tetchy about his condition: naturally he was. She'd have been the same herself – *would* be the same herself, if it ever happened to her.

Eric was sixty-eight now. He'd been fourteen years older than her when they married and she'd always told herself that she must be prepared for problems later. But much later, she'd hoped. Alzheimer's was a hazard for the eighties, she'd naively thought. It was only after he had been diagnosed that she found that people much younger than Eric could be affected.

He peered out now between the curtains, as he had never done until a year ago. 'There's someone at the door,' he said. 'Someone in a car.' She'd told him twice that the police were coming, but he'd forgotten twice.

'It's all right, Eric. They're from the police station in Brunton and I knew they were coming. I invited them to come, you see. It's about something that happened at Birch Fields after the summer ball.'

'The tennis club.' Eric nodded happily, as if congratulating himself on making the connection.

'Yes. I don't think it will take very long. You can stay here and watch the television and I'll take them into the dining room.'

'I want to come with you. I want to make sure it's all right.' His ageing features set into the pout of a stubborn child. She found that more moving than she could ever have imagined it would be.

She introduced him to the two policemen, then said that she would talk to them elsewhere. Peach sensed immediately that Eric was not a well man, though she had no idea how he knew that. He said much more gently than was his wont, 'We might need Mr Crawshaw to confirm your whereabouts early on Sunday morning.'

'That won't be possible, I'm afraid. He wouldn't be a reliable witness.'

'One o'clock. Time for the news,' said Eric cheerfully. He went over and switched the television on, even though it was in fact nowhere near that time. It was a Sky sports channel and a footballer raced briefly across the scene. 'We won the Premier League, you know,' said Eric. 'Everyone said we couldn't win it, but we did. I was there. Liverpool, it was. Even the Kop cheered when they heard we'd done it.'

Peach went over and looked him in the face. 'I was there too, Mr Crawshaw. It was a great day for Brunton, wasn't it?'

Twenty years ago, in 1995. He'd been nineteen then, watching his beloved Rovers triumph despite defeat at Liverpool on the last day of the season. He could remember feeling sick with excitement in the last minute as the news came through that Manchester United had only drawn at West Ham and the title belonged to Brunton Rovers. He grinned at Eric Crawshaw. 'We had Alan Shearer then. He scored on that day.'

Eric was delighted. He clasped his hands together exultantly. 'Running on to a cross from the right wing. Hitting it first time. He was the best we ever had, was Shearer.' As with many Alzheimer's sufferers, Eric's medium- and long-term memories seemed to grow sharper as his short-term one declined.

Percy said, 'He was that. The very best. A hundred and thirty goals in four years. The finest we ever had.'

'I can remember Ronnie Clayton and Brian Douglas,' said Eric proudly.

'Can you indeed? You're a lucky man, Mr Crawshaw. That's long before I was born.'

'I were nobbut a lad then.' Eric gazed fondly past his listeners and into the 1950s and 1960s of his childhood.

He'd lapsed from his previous standard English into Lancashire dialect with the last phrase. Olive said fondly, 'That's what his dad used to say when Eric was a child. I think he had a friend on the turnstiles who used to shove Eric underneath, when he was very small.'

She picked up the remote control from the television and switched to BBC One. '*Bargain Hunt* will be on soon, Eric. You like that. I'll have a talk with these gentlemen and be back soon.' Eric's eyes were on the television now, as if he had forgotten the visitors. 'I were nobbut a lad,' he repeated as they left him.

Olive kept her face studiously unemotional as she took them into the dining room and shut the door behind them. She didn't want to reveal her feelings to these strangers, still less to accept their sympathy. But she said to Peach, 'Thank you for that. It does him good to talk, even if nowadays it's always about the past.'

'I'm always happy to talk about the Rovers. DS Northcott

is useless on that. He's more into motorbikes. And tennis, of course. I'm told he has hidden talents.'

'I'm sure he has. But his tennis ones are going to become more public over the next year or two. I think Clyde has the potential to make the first team at Birch Fields, if he plays regularly and tests himself against our best players.'

Percy grinned, then moved swiftly into the business of their visit. 'We've been questioning people there, as you'd expect in these circumstances. They tell us that you didn't like Jason Fitton at all, Mrs Crawshaw.'

Peach was uncharacteristically gentle, almost apologetic for raising the issue. He was trying to rid his mind of the image of the sixty-eight-year-old man in front of the television next door.

'I'm not going to deny that. Fitton was a smoothie, when it suited him, but the more I saw of him the less I liked him.'

'This goes back some years.'

It was quietly spoken, but it was a statement, not a question. Olive responded with, 'We came from different worlds. He was the privileged Eton schoolboy and I was a passionate believer in the state education system and what it can achieve.'

Peach smiled, sensing that in this situation persuasion was going to bring more than bluster. 'We can't blame Eton for everything; the real faults lie with Jason Fitton. He was one of those who used a modicum of intelligence and a good education for bad purposes. Had you a particular reason to dislike him?'

It was almost casual, but Olive felt that they knew. She wondered which of the three major public spats she'd had with Fitton Peach knew about; perhaps it was all three. These CID people didn't miss much. Nor did they help her now, as the silence stretched. She said dully, 'I think sometimes that Jason Fitton started what you've just seen.'

It was Clyde Northcott, daringly using her forename for the first time, who said eventually, 'You'll need to enlarge on that for us, Olive.'

She glanced at them, then fixed her eyes on the Pre-Raphaelite print on the wall behind them as she spoke in the most even tone she could muster. 'Jason was scathing about our schools in Brunton when we met at the tennis club because he knew it annoyed me. But a few years ago he went more public. He told the local press that he employed all sorts of people at Fitton's Metals, "including even the scruffs from that grubby comprehensive down the road". The paper grabbed the quote and made the most of it, as you'd expect.'

Clyde glanced at Peach and then back at the strained woman in front of them. 'I can see how that would annoy you, Olive. But it wasn't personal, was it?'

'It was very personal indeed. Eric was the headmaster of that "grubby little comprehensive". He'd worked all the hours God sent to make it a good school and he'd succeeded, against the odds. The papers came to him and he responded to what Fitton had said, as he had to. It would have been taken as an acceptance of the insult if he'd refused to comment. He quoted some of the school's many successes, stressing his work with those academically less gifted as well as the Oxbridge entrants. The press set what he said against Fitton's comments and made him sound defensive. Fitton had funds and he used them. The dispute made the nationals and brought the sort of publicity you never want when you're working with young people.'

'And you think it prompted the troubles your husband has now?'

She sighed, forcing herself to be fair where she least wanted to be fair. 'It might be my imagination, but to my mind Eric never looked the same after that. He was getting near retirement. He was until that time a highly respected figure in the town. He's a shy man and he didn't like publicity anyway, even good publicity. He struggled to cope with all the press attention and journalists pursuing him into the school each morning, looking for statements. They even got quotes from the kids in the school, and they made the most of them. It's always the discontented and the troublemakers who are most anxious to speak up in situations like that.'

Clyde said daringly, 'It isn't your way to let people like that get away with things. You must have taken Fitton to task.'

She grinned bitterly. 'I always have to be head-on, don't I? I knew I couldn't win with a man like Fitton, but when he taunted me publicly one day at the tennis club, I told him exactly what I thought of him. I told him that he was a woman-izer and a crook and a hypocrite. I told him that Eric had done more for the Brunton community than he would ever do. I think that was when I told him that his overall influence was a baleful rather than a beneficial one, but I can't be certain of that.'

Peach spoke again now, softly but insistently. 'You said all of that and more, according to what people have told us. And please don't now seek out these people. They told us what they had to tell us, and their sympathies were all with you.'

'Thank you for that. I don't think you would lie about such things. Whatever else you are, Mr Peach, I don't have you down as a hypocrite.' She allowed herself a grim smile as she reflected on that thought.

'Thank you. That is a compliment from one as clear-sighted as you. As you are such a realist, you will see that this increases your motive for getting rid of Jason Fitton.'

'Drastically increases it, I should think. I'm glad he's gone. I shall never succeed in proving it, or even in convincing those close to me about it, but I remain convinced that Fitton began what you saw next door.' She stopped for a moment, her head on one side, listening to the strains of the opening music for *Bargain Hunt*, allowing her face to drop into the affection she felt for the damaged man she knew she was going to nurse. 'I'm heartily glad that Jason Fitton is dead. I didn't kill him, but I know you can't simply accept that and that I must be high on your list of suspects. In view of the character of the victim and the things he represented, I regard that almost as a compliment.'

'Have you come up with anyone who can confirm your whereabouts between one and three on Sunday morning?'

'No. I expect I'm not the only one. It isn't the easiest time to account for: there aren't many people abroad and observant in the small hours.'

'You must have thought about this since we last spoke. Have you any suggestions as to who might have committed this crime? Whatever you think of the victim, I must remind you that this was murder.'

'I don't need reminding that the law of the land must be upheld. It's one of our cornerstones. I still think that there are a lot of good things about this country, despite the flaws we hear so much about. If I'd done this, I should confess.'

Peach thought for a moment that that was probably true. Then he remembered the stricken man in the next room, and Olive Crawshaw's obvious desire to love and care for him. She needed to stay around, for Eric if not for herself. He said gently, 'You still haven't given me your thoughts on who could have done this.'

'I've thought about it a lot. I was in shock when you saw me on Sunday, but it's hardly been out of my mind since then. I know who I'd like it to be, but I haven't a scrap of evidence to offer you to connect him with this, so that's not much use to you.'

'Perhaps not. Tell us nevertheless.'

'Younis Hafeez. He's capable of murder, I'm sure. And he's creepy. He's not safe near young women and still less near young girls. I try to prevent my juniors in the club from getting anywhere near him. And before you say it, I know that doesn't make him a murderer.'

'It doesn't, indeed. But you are an intelligent woman and a long-time member of Birch Fields. You have seen Hafeez and others at close quarters for years. We appreciate your confidential views. Anyone else?'

She grimaced. 'I suppose you'd expect me to say Arthur Swarbrick, because we've been enemies for years. I chatted with him yesterday. Curiously enough, a murder at the club seems to have brought us closer together than we've ever been before. I'm aware from what Arthur said that he was around at the time and that he has no one to substantiate his alibi – he's like me in that, I suppose. We'll never be bosom pals, but I don't see Arthur as a murderer.'

Peach nodded. 'I've seen quite a few murders now, Mrs Crawshaw. In ninety per cent of the cases, the perpetrator was someone whom no one had seen as a murderer before the event.'

As they prepared to leave, the man in the sitting room looked up at them as if he had never seen them before. 'Hope the Rovers can pull it off on Saturday,' said Peach.

'You must come again,' said Eric with a smile.

Arthur Swarbrick might have been amused to hear what Olive Crawshaw said to the CID about him, but he was far away and he had other things on his mind. He had caught the ten past eight train from Brunton to London. Only his wife knew that.

It was bright and calm when he reached Euston. The Underground wasn't crowded at this hour. He didn't enjoy the journey, but he reached Harrow quite quickly. She was locked in the flat when he arrived. He smiled weakly at the eye that was distorted enough to seem scarcely human as it viewed him through the spyhole. It took her several seconds to turn the two locks and release the chain to allow him entry. He stood for a moment assessing her and then took her into his arms.

She did not resist him, but nor did she respond. She merely stood inert within his hug. He clasped her tight against him, running his large hands over the thin, sharp shoulder blades, willing her to give him some sort of encouragement. Eventually, she lifted her arms and set her hands briefly upon his back, but it was no more than a token response, an acknowledgement of the fact that if she wanted to be free of his clasp, she must offer him something.

She said, 'You shouldn't have come. There was no need.'

He wanted to say that he'd been up since six and thinking of her most of the time. He wanted to tell her that this was a cold greeting. Instead, Arthur Swarbrick said simply, 'You're my daughter, Clare. You weren't answering your phone. I felt I had to come.'

'I'm all right. I'll get through this.'

'But Jason's death has been all over the national press. I knew it would upset you.'

'It's strange, that's all. I suppose you'd say he had it coming to him.'

'I would. But that doesn't mean I don't feel upset for you.'

'You'd have killed him yourself years ago, if you'd felt you could.'

'I'm not sure I'd have done that. But I've only got one daughter, and I didn't like what he did to you. I hated him for it.'

There was a tiny pause, whilst both of them considered the question Clare did not dare to ask about how Fitton had died. Then she said, 'There are men like him doing the same thing to women all over the country. He's not unique.'

'Not many of them are as cruel as he was. Not many lead girls on to think they're going to be wives, and then simply laugh in their faces and tell them that they were fools for not knowing that would never happen.'

'Other men do it, and probably some women as well. I told you, Jason's not unique.'

She was speaking of him still in the present tense and Arthur didn't like that. 'He was unique to me, Clare. He was the only one who did that to my daughter.'

'I'm all right, Dad.'

'But you're not, are you? You're not at work, for a start.'

'I'm not off sick and I'm not pretending I'm bereaved. I've taken a couple of days of my annual leave.'

'But you wouldn't have done that unless you were upset.'

'I just didn't feel able to face people. I'm not even sure I'm upset, Dad. I'm not sure what I feel. I'm not pleased and I'm not sad. I just feel that my emotions have been deadened as far as Jason is concerned.' She got up and moved swiftly to where Arthur sat on the edge of his armchair. She bent and took him clumsily in her arms, kissing him and then pulling him against her. 'I'm sorry I gave you such a cold welcome, Dad. It was good of you to come. Quite unnecessary, but good of you.'

He smiled at her, feeling the same emotions as he had when he had been young and vigorous and she had been eight and had come home from school in tears. You never escaped from your children. He looked past her, across the tidy, rather sterile room and into the kitchen beyond it. 'I'll get us a sandwich, love. I'm not as good as your mother at food, but I'm not entirely helpless.'

She pushed him back into his armchair. 'I'll get us something, Dad. I'm not an invalid. I'm sorry, I should have realized sooner that you must be hungry. It's a long time since you had breakfast.'

'I didn't have much. I was too anxious about my daughter.' He called the words into the kitchen after her, happy that she should be working there, feeling that she would find a release in action.

She made them cheese on toast. It was surprisingly tasty. He was happy to see her eating the same quantities as he did himself. He suspected that it was the first food she had eaten in the day. She smiled at him, mocking his anxiety. 'Welsh rarebit was the first cooked thing I ever made, when I was eight, the first time I was allowed to use the stove and the grill at home. Mum was out and you stood over me from start to finish.'

'I remember now. I wouldn't have wanted to face her if you'd burned yourself, would I? That must be thirty years ago, now.'

'And it's seven years since Jason. Quite time enough for me to have got over it.'

'I suppose so. But it hit you hard at the time.' Clare had attempted an overdose, spent two separate periods in the mental wards of different hospitals. He was here because he didn't want any repetition of that. Both of them knew that, but neither of them felt able to voice the thought.

But they were easy with each other now and Arthur could see that she was much more relaxed than when he had arrived. They walked in her local park for a little while in the afternoon, enjoying the sun on their faces as they strolled between the flower beds and sat by the lake.

He said quietly, 'It's over now.'

'It was over a long time ago, Dad.'

'Yes. But perhaps your mind wouldn't accept that, until now. You're still a young woman. You need to get on with the rest of your life.'

He meant boyfriends, she supposed. She wanted to be able to tell him that she had moved on, that she had a new man, that things were beginning to come together for her. But she'd never been able to lie to him. He'd always seen through her and laughed at her when others had believed her girlish fictions. She watched a duck land, flap its wings, preen itself a little before it settled. Then she said, 'People talk a lot about closure, Dad. It's an overused word. But this death is a kind of closure for me.'

He nodded slowly, watching the now stationary duck, not daring to look at Clare. 'You'll need to work hard to make sure it really is closure, love.'

'And I will, Dad. Promise!' She clasped his arm and edged close to him, as she used to do as a girl and had not done throughout her teens, when small disputes that now seemed supremely petty had been ridiculously important to her.

The skies darkened quickly and there was thunder in the air. She put the lights on in her flat when they returned. Arthur thought it looked cosier in artificial light than in the natural light that had filled it when she had let him in three hours ago. Perhaps that was his imagination. As if she read his thoughts, she brought a photograph of her parents and herself when she was ten and put it in pride of place on the mantelpiece. In the picture, she had the serious smile of a child to whom the world is a mysterious and exciting place. 'I always liked that one,' Arthur said.

The rain fell from near-black skies as his train left Euston. He slept now, as he had not slept on the previous night or on the journey south. He woke as the train was running into Lancashire. It was dusk, but the skies were clear and blue here. He watched the western sky getting ever more crimson as the wheels took him towards home. Despite his sleep, he felt physically exhausted as they neared Brunton. But it was a pleasant lassitude, the kind he had felt as a boy after long Sunday walks with his father.

His wife heard his key turn in the lock and was waiting for him in the hall. Arthur Swarbrick said, 'I think she's going to be all right now. I think she's finally rid of Jason Fitton.'

'You look exhausted. There was no need for you to go, really.'

'There was, Shirley. I'm glad I went.' *For me as well as for her*, he thought.

*   *   *

Two hundred miles south, Clare Swarbrick too was glad that
her father had come to see her. She had resented his intrusion
for about a minute, but after that the visit had been first thera-
peutic and then pure joy. Perhaps she would sleep without the
pill tonight.

She just hoped that her father hadn't made the ultimate
sacrifice on her behalf.

FIFTEEN

When he was told that they wished to interview him for a second time, Younis Hafeez elected to meet the CID men at the police station. He didn't want them coming to his penthouse suite in the office block again. Word got around and it didn't do for the men you worked with in the underworld to divine that you were receiving police attention.

He knew how the police operated and he wouldn't let it get to him. He'd be left alone for five minutes or so within the claustrophobic walls of a police interview room. The idea was that he'd feel the pressure and become anxious. This he would obviously refuse to do. He maintained the supercilious smile he had worn ever since he entered the station as the uniformed constable ushered him into interview room number three and told him that DCI Peach would be with him very shortly.

They were peasants, these English policemen. And policewomen: they would never have employed women for this work in his country; women were for other things entirely. But the English were effete, in this as in other things. He'd seen one of the women officers as he'd passed through the reception area. Probably no more than twenty; she'd strip off quite nicely, he thought. But Younis didn't allow uniforms to turn him on, as they did some men. Except schoolgirls' uniforms, of course: they were a different matter entirely.

He gazed at the sage green walls and the square table and the single light high in the ceiling above him. The absence of any natural light after the brightness of the day outside would have unnerved some people, but it didn't disturb him, because he had prepared himself for it. Peach and that big, stupid black sergeant of his arrived at exactly the moment he had predicted. The fact that he had forecast all of this so accurately gave him extra confidence.

He said coolly, 'I've nothing further to offer you, Detective

Chief Inspector. The fact that you have asked me to come here suggests to me that you must be now quite desperate.'

'We didn't ask you to come here, Mr Hafeez. It was your suggestion. And you might be surprised to know how helpful you've already been. People are sometimes at their most helpful when they think they're being obstructive.'

Peach had played poker in his time, quite successfully, though never for stakes as high as this. 'If you've no objection, I think we'll record this conversation. You're not under arrest as yet, but we find that people sometimes recall things quite differently from the way they actually happened.' He flicked on the recorder switch and watched the cassette begin to turn. Rather old-fashioned, these days, but some subjects found the silent movement of the circling cassettes mesmeric, even disturbing.

Hafeez merely shrugged the expensive cloth on his shoulders. 'As you wish. Any playback will be desperately boring. But perhaps you may use it to study and refine your interview techniques.'

'We've collected some of Jason Fitton's files. We got there before you.'

'Nothing of Mr Fitton's would have been of any great interest to me.'

'Except his prostitution and his gambling and his loan-shark rackets, and the employees you have elected to take over from him. I told you at our previous meeting that we knew about that. We were moving in on Fitton, and we shall eventually have the evidence to convict you.'

He was shaken, despite his contempt for them. But the olive skin on his forehead did not crease and his smooth features kept their sardonic smile. 'I have no interest in such things: they are illegal. If it pleases you to stretch your imaginations, I shall not deny you that much-needed exercise.'

'Your English is very good, Mr Hafeez. A great contrast to your morals.'

'This is being recorded, CDI Peach, at your request. I should hate you to get into trouble with my lawyers.'

'Those lawyers are going to have other concerns in the coming months. They are going to be busy and they will need to be very good indeed. They will fail you, however skilled and unscrupulous they are.'

They were both exuding confidence, each trying to outmuscle the other mentally. Yet it was no more than a preliminary skirmish. It had a purpose, as far as Peach was concerned: he was trying to soften up his adversary and make him more vulnerable in the real exchanges that were imminent. 'There were two more arrests in Derby last night. It's only a matter of time before the special unit assembled for this investigation comes for you. The men arrested in Derby will talk, once they realize that they are cornered. They won't save themselves, in the face of the evidence against them. But they'll sell you to try to cut down their years inside. Their sentences will take into account the extent of their cooperation, as you know. Rats deserting a sinking ship aren't noted for their loyalty, Mr Hafeez.'

Younis maintained his smile with stiff lips and great effort. 'I seem to remember you telling me a year or so ago that the police don't do deals.'

'We don't. Especially not with the likes of you and where helpless children are involved. The evidence has accumulated and is now overwhelming: there is no need for deals. It's taken far too long, but the lot of you are going down. We'd have got Fitton for his part and we're going to have you for yours.'

'Empty threats, DCI Peach. Arrest me, if you think you have a case.'

'*I* shan't have that pleasure, Mr Hafeez. That is the province of the Vice Squad and the Serious Crimes Unit, who are closing several different nets at this very hour. I have nothing but contempt for the things you have done, but you're here this morning because I have narrower and very different priorities. I am investigating a brutal murder and you are one of the people with motive and opportunity and no alibi.' He gave his first real smile of the morning to exhibit his relish for that thought.

It was true and Younis Hafeez knew it. He didn't know what other suspects they had: perhaps none. He forced his practised urbanity back into his face. 'You have no proof of that and you won't be able to find any, because it doesn't exist. I didn't

kill my respected business colleague and acquaintance Jason
Fitton.'

'You'd be behind bars at this moment if we had that evidence,
Mr Hafeez. But we're patient people. Sometimes it takes us
rather too long, but I hope that won't be the case here. It is
still only four days since the discovery of Fitton's corpse and
we are making rapid progress. We have eliminated from suspicion almost all of the people who were around at the time of
this crime. I am happy to tell you that you remain in the frame.
You might even be what we often call the prime suspect.
Would you agree with that, Detective Sergeant Northcott?'

'I would heartily agree, sir. We mustn't make the mistake of
rushing towards the conclusion all of us would like to see, but
I think it would be fair to describe Mr Hafeez as our prime
suspect. He has many more things to worry about than this
single death, as you have indicated, and justice is going to
come to him from another quarter if not from us. But it would
be highly satisfying to us and a feather in the cap of Brunton
CID if we could arrest him for the murder of Jason Fitton.
There would be a kind of symmetry if we could arrest one
major criminal on our patch for the murder of another.'

The smile was gone now. Hafeez viewed the confident black
man with open hostility. 'You'd better be able to substantiate
these things, Clyde.' He delivered the forename as if it were an
obscenity. 'I shouldn't like to be in your shoes when they're
shown up as the fictions they are. The tennis club is not going
to take it kindly, and neither am I.'

Peach said grimly, 'Did you tighten that cord around Fitton's
neck in the car park of the club on Sunday morning?'

'I did not. I want that to be recorded formally, since you
seem unable to get it into your thick heads.'

'You have others available to do your dirty work, as Jason
did when he was alive. Did your men wait for Fitton in that
car park?'

'I do not employ such people. End of story.'

'On the contrary, you've just increased the number of your
bully boys. Not wise, that. Men like Abe Lockhart always talk
about their employers once they realize the game is up. As it
will be very shortly for you, Mr Hafeez.'

He was shaken by the fact that they knew the name of the man he had just taken over with Fitton's empire. He said as firmly as he could, 'Since you do not wish to hear what I keep telling you, I shall resort to the standard "no comment". I begin to see why policemen who will not see reason hear that phrase so often.'

'You had a dispute with Fitton two days before he died. A major dispute, with raised voices.'

There had been more than one. He couldn't be certain whether they meant the one at the tennis club or the one in Fitton's car. Probably the one at the tennis club: there was a greater possibility of them having secured a witness to that. He summoned his dismissive smile. 'You shouldn't believe everything you hear, Peach, especially if it's from women. They build up a normal exchange of views between friends into a major dispute.'

Peach arched his black eyebrows. The dark eyes beneath them seemed to Hafeez to glitter in the harsh artificial light of the interview room. 'That jacket you're wearing today. The one you've slipped off and put on the back of your chair. Were you wearing that at Birch Fields on Saturday night?'

'I may have done. I can't remember now.'

If he didn't deny it, he'd been wearing it: both the men watching him from the other side of the small, square table knew the score. Peach walked round behind the man, took the lightweight woollen jacket between finger and thumb, and removed a single fibre from it. He walked back to his chair, pulled a small plastic envelope from his pocket and put his almost invisible trophy carefully inside it. 'You don't mind volunteering us a sample from your jacket, do you, Mr Hafeez? An innocent man wouldn't.'

'An innocent man doesn't.' Younis was pleased with his snappy reply, but more fearful than he wished to show beneath the surface calm he still maintained. He knew that he was at liberty to refuse them, but he couldn't do that without seeming guilty. He wanted to be away from here and making his own enquiries. He was more disturbed than he could afford to show by what they had said earlier about the arrests in Derby. The dangerous, lucrative trade which had so excited him and brought him so much profit seemed now to be collapsing around him. 'Why on earth are you picking bits off my jacket? Is this an attempt to fit me up?'

'We don't fit people up, Mr Hafeez, not even people like you. Our forensic teams have examined certain fibres taken from the passenger and rear seats of Jason Fitton's car. From the murder scene, in other words. If we find a match with the fibres you have just volunteered to us, I have no doubt that a court would find that significant.'

'I have certainly been in Jason's Bentley on occasions. I wasn't there on Saturday night or Sunday morning.'

'That is a contention you may have to justify in court, in due course. In the meantime, have you any other candidates to offer us for this crime?'

'Anyone who was at the summer ball at Birch Fields on Saturday night, as far as I'm concerned. You should by now know much more than I do about this. I gather from the confusion you have exhibited this morning that you have made little progress.'

'You are at liberty to go whenever you wish. Please don't leave the Brunton area without informing us of your movements.'

Once Hafeez was gone, Peach sat looking in silence at the small plastic envelope and the sample he had secured. 'I think we'll find a match between this and fibres extracted from the Bentley.'

Clyde looked at Peach's almost invisible trophy, willing it to give them more than it possibly could. 'We know now that the car was thoroughly valeted on the Tuesday before Fitton died. This could prove that Hafeez was there after that, but not necessarily after the dance was over.'

'True. It will be up to Hafeez to show that his presence in Fitton's car pre-dates the death hour.'

'Innocent until proved guilty. The onus of proof will be on the prosecuting counsel.'

Peach nodded almost gleefully. 'There are all kinds of other things mounting in the case against Younis Hafeez. I hope this will add to the pile.'

*   *   *

Lucy Peach's own GP wasn't immediately available, so she took the only doctor available: a man who had officially retired but still did one day a week in the practice. Lucy had never realized how vulnerable you were when you were pregnant. She lay flat on her back on the table with her tiny bump feeling enormous and stared up at the male doctor. It wasn't much fun lying half naked and being prodded and asked intimate questions about the behaviour of your anatomy. It was, she supposed, preparation for being old and ill. Her thoughts flashed suddenly to her mother, Agnes, when she knew she should be concentrating hard upon the present. This was the moment to ask questions, to acquire answers to all the queries she and Percy had discussed.

Yet it was this overweight man with the cigar-smoker's breath and the air of impatience who seemed to be asking all the questions. He'd been brisk and dismissive, even rude, to her. But when you were lying on a hard surface it wasn't easy to be aggressive. She said, 'The morning sickness has been quite bad. That's OK, isn't it?'

'It's not abnormal. Some people say that means it's probably a boy, but that's an old wives' tale.' Like most medical men, Doctor Tierney was very strong on old wives' tales. He summoned them up at every opportunity so that he could dismiss them.

Lucy tried to show a little spirit and humour. 'Awkward little sods, boys. We call this one Horace – not that we know that it's a boy, of course.'

'Not many kids are called Horace nowadays, are they? Still, it's your own choice, I suppose.'

'No, I don't really intend to call him that. It's just that you have to call your bump something, don't you?'

'Do you?'

'Well, we do. "Horace" seems better than "it" to us.'

'Does it really? There's no accounting for tastes, I suppose. One meets all sorts of women in this job.' The great man spoke as if that were a definite disadvantage. 'You troubled much with flatulence?'

Lucy wondered if she had made some embarrassing emission since she had stripped off and climbed on to this unyielding

surface. She didn't think so, but Horace was making all sorts
of assaults upon her dignity. She was tempted for a wild
moment to say, 'No, I rather enjoy it!' but this man didn't
look as if he would welcome humorous rejoinders, and she
was still stretched out on her back and at his mercy. So she said
only, 'Not much, no. Nothing I can't cope with.'

Dr Tierney seemed rather disappointed. 'It's your first, of
course. You may find things become a little looser, with the
passage of time.' He did not enlarge on what seemed to his
patient a vague and wholly alarming prospect. He looked at
her notes, as he should have done before he saw her. Medics
always did that: Lucy thought it was a very inefficient way of
going about things. But she was literally in no position to
criticize him. He said accusingly, 'You're a police officer.'

'Yes. A sergeant in CID, actually.'

That usually seemed to impress people, but he frowned at
her over her file. 'Do you spend much time on your feet?'

She was ready for that one, because her own doctor had
already raised it with her. 'It varies from day to day. I've found
the exercise has been good for me, so far.'

He frowned and shook his head, but offered no comment.
'Are you intending to go back to work after your baby? To
just take maternity leave?'

'Probably I shall, yes, if everything goes smoothly. We
haven't made a final decision.'

She had discussed it with Percy, but aborted the conversation when it had become an argument. Tierney didn't say
anything, but he nodded his disapproval. The only other person
she knew who could nod disapproval was Percy, who used it
as part of his interviewing technique with seasoned criminals.
Most people shook their heads to indicate disapproval, but Dr
Tierney and Percy Peach could do it with a nod.

He now said almost reluctantly, 'Everything appears to be
proceeding satisfactorily.' It was what she most wanted to hear,
and he had kept it until the end. She had begun to think whilst
his cold hands prodded at her nether regions that Horace was
misbehaving. Tierney said, 'You can get dressed now. You'll
need to make appointments to see the midwife. In due course,
you'll be able to see the sex of your baby and report it to your

partner.' He sighed on that word: you'd had to say 'partner' for twenty years now, but the word still occasionally stuck in his throat.

'We don't want to know the sex. We've decided to take whatever arrives when the time comes,' she added nervously. 'I suppose that sounds a bit old-fashioned.'

'It's your choice, Mrs Peach. If you choose to ignore what modern science has worked hard to produce, that is entirely your choice.' He peered at her notes again. 'I see that your husband is a Denis Charles Scott Peach. A detective chief inspector.'

'Yes. I used to work with him before we were married, but nowadays I'm—'

'I've played golf with a Percy Peach. I think he's a police-man.'

'That's my husband. Everyone calls him Percy.'

'Used to be a good cricketer, this one. Played for East Lancs.'

Her mother would have liked that, Lucy thought. 'That's the one.'

'He's a very promising golfer. Only needs to play more to be very good indeed, in my opinion. I hope you won't restrict his appearances at the club when you have a family.'

'I shan't do that. I might even take up the game myself, in due course.'

He looked at her sternly over his glasses, as if he needed to check how serious this aspiration was. 'I expect you'll find you have very little time to yourself when Horace makes his appearance.'

He'd remembered that name and he'd smiled upon it. It was his first hint of humour or humanity. Lucy felt that she should congratulate him upon it for the sake of others. But she was too happy to climb stiffly down from that cold, hard base where he had examined her. As he sprayed his hands with cleanser, Lucy said meekly, 'Thank you, Doctor Tierney.'

The morning had gone well, Anne Grice thought. Like all good PAs, she judged its success by the performance of her boss and the results he had achieved.

Robert Walmsley had been at his very best during the meeting that had taken place in the managing director's office during the morning. Representatives from all sections of the company had been pleased with what they heard. The firm was going to have a new lease of life. The new owners wanted to see it run as it had been run in the old days, with a generous proportion of the profits being ploughed back into the new technology that would ensure continuing success. They were happy to entrust all but the largest policy decisions to their managing director and his senior staff, and Walmsley would keep them in touch with developments through a weekly verbal report.

Bob's own relief and delight had shone through the exchanges with his senior staff. He had looked a good five years younger today, Anne thought, and his renewed drive and enthusiasm had been communicated to the people in the meeting, all of whom he had known for many years. They had gone away imbued with optimism and energy, and Anne had no doubt that was now being passed on to staff down the line. The week had begun with tragedy and crisis. It looked as though it would end with the beginning of a new and more successful era at Fitton's Metals.

Anne Grice was alone in her office, feeling something very near euphoria, when the CID men arrived. She said breezily, 'Mr Walmsley won't be available for the rest of today. He has an important meeting with the firm's solicitors which he anticipates will take all of this afternoon. I can probably squeeze you in for an appointment some time tomorrow.' She reached for her desk diary.

Peach sat down without being asked on the chair in front of her desk. Without taking his eyes off her, he gestured to Clyde Northcott, who brought another chair from the corner of the room and sat down beside him. 'His absence is really quite opportune, Ms Grice. We wished to speak with you alone.'

'Really? That is flattering, I suppose, but mistaken. I can tell you very little about the late Mr Fitton and still less about the history and structure of Fitton's Metals. Perhaps you forget that I have still only been here for a few weeks.'

'No, Ms Grice, we do not. I am aware of exactly how long you have been here. More pertinently, I am now aware of exactly how well you knew the late Jason Fitton.' Peach's normally mobile face was stony: he did not even accord her one of his vast array of smiles.

She knew now what was coming, but she brazened it out for a little while longer, buying herself time to organize her mind, to determine just how much she must give them and how she should deliver it. Better to be questioned than to roll out a long prepared speech of her own, she thought. If she drew the questions from them and made her answers, she'd discover just how much and how little they knew. She wouldn't need to reveal any more than was absolutely necessary.

She said calmly, 'I prefer "Mrs Grice" to "Ms". I was working full-time and quite intensively as a PA in Preston before I came here. I live in Brunton and I knew of Jason Fitton as a prominent local businessman, as you might expect. I knew him largely by reputation. I can't see how that distant and third-hand sort of acquaintance can help you at all in solving the mystery of his death.'

She was good, Peach thought, and cool, or apparently cool. Perhaps that came with her training and experience as a PA. He said grimly. 'We know all about your relationship with Jason Fitton, Mrs Grice. It's time for you to come clean.'

Her brown eyes were wide and serious between the immaculately styled short dark hair. She forced a smile she did not feel into the alert, attractive features. 'All right. I did at one time know Jason Fitton quite well. I suppose this is what you call a fair cop.'

'It is an instance of someone attempting to deceive us about a close relationship with a murder victim. That is of great interest to us. You have a lot of explaining to do, Mrs Grice – if, of course, explanation is possible. Confession would be more appropriate, perhaps.'

'The explanation for my reticence is simple. When you hear that someone has been murdered, you are not inclined to declare a long-term relationship that ended in bitter acrimony. You panic and conceal that intimacy.'

'You don't strike me as a woman who panics easily, Mrs

Grice. Having said which, you had now better give us a full account of your relationship and dealings with Jason Fitton. Leave nothing out, please.'

It was an absurd phrase, that, Anne thought. Was she to give the details of their tumblings and wrestlings and sweatings in bed, for instance? Did they want to know what she'd shouted and he'd promised? Recollections that were never going to be made public flashed across her mind. 'I did know him, as you've obviously discovered. I should have realized that you would, but I didn't realize the extent of the questioning that goes on in a murder investigation. You've been back to people who worked with me in my old firm in Preston, haven't you?'

'Members of our team spoke to them and to others after we'd talked to you on Tuesday morning. You brought this upon yourself by not being frank with us then, Mrs Grice.'

'I met Jason Fitton socially whilst I was still married. My marriage ran into a few problems and Jason could be very charming. I began an affair with him. It went further than I'd ever intended. I suppose you've heard that phrase quite often.'

'We seek significant facts, Mrs Grice; we don't strike moral stances. How long ago was this?'

'It began five years ago. It took me more months than is nowadays fashionable to go to bed with him. Once I'd done that, things moved fast.'

'How fast and how far?'

'Jason was genuinely attracted, I believe. I like to think that wasn't surprising: I scrubbed up quite well, five years ago.' She gave a bitter smile. She was a highly attractive woman now, at forty-four. It was indeed not surprising that even a practised womanizer like Fitton had found her irresistible. Probably the very fact that she hadn't been an easy conquest had added to the excitement for him. For men who pursued women relentlessly and unscrupulously, resistance was often exciting. 'Things moved fast once he'd won me over, as I said. It didn't take long to finish my marriage.'

'Do you blame Fitton for that?'

'I blame myself more than anyone. I lost all sense of reasonable behaviour for a time. I was in love with Jason and I thought he was in love with me. He said consistently that this wasn't just another affair for him, that he wanted to marry me. I took him at his word and didn't bother to conceal the things I was doing with him. Richard, my husband, sued for divorce and I didn't contest it. He was given custody of our two teenage children – one of them is now in her third year at university and the other one goes at the end of next month. They come to see me regularly and I'm grateful for that. Sorry, that isn't something which interests you, but it's important to me.'

'What went wrong with your relationship with Fitton?'

'Nothing I couldn't have seen coming. Nothing other people wouldn't have warned me about, if I'd cared to listen. We women are stupid when we fancy we're in love.'

'No more stupid than men, I can assure you. We've seen men do some pretty stupid things when they thought that infatuation was love, haven't we, DS Northcott?'

'Indeed we have, sir. Ours might be the more stupid of two unpredictable genders, if we count heads. But in our game we see more of stupid men than we do of stupid women. And you're certainly not stupid, Anne.'

She had so set herself upon a contest with the aggressive Peach that she was disconcerted by the quiet and much deeper tones of the big black man and still more by his use of her first name. She didn't welcome it, but it was almost as if by calling her Anne he had declared his sympathy for her. She smiled ruefully. 'I'm not sure I find that consoling. When I look back on it now, I was certainly very stupid. I took Jason at face value and accepted his assurances, when any rational assessment of his previous philandering would have warned me against doing that.'

Clyde nodded. The pen looked absurdly small in his huge hand as it was poised over his notebook. 'When did the relationship end?'

She was sure that they knew the answers to most of these questions now, after the research they had clearly done on her and Jason. Perhaps they wanted her to get the details wrong or to conceal things, but she wasn't going to do that. 'Two years ago. I challenged him to set a date for our marriage and he laughed in my face. He said that I was a mature woman, not a stupid little tart, and that I should have known from the start that there would be no permanent arrangement. It had been good in bed, but it had now run its course. It was time for me to find myself a new prick to sit on. That was his very phrase. It seemed pretty dismissive to me at the time and it still does.'

Clyde made a note of the phrase and said calmly, 'It sounds very cruel as well as very final to me, Anne. You must have felt very bitter indeed towards him.'

It was an open-ended observation which invited further revelations from her, and it brought them. 'I denounced him to anyone who chose to hear me. I told my friends and work-mates – anyone who would listen, I suspect – that I would get even with him for what he had done to me.'

'Did you say you would kill him, Anne?'

'I might have done. Probably I did. If I could have torn his face with my nails at that time, I would have done it.' She was breathing hard, wondering if she should say these things. But perhaps they knew them already. 'I wouldn't have killed him, not even then. And certainly not now, when things have cooled down and I can look back at myself as the fool I was. I said all sorts of things in that situation, but I don't have the stuff of a killer in me.'

'I sometimes think all of us have the stuff of a killer in us, if we should be placed in a particular situation.'

'Do you, Detective Sergeant Northcott? It's an interesting thought. I'd need to consider it for a lot longer before I could tell you whether I agreed with it.' Anne was pleased that she'd remembered his name and rank: it seemed to assure her that she was still in charge here, despite the things she was revealing to them.

Clyde flicked to a new page in his notebook. He watched her as closely as ever as he said, 'Tell us exactly where you were between one and three on Sunday morning, Anne.'

She could feel her pulses racing now, even though she knew what she was going to say. She paused, took a deep breath and set herself for the obstacle, like a high jumper staring hard at a raised bar. 'I told you on Tuesday. I was safely tucked up in bed at home. Nowhere near the place where Jason died.'

'With no witnesses.'

'I cannot help that. The innocent do not plan alibis.'

Peach came in again now, having watched his bagman with approval for the last few minutes. 'That is true, Mrs Grice. It is very inconvenient for us, because we like to proceed by elimination. Your being alone makes it very difficult for us suspicious coppers to eliminate you from consideration.'

'I'm sorry about that, but I don't see what I can do about it.' The dark eyes were earnest, the heart-shaped face enhanced by a regretful smile.

'I'm sure you can see our difficulty. You have just declared a hatred for our murder victim. You have admitted that you declared publicly two years ago that it was your intention to kill him.' Peach wore now an apologetic smile, a great rarity on that mobile face.

'You're not going to give me that old cliché about hell having no fury like woman scorned, are you?'

'"Nor hell a fury like a woman scorned" are the exact words, I believe. It's often misquoted, but I sometimes think Congreve would have preferred your version if he'd had longer to think about it.'

'A literary policeman? The world is full of surprises, Detective Chief Inspector Peach.' Her full lips slipped for a moment into a taunting smile. She had thrown the full rank at Peach this time, and she was ridiculously pleased by it. The adrenalin must be working overtime in her veins.

But Peach seemed to play along, to enjoy this as much as she was doing. 'Clichés become clichés because they reflect reality, Mrs Grice. You're a very efficient woman: everyone tells us that. I think part of your efficiency is to be cool and well organized. I think I would dispute your view that you do not have the stuff of a killer within you.'

'Then I would quote your sergeant back to you: he says that almost everyone could be a killer in a particular set of circumstances.'

Peach's smile became now puzzled; his forehead puckered into a fierce frown beneath the baldness above it. 'Have you had many relationships since the one with Fitton hit the rocks, Mrs Grice?'

'I don't think that's any of your business.' She sighed. 'But I suppose you'll tell me that in a murder enquiry everything is your business. There have been one or two short-term things. I'm not a nun and I don't aim to live like one. But there's been nothing serious.'

'I see. Nothing that would have any connection with this death, then?'

She looked at him for a long moment. But he wasn't going to offer her anything more specific. 'Nothing that would have any connection with Jason's death, no.'

Peach glanced at Northcott, arched his black eyebrows for a second and said, 'Tell us again how you get on with your new employer.'

'I told you all you needed to know on Tuesday. We work together very well. So well, in fact, that we have become friends.'

'All we needed to know, or all that you wanted us to know at that point? Do you have a sexual relationship with Robert Walmsley, Mrs Grice?'

The question had come abruptly at last, like a slap in the face. Anne looked very shaken by it. She eyed the carpet rather than her questioner. It took her a long time to say, 'How did you know?'

He hadn't known, of course. But things had led logically to this. He didn't answer her question but said instead, 'You are now going to tell us about it, Mrs Grice.'

'It's only recent. I'm a free woman, but I would remind you that Bob Walmsley is a happily married man and I don't wish to destroy that marriage. He's been operating under a lot of strain, with Jason Fitton running down the business and using its profits for other purposes. And I've been under strain, too, of a different sort. I wasn't tucked up alone in bed last Saturday night, as I told you I was. We knew several days beforehand that Bob's wife was going to be away at her mother's that night. It seemed too good an opportunity to miss. I was in my bed all right, but I wasn't alone. Bob Walmsley was with me.'

'An alibi, then, for both of you. Why did you not reveal this earlier?'

'I don't think you really need to ask that. It's merely embarrassing for me, but potentially disastrous for Bob. And as neither of us had anything to do with Jason's death, we thought for a long time that this could remain our secret.'

She sat still with her head in her hands for a while after they had left her, then tried Robert Walmsley's mobile. It was switched off during his meeting with the solicitors, as she had anticipated. She texted the simple message Bob must have been half expecting. 'I had to tell them.'

SIXTEEN

Younis Hafeez was not used to being fearful. Fear was a tool he used with skill and for his own purposes. Fear made others do his bidding. On the evening after he had spoken with Peach and Northcott, he experienced real fear himself, as he had hardly done since he was a boy.

A sound English education had been a great help to him. It had enabled him to make his way in business, to establish trust with people who should not have trusted him. The English establishment appreciated education amongst its former colonials. If you joined their system and did well in it, the mysterious people who operated the establishment made exceptions.

It all went back to Oxford and Cambridge and their acceptance of rich Indians early in the century. Indians like Ranjitsinhji had been accepted there, even welcomed. Had not Ranji even played cricket for England and been considered one of the greats? That had been long before India gained independence, long before Younis's country of origin, Pakistan, had even existed. Ranji had been an Indian prince, which must surely have sugared the pill for the reactionary English peerage. Even that arch-agitator Gandhi was for a long time afforded an amused tolerance by the English toffs because he had studied law in London.

Now people like Younis Hafeez were taking advantage of the English tolerance to achieve wholly other things. He had never been a prince, but he was richer than he had ever imagined he could be. He had begun by supplying men who could afford it, many of them Asians like himself, with all sorts of pornographic pictures of young girls, some of them very young indeed. He'd found a surprisingly large demand for pictures of boys too, and had succeeded quickly in meeting it. Things had moved rapidly after that. He provided girls in large numbers and people had paid him handsomely for them. When he found that there was a demand for young and inexperienced girls, he found it surprisingly easy to recruit them from care homes.

He'd drawn a blank in Brunton, but it was surprising how lax had been the supervision in many care homes in the north and the Midlands. In many cases, the police hadn't wanted to know about what was going on, even when local busybodies had brought it to their attention. Where Asians were prominent members of local councils, the police and others were afraid of accusations of racial prejudice. Money gives you all sorts of influence: for a thousand quid or so annually, you could fee an officer in many of the police forces. He would then keep you well abreast of the latest thinking and action. Hafeez was very rich now: he had acquired millions far more quickly and easily than he would have believed possible when he set out on this road.

But Younis Hafeez began to miss Jason Fitton less than a week after he had been killed. He'd been glad to see him dead, eager to take over his local criminal enterprises. But he realized now that Jason had been a useful middleman, arranging the transfer of girls whilst Hafeez remained in the background. He'd been handsomely paid for that, but he had been a buffer which had made it difficult for the large police squad now investigating the procurement of young girls across the country to pin anything on Hafeez. Younis had financed the recruitment and movement of the desired sort of girls and boys, often little more than children, whom the press were now getting so indignant about. He had passed out a lot of money and in due course taken twice as much in return.

But things were getting dangerous for him now, and Jason Fitton was no longer around to provide a cushion between him and the police. Peach, with his confident assertion this morning that Hafeez would be in court within months, had scared him more than he had cared to reveal at the time. It was because of that that he had chosen to meet the man from Oxford in his home this evening. It felt more private and thus safer than his penthouse office: the police might have that place and the comings and goings of his visitors under surveillance. Or was he becoming paranoid? Was there less threat than he had felt there might be earlier in the day? It was difficult to tell with Peach. And also, more surprisingly, with that big black sergeant of his, who had joined the tennis club and might now be active as an unwelcome spy on Younis's activities there.

The man came precisely at the time arranged. But it was the wrong man. A heavily built Pakistani in his fifties, with a moustache and a shifty air. He did not have the appearance that would allay suspicion in anyone who might observe him. 'Where's Afridi?' said Hafeez immediately. He could hear the nervousness in his own voice.

'He couldn't come. He sent me. He's keeping a low profile. He advises you to do the same. He thinks the police have him under surveillance.'

This wasn't good. Afridi was a rich man, like himself. If he felt the police net closing around him, he was probably right. It was time to get out, to cut ties. Younis said, 'Does he want the usual next month?' It was a crude evasion they used, almost as though they were superstitious. Perhaps they did not want to confront the fact that they were trading in young lives. But it couldn't be that sort of squeamishness in his case: he'd laboured long and hard to make himself immune to any such sensitivity. Sex was a lucrative commodity to retail, as long as you closed your mind completely to the lives of the young-sters you were committing to a kind of slavery.

'He doesn't want the usual. He says it's too dangerous. I'm to tell you that all trade is suspended until further notice.'

'But I've laid out money. I have the goods ready to convey to him. He's committed to this.' But he knew even as he spoke that you couldn't argue with an emissary. This acolyte wouldn't have been given the authority to wheel and deal. Hafeez and Afridi would have exchanged views as equals, but this man had been sent to close down the enterprise.

'He's committed to nothing. He says don't make any contact with him whilst you're involved in this murder case. He'll get in touch with you if and when he sees fit.'

So they knew about Fitton. Of course they did. He should have anticipated that. He suddenly wanted to be rid of this heavy-breathing, overweight man, who was no more than a negative mouthpiece for his boss. Younis wanted to refuse to accept what he said, to tell him that he'd get in touch with Afridi when it suited him, not wait for a contact from him. But he didn't know what sort of pressure the man in Oxford was under. He mustn't make an enemy of Afridi. If the Vice Squad were on to him, he might give them other names, as he strove to preserve his own skin.

Younis Hafeez ignored the refreshments he had set out ready on the low table in his living room. 'Don't take your coat off; you need to get moving. Tell your boss his decision is going to cost me a lot of money. Don't hang about around here, unless you want to be dragged into a murder investigation.'

Hafeez normally slept soundly and woke refreshed. He often boasted that he slept well whatever concerns he had and wherever he had to lay his head. That night he slept fitfully, waking several times with a sense of impending doom.

He awoke in the morning to the news that Afridi had been arrested in Oxford.

For a retired man, Arthur Swarbrick was up early on Friday morning. He had finished his breakfast before nine and told his wife, 'I need to get down to the tennis club. We've a first-team match at the weekend. I want to make sure everything is ready.'

Shirley was usually happy to see him involved at Birch Fields. It was his hobby and his pleasure, and it had taken him out into the world and filled his days since he had left his real work behind two years ago. It got him out of the house and ensured he was not under her feet all day. She had been married for a long time now, but she had no illusions about their union. They needed to get away from each other if they were to remain contented. But this morning Arthur could not go to the tennis club. Not yet, anyway.

She said, 'You still look tired, Arthur. You should let other people do more at the tennis club; you can't take responsibility for everything. I think it took it out of you going to see Clare on Wednesday, whatever took place between the two of you. You haven't told me much about it, you know.'

It was true. He wondered why they found it so difficult to

communicate about important things. Shirley loved Clare as much as he did, but in a different way. They should be able to talk easily and naturally about such things, but they did not. Giving each other space, people called it, but that was just an evasion here, he felt. As if he were speaking to a stranger, he said, 'She was very tight when I got there. But she loosened up during the day. We had cheese on toast for lunch, made the way you taught her when she was a girl. We walked in the park during the afternoon.'

'You told me that – well, except for the cheese on toast bit. But you didn't explain why you thought she was neurotic when you arrived but relaxed when you left.'

He wouldn't have used those words and Clare wouldn't have accepted them. They seemed clinical, not personal. Not the kind of words to be used between parent and child. But then Shirley had never been as close to Clare as he had. Or was that notion just part of his selfishness, the means he chose to deny her access to that precious bond between father and daughter? 'We talked about Jason Fitton, the way we hadn't been able to do for a long time. It was as if his death had brought a kind of release for her. "Closure" was the word Clare used herself.' He felt he had to apologize for such a conventional word. In a more intimate marital relationship he would not have done that.

'But you think she's going to be all right now?'

'I do. I'm not saying that she was happy when I left her. But happiness wouldn't be quite natural, would it? She was quiet and resolute and she had a sort of calm about her.' He felt an irritation he should not have felt about struggling to put this into words for his wife. It was quite illogical, but he felt that articulating this might fracture the rather brittle calm that he had brought to Clare.

Shirley wanted to push him further, but sensed now that she must not do that. She said, 'That trip was more tiring than you realized, you know. Perhaps you shouldn't go to Birch Fields today. Not this morning, anyway.' Now it was she who was fumbling for the right words. She was evading the issue, when that was not her way of doing things. She said abruptly, 'You can't go to the tennis club – not this morning, anyway. The police are coming to see you again at ten o'clock.'

Murder overrides most things. Even young love suffers in the course of a murder investigation. PC Elaine Brockman had hardly seen DS Clyde Northcott since Sunday, when the news of Jason Fitton's death had demanded his attention.

She could have rung him on his mobile, of course, but she was not sure whether their relationship had gone far enough for that. He'd been a very welcome mentor to her at the station, where graduate entrants had to tread very carefully, and she'd helped him along a little with his tennis and with the early trials of his membership at Birch Fields. They had been useful to each other in these different fields, but did what they had between them go further than usefulness? That Friday morning, she had the chance to answer that question and she was determined to take it.

They were together for a few minutes after Peach's briefing to the team had dispatched their fellow officers in various directions. She said nervously, 'I don't think the house-to-house is going to bring us much more, now.'

'No. I think Percy will shut it down after today. You can never tell what house-to-house will bring. It throws up unexpected nuggets sometimes, so it has to be done.'

Clyde seemed to be apologizing for the boring and repetitious work in which she'd been involved in the earlier part of the week. Promising, she felt. 'I didn't mind it. Everything is good experience when you're as raw as I am in the job.'

He grinned at her, his rather solemn face lighting up suddenly in that way that had first drawn her to him. 'Percy says you'll be ordering all of us around in a few years.'

'Is that his way of saying that he doesn't approve of graduate entry?'

'No. He's in favour of it really, though he'd never dream of admitting it publicly. Just as he allows me to have a mind of my own and to question suspects, though he describes me to anyone who will listen as just the hard bastard in his team.'

She took the plunge. 'Mum wondered if you'd like to come round for tea.'

He looked hard at her. The smile had disappeared as quickly as it had arrived. 'Are you sure she'd want the hard bastard in her house?'

'I'm not at all sure that she would. I think she'd like to meet the big daft bugger, though. I think she might quite like him.'

He frowned. 'I'd like to come, But—'

'That's good, then. Around six be all right?' She was in before he had finished his acceptance, eager to clinch the deal.

'I was going to say that it's difficult to make firm arrangements when there's a murder investigation going on. I don't want to let you down and get off on the wrong foot with your parents.'

He thought that this was the beginning of something, then, not just a one-off. That was good. And he must be anxious to come, because he hadn't used the excuse that the case could give him to fob her off. Elaine said, 'I'm sure Mum and Dad would understand that. I'll tell them what an important person you are.'

'I'm not and you mustn't. Just ask them to make it something that won't spoil if I'm not there on time.'

'That might mean salad. Mum's big on salads when the days are long and the weather's warm.'

Clyde grinned weakly. 'Whatever. I'll be there as near to six as I can. And thank you for the invitation.'

It was a long time since he had received a formal invitation to a meal in a middle-class house. In fact, he wasn't certain that it had ever happened to him before; he had certainly never accepted before. He hoped he wouldn't get the cutlery wrong.

Elaine Brockman wondered quite what it was that she had set in motion. Inviting a man round to meet your parents was another step along the way and Dad at least would make sure she was aware of that.

Arthur Swarbrick took the CID visitors into his study when they came: he didn't want Shirley to hear this. The room was larger than most studies. The estate agent had called it a 'playroom' when they had bought the house, one of 'three spacious downstairs reception rooms'. He didn't use it a lot now. He kept some confidential papers and files from the tennis club there, but most of his chairman's stuff was stored in his office at Birch Fields.

He sat them in armchairs and pulled his own one close to them. 'I hope you're getting closer to an arrest. This business has been the talk of the club, as you can imagine.'

'I can imagine, sir, yes. And we are getting closer to an arrest. Have you picked up anything that might be useful to us?' Peach was watching with the attention a young cat affords to a newly captured mouse.

'No. I've heard lots of gossip and speculation around the tennis club, but it's been no more than that. Most of it centres on your activities and how assiduous your team has been in questioning everyone.'

'We try to be thorough, sir. That makes it difficult for people to conceal things, you see. When they try to do that, we usually pick up from others what they are trying to hide. Concealment always excites our interest. We ask ourselves why people are trying to deceive us. And we come up with some interesting answers.'

'I see.' Arthur Swarbrick was filled with a foreboding that he did not succeed in masking. 'I suppose you're now going to tell me that some of my members at Birch Fields have been trying to hide things from you.'

Peach nodded gravely. 'Including the chairman himself. A man who really should know better.'

Arthur tried to look surprised, but he was trumped in this by Peach's eyebrows, which rocketed upwards more dramatically than should have been possible beneath the bald dome that topped them. Those dark arcs seemed to dominate Arthur's vision, like moving black slugs that prevented his mind from operating rationally. 'You mustn't think that I've deliberately tried to deceive you. If I've held anything back which you think you should have been told, it was quite unwitting on my part. Does this concern one of my members?'

'No, sir. It concerns you yourself and no other person, as far as I am aware. Of course, I am not as aware as I should be, because you and others have chosen to try to keep me unaware. Deception is counter-productive, Mr Swarbrick, as you are about to discover. It draws our attention and makes would-be deceivers highly suspect. Especially when we had them in the frame for this crime already and they are without convincing alibis.'

Peach clasped his hands together and set them in his lap, as if to emphasize the satisfaction this thought brought to him. Arthur felt very pale and was sure that he looked very pale. 'It is not my fault that I do not have an alibi. Neither is it my wife's fault, but her departure left me without anyone to substantiate my account of my actions and whereabouts at the time Jason Fitton died. Shirley left the summer ball before its end because she wished to get home and go to bed.'

'Or she was dispatched home to leave you free to do what you had planned for some time to do. Her absence left you free to wait for Fitton in his car and kill him quickly and efficiently with the cord you had prepared for the purpose.'

'That is ridiculous. It was nothing so sinister.'

'We have to consider the ridiculous, Mr Swarbrick, when the obvious offers us no solution. It's what we're paid to do – amongst many other things. You were not at Birch Fields on Wednesday. Where did you go on that day?'

The question was rapped at him so bluntly that it destroyed what little coolness he had retained. Perhaps they knew all about where he had been and were trying to trap him. Or perhaps they didn't know and were prepared to put some much more sinister interpretation upon his absence. 'I went to see my daughter in London.'

'The one who had had the affair with Jason Fitton.'

It was a statement, not a question. Nothing was sacred to these men. 'Clare was involved with Jason at one time, yes.'

'Seriously involved.'

'Yes. As far as she was concerned, it was *very* serious.'

'But it wasn't for Fitton. And when he broke it off, it affected her badly.'

'Yes. Deep clinical depression, the doctors called it. As far as my wife and I were concerned, it was a serious mental breakdown. Clare had spells in two different hospitals and we were warned that her mental health was still brittle when she was discharged from the second of them.'

Without any visible sign from Peach, Clyde Northcott took over the questioning. 'Is Clare your only daughter?'

'Yes. Our only child, in fact.'

'You must have been very upset. You must have felt very hostile towards Fitton, in view of the way he had treated her.' Northcott's voice was deep, soft and reassuring, inviting confidences that his demeanour implied would be treated with understanding. Arthur was glad for the first time that they had accepted this imposing black man as a member at the club.

Swarbrick's voice was almost inaudible as he said, 'We thought for many months that Clare might die. She attempted suicide once and we feared that she might do so again.'

He hadn't resorted to any of the normal conventions like 'do something silly'. In this most conventional of men, that made his concern more touching. He looked older than his sixty-two years now, but his distress for his daughter had brought to his lined face a dignity that it had not had earlier. Clyde said softly, 'You were concerned for her welfare after Fitton's death at the weekend.'

'Yes. That's where I was on Wednesday. I went to see Clare in London. That's where she lives and works now. It seemed better for her to make a complete break when she came out of hospital. I knew Clare would have heard about Fitton. I wanted to make sure that she was all right.'

'That she wasn't feeling suicidal.'

Arthur glanced up quickly into the large black face, but saw only sympathy for him and his plight there. 'That's true, I suppose. I just wanted to be with her, to make sure that she was safe. She'd heard, all right, once it was in the papers and on the radio. I don't think she watches television much, since she came out of hospital.' He stared bleakly at Northcott, refusing to contemplate Peach.

'Did you find her well?'

'Yes – well, better than I'd expected, I suppose. She seemed to get better whilst I was with her. I was glad I'd gone down there.'

'You should have told us about Clare when we spoke with you on Monday, Arthur.'

'I suppose I should, yes. Well, I can see that I should certainly have done that, now that you've found out. But it seemed to me a private thing. I didn't want to broadcast the trouble she'd had with Fitton, or to tell you that we'd even feared for her life.'

Clyde nodded, but pointed out gently, 'You don't broadcast things when you tell us about them, Arthur. Everything we hear is treated as strictly confidential.'

Peach came back in now, strident and insistent where his bagman had been quiet and understanding. 'And everything you don't tell us is treated as suspicious, Mr Swarbrick. If you can view things for just a moment from our point of view, you'll see why.'

Swarbrick turned his attention reluctantly back to his nemesis. He nodded reluctantly. 'The fact that Fitton did this to my daughter gave me a greater incentive to kill him.'

'The fact that you tried to keep the knowledge from us certainly makes you a more probable candidate, as far as we're concerned. You must have wished him dead many times over the last few years.'

'I have. Many times.'

'And those years gave you ample time to plan his death. The annual summer ball at the tennis club, where you were in control and you knew he would be in attendance, was an ideal opportunity. You know every inch of the Birch Fields complex and you know the preferences and probable movements of most of your members, including Jason Fitton. You probably even knew where he would park his car last Saturday night.'

Arthur merely shrugged his shoulders. There was no point in a denial. 'I know all these things. I'm glad he's dead. I've considered killing him a few times in the last few years, for what he did to Clare, but he was a powerful man and I didn't have it in me. Do I look like a murderer?'

He raised his arms a few inches and let them drop limply by his sides. He certainly didn't look like a killer. Not many men in their sixties, with glasses and thinning grey hair and pot bellies and neat, slightly out-of-date suits, look like killers. But Peach told him with a grim smile, 'If we considered only the people who look like murderers, we'd have precious few suspects. And I'd have missed a lot of arrests over the last ten years.'

Clyde Northcott said thoughtfully in the car, 'Arthur Swarbrick opposed my application for membership at Birch Fields.'

'He's not unintelligent, then. Perhaps a big daft bugger like you wasn't part of his plan.'

'I thought he and I would always be enemies, but I had a lot of sympathy for him in there this morning.'

'A big daft *soft* bugger, then.'

'He had a right to be upset. I wouldn't like to be on the end of a hostile interview from you.'

'Entirely professional, DS Northcott. Anyway, you've been there, in the past.'

'Yes, but you were on my side, once you'd got further into that case. I think *you* must be a little daft soft bugger inside.'

'A long way inside, DS Northcott. And don't you dare go public with your opinions.'

Clyde's smile lasted all the way back to the station.

SEVENTEEN

P each spoke to the team at four o'clock on Friday afternoon. They were pleasantly surprised by what he had to say. They had anticipated losing much of their weekend, but he reported that the routine work was more or less complete and congratulated them on the thoroughness of their efforts. He and DS Northcott would conduct at least one interview on Saturday, but most of the team could take the weekend off.

Clyde was released in plenty of time for his assignment for tea at the Brockman household. He wasn't entirely sure whether he was pleased or disappointed by that. He was able to journey there with PC Brockman herself, which he supposed was a good thing. He hadn't been looking forward to arriving at the house on his own. He put on the suit he had worn for his interview at Birch Fields Tennis Club, and she changed out of uniform as she always did before leaving the station.

Elaine drove him to her home in the old green Toyota she had taken over from her mother when she came down from university. Clyde was glad that he did not have to arrive on his treasured Yamaha. That would have involved removing helmet and leathers at Elaine's home, which he felt would not give the best first impression of him to her parents. She was their youngest child and had come quite late, and they were now in their early sixties.

She slid the car expertly out of her parking space and into the stream of rush-hour Brunton traffic. This swift exit would mean that fewer people saw her with what many of her colleagues regarded as the most eligible bachelor in the station. Clyde had not taken on a permanent partner since he came here, though there had been several opportunities for him to do so. The tight-knit community of a police headquarters is as subject as any other workplace to the vagaries of gossip.

They were queuing at the traffic lights when she said to him, 'What progress, Clyde?'

She'd been involved in this case from the start, since Peach had said it would be a valuable part of her experience as a fast-track graduate entry. She'd done three days of house-to-house and minor witness interviews; she'd spoken with many of those who'd attended that fateful summer ball at Birch Fields, since she had been a member of the tennis club since she was ten and already knew many of them.

Clyde, whose inclination was always to keep things to himself, even with his colleagues (too many coppers were tempted by the prospect of easy money from the media in exchange for information), decided that she was a member of the team for this case and that he could speak frankly to her. That was good, because he found he didn't want to have secrets from Elaine; he must be a big daft soft bugger, as Percy Peach had said.

'I can tell you what I think. It won't necessarily be what Percy thinks, because he tends to keep his thoughts to himself in the early days of a case.'

'Not wishing to influence you, I expect. Wanting your great mind to operate independently, so that he can have two informed views on the subject.' She had her attention on the traffic around her and no trace of a smile. She was an expert piss-taker: that was one of her attractions for him. He wondered how much that was natural to her and how much a university education had developed it. He also wondered for the tenth time whether he would be out of his depth in her household, having volunteered himself eagerly to enter this lions' den.

'You know most of the people in the frame for this one. I should think it's almost certainly someone who was at the summer ball with us on Saturday night.'

'Oo-er!' She shivered extravagantly behind the wheel. '*Almost* certainly?'

'Well, we've unearthed a couple of others who've covered up their feelings about Jason Fitton, but as they were nowhere near Birch Fields on Saturday night and were tucked up in bed together at the time of the murder, I don't see how they can be involved.'

'Anne Grice?'

He was struck yet again by the sharpness of this surprising girl. 'Yes. She's the PA to the managing director at Fitton's Metals and she—'

'She was Fitton's mistress for quite some time. Until about two years ago, if I remember right.'

'You do.' Clyde was tremendously impressed – and also a little irritated. You didn't want a girlfriend who was cleverer than you – and he was sure now that he wanted Elaine as his girlfriend. He said resignedly, 'How did you know that?'

'I was sent to ask questions at her old firm in Preston. It seems to have been quite a torrid affair they had, and long-term by Jason Fitton's standards. She was very angry when it ended, according to the people who worked with her in Preston.'

'Yes. She more or less admitted to us that she took the PA job at Fitton's Metals just to get near to him – not that Fitton was around much there. He was milking the profits to spend elsewhere, according to his MD. That's Robert Walmsley, the man who had recently become Anne Grice's new boss.'

'And new lover, apparently.'

'Yes. We had to prise that out of them and I don't know how serious it is. She's a lot younger than he is and she claims he's happily married. The only thing they have in common seems to be a hatred of Jason Fitton, she for what he did to her and he for what Jason did to Fitton's Metals.'

'But you think they were concerned with altogether other things at the time of the murder. So proceed, please, to your real suspects.'

Clyde decided to begin with the one he thought least likely. *Take the bones out of this, you clever little minx.* 'Olive Crawshaw.'

'She taught me when I was at school.'

'Perhaps she could offer that as extenuating circumstances, then, if we nail her for murder.'

'And she introduced you into the tennis club. Insisted that you should be accepted, in fact, no doubt against strenuous opposition. Perhaps she did that so that she could plead insanity if she should be arrested for murder.'

'She had motive and opportunity.' Clyde fell back stubbornly on the old copper's watchwords. 'And she has no one who can vouch for her whereabouts at the time of the killing.'

'Can't Eric do that?' Elaine had known both of them since her early teenage years and she couldn't picture either of them as a criminal.

'No. He wasn't at the dance and he was fast asleep when she came home from it. He's got the beginnings of Alzheimer's, but I shouldn't think Olive wants that broadcast.'

'I'm sorry to hear that. He's a nice man, Eric.'

'Yes. Percy was very good with him. He talked to him about the Rovers.'

She smiled and motioned to an elderly woman to cross the zebra crossing in front of them. 'You like your boss, don't you?'

'Yes. I like the fact that he's good at his job and that he's full of surprises.'

'Like asking you to be best man at his wedding.'

'Well, yes. I was thinking more of the things he seems to know, when we're interviewing people.'

He sounded apologetic. She wanted to tell him that he didn't need to apologize for liking the formidable Percy Peach. Instead, she said thoughtfully, 'This Alzheimer's would put Olive under a lot of strain: they're not at all like each other, she and Eric, but they've always been very close, I think. But I can't see her as a murderer, strain or no strain.'

Clyde nodded, then recalled what Percy had said. 'Olive Crawshaw has the capacity for murder: she's well organized and very determined when she thinks she's right. And she certainly had no liking for Jason Fitton. She thought that he was a spoilt brat who had grown up into a villain and was doing untold damage to the town and the community she and Eric have worked so hard to nurture.'

Elaine surprised herself by what she now recalled. 'Eric was a very good headmaster in the comprehensive that handled most of the town's problem kids. Jason caused him a lot of grief by attacking his school. I'd almost forgotten that.'

'Olive thinks that her husband's trouble with Alzheimer's

stems from that episode. She may or be not be right, but the important thing for us is that she believes it. It certainly increased her hatred of Jason Fitton and her desire to be rid of him.'

Elaine wanted to say that she still couldn't see Olive as a murderer, but her brief experience of the police service had already taught her that that would mark her as a naive amateur. 'Who else?'

'Arthur Swarbrick, your chairman.'

'Not *my* chairman, you silly sod. The Birch Fields Tennis Club chairman, who you think had the good sense to oppose your entry. Arthur's a pig-headed bigot, but hardly a murderer. He's ultra-conservative and opposed to anything even vaguely liberal, and I'm sure he didn't like Fitton. But would he murder him?'

'I might, in his shoes.' Clyde paused to consider that rather alarming possibility. 'Jason had an affair with Arthur's daughter, before he became involved with Anne Grice. He might even have been running the two in tandem, for all I know. Maybe it was the charms of Anne that made him dispense with Swarbrick's daughter, Clare. The important thing for us is that it almost destroyed Swarbrick's only child. Clare was in and out of mental hospitals and is still on medication for depression. Arthur went down to London on Wednesday, to make sure she was handling the news of Fitton's death without mishap. He has far more reason to be bitter about Fitton than we thought at first.'

'Do you think he did it?'

Clyde smiled grimly. 'He's no friend of mine, but I rather hope he didn't. I found myself very sorry for him when we prised all this out of him this morning.'

'Very unprofessional, DS Northcott, to let personal feelings obtrude on your judgement like this. I'm with you, though. I see Arthur Swarbrick, *your* chairman as he is now, as a racist and sexist bigot rather than a ruthless killer. Can you offer me anyone more likely?'

'Younis Hafeez. Even to a resolute non-racist like me, he's a kettle of stinking fish.'

'You infest things with a kind of poetry, DS Northcott. But

I agree. That man has given me the creeps ever since he tried to slide his hand up my tennis skirt when I was thirteen.'

Clyde thought unworthily that he would very much like to slide his hand up that same thigh nine years later, though he would never do it without invitation. He strove to concentrate. 'Hafeez has been trafficking young girls from care homes for the pleasure of middle-aged perverts many miles south of here.'

'And did he kill Fitton?'

'Admirable question. You are properly focused on the matter in hand. Brunton CID isn't even directly involved in the procurement case, though we've cooperated throughout it with the Serious Crime Squad. The question for us, as you rightly state, is whether Hafeez garrotted Fitton in the early hours of Sunday morning.'

'And did he?'

'I'd like to think so. And so would Percy. That's unusual, because he's usually determined to be completely objective about these things.'

'I'd also like it to be him. Younis Hafeez is an oily perv.'

'If I'd been to university, I might have been able to produce balanced judgements like that.' Clyde was uncomfortably conscious that they were getting close to the Brockman residence and that he hadn't been able to concentrate in these last minutes on the impression he wanted to make.

As she swung the Toyota expertly into the drive, Elaine said, 'Don't worry. It will be all right.' Clyde thought that there might after all be something to be said for this notion of female intuition.

Mrs Brockman welcomed him with the studious politeness which all black men are accustomed to meeting from liberally inclined middle-aged, middle-class women. He didn't mind that: he knew that she meant well, and he was equally careful, polite and slightly artificial in his response. 'It's very kind of you to invite me here, Mrs Brockman.' She hadn't met anyone quite like him and he had met very few quite like her.

Elaine's father tried hard to be breezy: it was what he usually did when he was nervous. 'And how's our little girl been getting on in the big world outside, Clyde?' He added the forename after a tiny pause, which made it obvious that he'd had to work hard to produce it.

'She's doing very well, Mr Brockman. I think we could almost say exceptionally well.' It sounded patronizing, but Clyde couldn't think what else he could have said.

'Quite well for a girl, at any rate,' said Elaine. She glanced sharply at her father and the two smiled; Clyde felt excluded from what was obviously a long-standing matter of contention.

It was salad, as she had threatened. Clyde picked up his knife and fork carefully and embarked on his trial. He managed to eat quite delicately, though the effort involved meant that he trusted his fork only with small fragments and fell behind the others as the meal progressed. There was much false bonhomie. Clyde failed in his contributions to this, as he found that he could not respond to questions and down his salad at the same time. He was confined to monosyllables and inane smiles: they must surely consider him very stupid indeed.

They had home-made scones with jam and cream after the salad: he was much happier with these. He remembered to compliment Mrs Brockman on her scones and downed two of them with relish, though Elaine seemed to find it very amusing that he unwittingly acquired a blob of cream on the end of his nose as he did so. Then there was tea in delicate china cups, with his hand ridiculously large upon the handle and his little finger flickering uncertainly as he drank.

He insisted on helping to carry crockery back into the kitchen. There he watched the family's amiable golden Labrador demolish its meal with gusto in thirty seconds and marvelled that eating could be so brisk and uncomplicated.

Mr Brockman seemed to be striving hard to approve of him. When they were all sitting in comfort in the lounge, he said, 'Elaine brought a chap from the university here last year. We didn't take to him.'

'That's hardly fair,' said Mrs Brockman hastily. 'We never got to know him, really.'

'He lived locally. He wasn't really a boyfriend,' said Elaine, equally hastily.

'Bloke was on drugs!' said her father. He shook his head disgustedly.

It must have been nervousness that prompted Clyde's reaction. He reviewed it many times later, but he could offer no other explanation to himself or an equally bewildered Elaine. 'I sold drugs once,' he said.

The silence was profound and extended. Clyde looked even more aghast than the other three in the room. Eventually, he managed to falter, 'It was a long time ago and in a different life. I find it difficult to believe that it was me, now.'

Elaine said eventually, 'Everyone respects Clyde at the station. He's made DS very quickly and he works alongside DCI Peach. I'm sure you've heard of him.' Her father's face was still set in stone and her mother shook her head slowly. Elaine added desperately, 'Clyde's been really helpful to me. There's a lot of resistance to graduate entry in the police.'

Her father found his tongue and said dully, 'We didn't want you to go there.'

'It's been wonderful for me to have Clyde's advice. Everyone respects him, you see, and no one dares to be horrid to me with him on my side.' She grinned hopefully at her father, then stared more fiercely at Clyde, willing him to say nothing about his role as Peach's hard bastard.

Mrs Brockman eventually managed to say, 'I hear you've been working on this murder at Birch Fields Tennis Club, Clyde. Is there any progress?'

'Clyde can't talk about that, Mum,' said Elaine hastily. 'We're not allowed to talk about our work at home.'

'No, of course not. I shouldn't have asked.'

'We're making progress, Mrs Brockman,' said Clyde, wanting to offer something but picking his words very carefully. 'In fact, I should be off now. Detective Chief Inspector Peach has an interview lined up for the two of us tomorrow morning.'

'Working on a Saturday, eh?' Mr Brockman seemed mildly impressed by this diligence in his visitor. 'Do you think you're near to an arrest?'

'We could be,' said Clyde Northcott mysteriously.

He'd no idea why he'd said that, beyond some vague desire

to raise his standing in what was to him an alien but important environment. He'd no real conviction that Peach knew any more than he did about this baffling mystery.

Within the next twenty-four hours, however, his standing in the Brockman household would be gloriously elevated.

EIGHTEEN

'Why did they want to see us here?' Anne Grice looked nervously round the managing director's office.

'I don't know. They just said that it would be quiet here on a Saturday morning. Peach said that we wouldn't be disturbed.' Bob Walmsley helped her as she moved chairs into position. Any action was a release of tension as they waited.

'Does Peach usually make his own appointments?'

'I don't know. How should I know?' He was sharp with her, when he did not mean to be. It was getting to both of them, this waiting and wondering. 'Sorry.'

'You wouldn't make your own appointments. You'd leave it to your PA.' She gave him a weak grin, striving to convey to him that this was an attempt at humour. 'And why did he specify we should be together? They've been happy to speak to us separately previously.'

'I don't know, do I? I don't know why they wanted to see us together. I can't read their minds, can I? Peach just said that he and DS Northcott needed to speak with us. And that we wouldn't want to be disturbed.'

'DS Northcott's that big black officer who takes notes.'

'I know that. I'm not entirely stupid.' He forced a smile. 'Even though I need an excellent PA to support me.' They needed to be relaxed, or at least to seem so, when the CID men arrived. He tried hard to think of something neutral and unthreatening to offer her. 'He didn't say much when they questioned me, the big black guy.'

'He did with me. He took over for a while and asked quite a lot of questions. He seemed more sympathetic than Peach.'

Bob's smile this time was genuine, but rueful. 'That wouldn't be difficult. Do you think they use the good cop, bad cop technique?'

'I don't know. I've never been questioned by the police before.'

'Neither have I. Well, once, years ago, but that was about what someone else had done, not about my own actions.' He came round his desk and stood facing her. Then he put a hand on each of her shoulders. 'This is unnerving, isn't it?'

'Yes. I should have realized it would be. I hadn't even thought about being grilled by the police, when I . . . when we . . .'

Her voice tailed away and she looked for a moment as if she might cry. She was very pale this morning, he thought. Still attractive and well groomed, but quite wan. She was normally so efficient in all her actions that he hadn't realized the strain all this must have put upon her; that was very stupid of him. He gripped her shoulders more tightly and said, 'The important thing is that we stick together. If we give them nothing, they won't be able to do anything, whatever they might think.'

'I suppose not.' She brightened determinedly. 'We can present a united front and send them off to look elsewhere, can't we?'

'Of course we can. And then we can get the show back on the road. This firm has needed to be rid of Fitton for years!'

'Just as this woman has.'

He leant forward and kissed her chastely on the forehead, feeling the cool smoothness of her skin against his lips. 'We can do this, Anne, and we will!'

There wasn't much else to say. They would merely have slipped into repetition. They arranged the chairs with elaborate care and did not look at each other directly again. It was almost a relief when the two detectives arrived. There were two cars: the Mondeo they had seen before and another, more official-looking car behind it, with police markings and uniformed officers. The uniforms stayed behind when the plain-clothes men moved into the nerve centre of Fitton's Metals.

Peach looked at both of them hard before he accepted the seat offered. No change there, then, Bob told himself. He deliberately avoided looking at Anne, feeling that would show some sort of weakness. Clyde Northcott was the last of the four to sit. His height and his size seemed ominous as he towered above them, but he eventually folded his long limbs into the chair provided and offered what might have been the slightest of smiles. Behind that studiously impassive face, he was thinking about what Peach had told him on the way here and of the part he must play in the drama that was about to unfold.

As usual, it was the most nervous person in the room who spoke first. Bob Walmsley said, 'This is all very intriguing, Mr Peach. Both Mrs Grice and I have had a very busy week, as you can imagine, but we're happy to offer you whatever help we can.'

Peach made no acknowledgement of this. Politeness, even that meaningless politeness that humanity uses to oil the social wheels, relaxes tension, and he had no wish to do that. People make mistakes when they are tense, and he needed mistakes. Evidence was still thin upon the ground, but these two would give him all he needed before the day was out. With any luck, before the hour was out.

He said, 'You and Mrs Grice have had a very busy week, as you say. It began early last Sunday morning and has been hectic ever since then.'

'Since you called at my house with the news of Jason Fitton's death, yes. That set off a whole train of events here. But I flatter myself that I've coped pretty well, with the unselfish and highly efficient support of Mrs Grice.' He reached out a hand towards the chair beside him. After a moment, Anne Grice took it and held it.

They were curiously diffident for lovers, thought Clyde Northcott. It was almost as if they were feeling their way with each other. They behaved as though they were embarrassed to display their feelings for each other in public, as many people are.

Peach watched them until their hands fell limply apart. He looked from Walmsley's face to Grice's. The PA seemed attentive but quite calm. It was Bob Walmsley who looked more disturbed. He looked expectant, in the manner of someone anticipating bad tidings rather than good ones – rather as parents or spouses had looked years ago, when, as a young copper, he had needed to give news of road accident deaths. Apprehensive rather than merely expectant, in other words.

Peach focused his attack upon the managing director. 'Your reception of the news of your owner's death on Sunday morning was abnormal,' he said bluntly.

'I wouldn't know what is normal, Detective Chief Inspector. My mind was reeling with the news. And at the same time as I was trying to work out its implications for the firm I serve and control.'

'You were very anxious to convince us that the news was a surprise to you. You told us four times how shocked you were.'

'It may be news to you to hear that ordinary, innocent people very often are shocked by death, DCI Peach.'

'Indeed they are. I have the advantage of you in this: I have had to bring the news of sudden death to people on many occasions and in many different circumstances. I have seen innocent people suffering all kinds of shock and reacting in many different ways. They very rarely comment on how shocked they are. You told us repeatedly what a surprise this death was to you, as if it was important to you that we should be convinced of that.'

'Fanciful, Mr Peach. Imaginative, but hardly convincing.'

'It was a quarter of an hour before you asked us how Fitton had died, Mr Walmsley. People normally wish to know immediately how someone has died. It is a reflex action to ask that question.'

Bob tried to muster sarcasm. 'I'm sorry if I disappointed you. Perhaps I was more concerned with the implications for the firm than with the details of the owner's death.'

'When we asked you to give us some account of the dead man's character, you enlarged upon several major defects – you certainly didn't seem concerned to protect his reputation. Yet you did not tell us that he was a serial womanizer, which is a trait that invariably brings us multiple suspects. Why was that?'

It was one of the sudden, almost violent questions that had become Peach's trademark: one of those shafts that plunged him into violent confrontation with the recipient. Bob Walmsley said hopelessly, 'I don't know, do I? My mind was reeling. Perhaps I felt some obligation to protect *some* shreds of my owner's reputation from public perusal.'

'Or perhaps you wished to keep us away for as long as possible from the knowledge of Mrs Grice's involvement in a passionate affair with the murder victim. An affair that would inevitably have focused our attention upon her.'

'Anne had nothing to do with that death, and neither did I.'

Clyde Northcott spoke now, his attention upon the only woman in the room. His voice was deep, persuasive, but at the same time ominous. 'You never gave us a satisfactory explanation of why you came here, Anne. Everyone we spoke to at your old firm in Preston told us that you seemed very happy there and had excellent relationships with your boss and the other people in your office. That firm was on the up, whereas when you came here Fitton's Metals seemed to be heading for a bad period, largely because its owner was milking the profits and starving it of research and development funds.'

'I wanted to get near Jason Fitton. I wanted to damage him in any way I could.'

It was the first time she had made any sort of concession. Bob Walmsley glanced a sharp warning at her. DS Northcott said quietly, 'You should have told us that when we spoke on Tuesday, Anne. You told us several times in the first five minutes of our chat that you'd never met Jason Fitton. You'd no real chance of concealing your affair with him, once we spoke to the people you'd worked with in your previous post.'

'I didn't know that. I've never been involved in anything like this before. I didn't know how many police were involved or how thorough the questioning would be.'

'Once we heard about your affair with Fitton and how bitter you were about the break-up with him, you were bound to be at the centre of intensive enquiries. The fact that you tried to conceal what had happened previously only made your conduct more suspicious.'

Walmsley spoke up sharply before she could respond to this. 'So we concealed things. It may have been foolish, but it doesn't make us killers.'

Northcott glanced at Peach, who said unsmilingly, 'Certain fibres have been extracted from the car of the deceased. Human hair was also collected, from the headrest of the passenger seat. We shall have no difficulty in obtaining a warrant to examine your clothes, once the two of you have been arrested.'

It was the first time there had been mention of an arrest. Anne Grice looked sharply sideways at her boss, who kept his eyes on Peach's face as if hypnotized. It was Grice who said, 'That hair could have been from a long time ago. He bought the Bentley three years ago. It wasn't his only car, but he liked it. He had it when I was with him. I rode in it with him quite often. I even drove it myself, on occasion. I'm sure I left fibres from my clothing and hairs from my head in there.'

'It's interesting that you know how long the car had been in his possession. No doubt you had a key to it when you were close to him. A key you used to gain access to the car in the early hours of last Sunday morning.'

'That is a ridiculous idea! As is your production of hairs and fibres that have probably been there since I was with Jason.'

'That car was valeted regularly and thoroughly, as you no doubt remember from your time with Fitton. It was last cleaned on Tuesday the fourth of August, less than three days before his death. Forensic scientists are very clever nowadays: I think they will be able to put a recent date on the single hair extracted from that headrest.'

Walmsley now spoke, without any obvious emotion, like a man delivering the words of a script he has learned to prove that he knows it, rather than with real expression. 'We were nowhere near the scene of this murder. Anne told you on Thursday where we were and I now confirm that.'

'Yes. Your fallback position. You'd set that up for us, dropped us useful clues to the idea that there might be more than a professional link between the two of you. You told us in that first meeting, Mrs Grice, that you and Mr Walmsley were "almost personal friends". Unusual for a PA to assert that, even when it's true. Preparing the ground for your later contention that you were tucked up in bed together and indulging in carnal delights at the time of the murder. You'd dropped hints of a liaison when we spoke to you on Tuesday. You wanted us to pick up on the notion of an affair, to think that we'd prised the information out of the two of you.'

'I'm a happily married man, DCI Peach. I'm not in the habit of conducting affairs.' He reached his hand sideways towards Anne Grice again. She took it without looking at him.

Peach shook his head. 'The fallback position, as I said. From the start, neither of you shut the door on the possibility of a personal liaison. That is the opposite of the normal attitude. But you needed to keep that suspicion in our minds: if it looks as though we are getting close to what happened in that car park, you need a Plan B. So you claim that you were in bed together at the time. Show an appropriate embarrassment about it, but claim an impregnable alibi.'

Walmsley shifted his chair a little closer to his PA and took both of her hands in his. She acquiesced in that, but when he tried clumsily to slide his arm round her waist, she detached it gently and said with bleak finality, 'It's over, Bob.'

Clyde Northcott said, 'There never was a sexual affair between you, was there, Anne? You were in that car park together in the early hours of Sunday morning, not in bed together.'

She gave a sad smile. 'I don't suppose it was ever convincing, was it? Bob has a happy marriage and far too much good sense to jeopardize it. I like him very much, but I've never wanted to go to bed with him. I prefer younger models.' She detached Walmsley's hands from hers and looked at him with affection as she shifted her chair a fraction away from him. 'We were in that Bentley from one a.m. onwards, waiting for Jason Fitton. I still had my key and it was too good an opportunity for us to ignore.'

Walmsley glanced at her sharply. It was the phrase she had used repeatedly when she was persuading him to do this. He said quietly, 'I killed Fitton. It wasn't Anne.'

'It was both of us, Bob. You for what he'd done to this firm and me for what he'd done to me.'

Peach said evenly, almost apologetically, 'You've given us what we need. We'll ask you to put the details into statements at the station and sign them.'

Anne Grice continued almost as if he had not spoken. 'I opened the car with my old key and sat in the front passenger seat. It seemed quite a long wait, but it wasn't cold. Jason didn't hesitate to get in beside me. Probably he thought he was on for an easy shag for old times' sake. He was incredibly vain about his sexual attractiveness.' She allowed herself a bitter smile. 'I let him think for a moment that I was there for the taking. Bob was crouching in the back behind the driver's seat and the fool never knew he was there. He had the cord round his neck and the deed accomplished in a few seconds. Jason didn't make a single sound.' Her voice was filled with admiration, as if she was complimenting a craftsman on his work.

Clyde Northcott pronounced the final words of arrest and the pair were handcuffed and stowed without any hint of resistance into the police car brought there for that purpose. He slid the Mondeo quietly into line behind it and followed it through the gates of Fitton's Metals and back towards the police cells in Brunton.

'Too much love,' Clyde said after half a mile. 'A crime of passion, in a way. She killed because of an excessive love for a scoundrel, he because of an excessive love for the firm he had served so well.'

'But a carefully planned and coldly executed crime. We'll let the lawyers argue about how much passion came into it. Give the buggers something to do for their money.'

They were almost at the station when Peach added, 'Dangerous thing, love, when it gets out of hand. Just you remember that with PC Brockman, young Northcott.'